COMING HOME TO HIDEAWAY BAY

MICHELE BROUDER

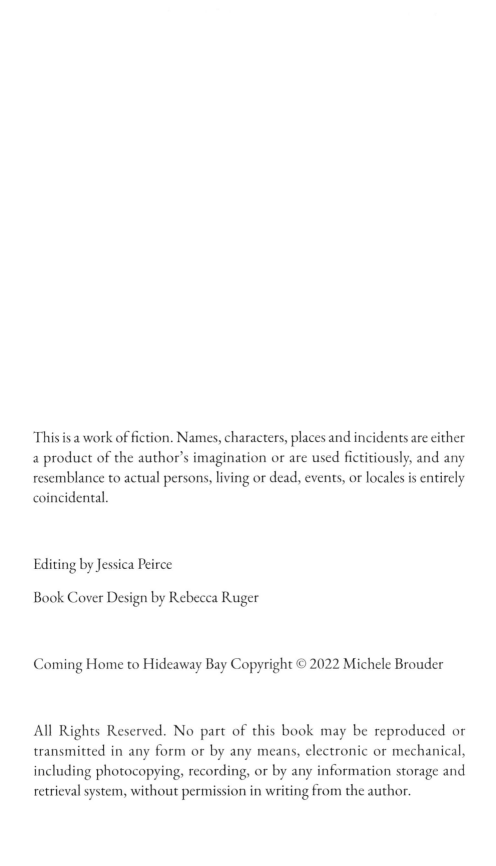

Editing by Jessica Peirce

Book Cover Design by Rebecca Ruger

For Jessica Peirce,
who waved her magic wand
and allowed me to go to the ball.

Hideaway Bay, New York is a fictional town that is solely the creation of my imagination based on all the beaches and beach towns I've been to in my life. I had to redraw the coastline of Lake Erie a bit to suit my story, so apologies. Although some street names are actual streets in Buffalo, New York, the people and situations are fictional.

If you'd like to read Sue Ann's story, sign up for my newsletter at www.michelebrouder.com and receive a free novella, *Escape to Hideaway Bay*.

CHAPTER ONE

Present Day

May

Lily

Lily Ford whistled for her dog, Charlie, a gray merle Great Dane, who was playing with a group of other dogs at the far end of the dog park. He lifted his head, made eye contact with Lily, and broke away from the small pack and trotted toward her with that easy lope of his. The sight of him always made her smile. And smiles were in short supply these days.

"Gosh, I wish my dog responded to commands like that," said her friend Diana. She'd been calling her yellow lab for the last five minutes, but he was busy at the fence line, sticking his nose into something.

Their other friend, Cheryl, approached them after speaking to another park-goer. Her dog, a Corgi, walked as fast as he could to keep up with Cheryl's long strides.

When Charlie arrived at Lily's side, she clipped the lead onto his collar. She patted him on his head and said, "Good boy."

Diana smirked. "Charlie, can you teach Pepper how to listen?" The three of them glanced over at the dog, who now had both his forepaws digging into the ground, dirt flying everywhere.

"Ugh! Pepper!" Diana called, hands on her hips. "I better get him, or I'll have a hole to fill in. Again." She marched off, arms swinging at her sides as she called out again, "Pepper!" Her dog never lifted his head.

Lily and Cheryl laughed. The dog park on Saturday mornings was Lily's highlight of the week. It was a chance to relax and spend time with Charlie and her friends. She'd met both women at the dog park within the last year.

Cheryl bemoaned the fact that she had to spend her afternoon ferrying kids back and forth to baseball practice, music, and dance lessons. Although she complained, Lily knew she loved it, loved being a mom to three kids.

Diana had a similar tale of woe. Her two college-age kids had returned at the end of their semesters with enough laundry to keep Diana busy for a week, but as she complained she also told Lily about the favorite dishes she was cooking and baking for each of them.

Diana rejoined their group with her naughty lab at her side.

As the three of them walked toward the parking lot, Diana said, "Where will we go for coffee?"

"How about that new place over on Locust Street?" Cheryl asked.

"I drove by that the other day and I thought the same thing: that we might try it out for coffee," Diana said.

Lily hesitated. She hated to let her friends down, and there was nothing she'd enjoy more than to spend some time gabbing over a cup of coffee. She'd seen that place too and thought it would be perfect as they had picnic tables outside, and she'd spotted a dog or two. But her budget was so tight she didn't have room to breathe, much less have a cup of coffee.

"I'm going to have to take a pass," Lily said, feeling a flush creep into her cheeks.

"Why? Aw, come on, this is my last chance for adult conversation before I'm forced to listen to preteen girls' conversations in the back of my car," Cheryl said.

Lily smiled but held firm. "No, really. Next week for sure."

"Come on, my treat," Diana added.

"No, thank you," Lily said. She loved her friends, but they'd been taking turns the last few weeks treating her, and although she was touched by their generosity it made her feel like a charity case.

"I don't mind," Diana said.

"I know and I'm grateful," Lily said. "You two can't keep picking up the tab. That's not fair." It would begin to cause an imbalance in their friendship and Lily didn't want that.

Cheryl went to protest—it was like they were tag-teaming her, but Lily held up her hand and said, "Next week for sure."

"Promise?" Cheryl said.

"I promise," Lily repeated.

Diana reached out and rubbed her arm, giving her a reassuring smile. "It's a tough time but you know we're here, right?"

Lily nodded. "Of course I do! But there are some things I have to figure out and do for myself."

"Okay," Cheryl said. "I'll text you during the week."

"Me too," Diana added.

Each of them drifted off to their own cars, and Lily waved goodbye. She hit the button on her keyless fob and heard the familiar beep that indicated her car was unlocked. Charlie jumped into the back seat and settled down against the opposite door, staring out the window.

Once Lily was buckled in, she glanced in her rearview mirror and then over her shoulder before reversing out of her parking space. As her friends pulled out, they waved again, and Lily smiled. But when they were out of sight, Lily's smile disappeared, and she sighed.

There had been a time in her life when she could grab a coffee or lunch whenever she felt like it, without a thought to what was in her wallet or her bank account or what bill was due next. But her late husband, Jamie, had robbed her of that. He'd died tragically six months earlier and as if that weren't shock enough, his death had unexpectedly saddled her with a debt that hung around her neck like a millstone.

Ten minutes later, Lily stepped into the hallway of her ranch-style home, the sound of her sandals echoing off the white tile floor. In one hand she held the mail she'd picked up from her box, and in the other was the leash that tethered her to her dog. She unclipped the lead and laid it, along with her sunglasses, on the small console table. Quickly, she leafed through the day's mail, determined that nothing needed her immediate attention, and placed it with the rest of the growing pile of unopened envelopes. She placed her shoulder bag on the floor next to the table. Charlie's nails scrabbled against the tile floor as he made his way down the long hallway toward the back of the house.

Her home was quiet. Unusually so. She didn't know if she'd ever get used to it. Although she didn't miss the three televisions blaring with different sports games. No, she didn't miss that at all. Or Jamie shouting in jubilation when his team scored or, worse, begging them to pull it together when they were losing.

She walked past the closed door of the spare bedroom. There had been no children in her short marriage. The extra bedroom had been used as a place where she could do her crafts. She used to dabble in all sorts of things—sewing, painting, knitting—loving the feeling of getting lost in creating something. It had been an outlet from a job that no longer excited her, a marriage that was less than stellar, and an overall feeling of dissatisfaction with the way her life had turned out. But when Jamie died, she'd closed the door and had yet to pick up any of her old hobbies. She lacked the energy for it.

The open-plan kitchen and family room were at the end of the hallway. Sliding glass doors looked out over a fenced-in backyard. She'd always wanted a pool, but that wouldn't happen now. The kitchen walls were painted a dark gold, and the woodwork was white. The glossy white cabinets were contemporary in style. Beige sofas and chairs were grouped around the television, and art prints in bright colors of red, orange, and purple adorned the walls, giving the space a splash of color.

Charlie stood next to her, waiting, his gaze on her.

Lily bent down and buried her face in the dog's neck, hugging him. In response, Charlie wagged his tail, thumping it against the cabinet door. He'd been an amazing companion and comfort these last six months. If it hadn't been for him and his need to be fed and walked, she doubted she would have gotten out of bed.

"Come on, let's get a snack," she said.

The pantry was nothing more than a deep closet in her kitchen. She pulled the box of treats off a top shelf—Charlie had learned how to open bottom cabinets—pulled one out, and said, "Sit." Charlie promptly sat, and Lily handed him the biscuit.

She should probably eat something herself. Without giving it much thought, she grabbed a yogurt from the shelf in the fridge and peeled back the lid. She rooted around in the drawer for a spoon, then took a seat at the small table against the wall. She leaned against the wall and sighed, scooping yogurt out of the plastic container. The clock above her ticked. The rest of the day stretched out before her with no immediate plans, like every other weekend and day off. She yawned.

The place had suited her and Jamie, but now she wasn't so sure. Everywhere she looked were memories. She still had a hard time believing she was a widow at the age of thirty-seven. She felt as if she were operating in the midst of a thick fog. It certainly wasn't how she'd thought her life would turn out.

After she finished the yogurt, she set the empty container aside and stared at the wall. She wondered how long she would feel like this. How did you grieve for a husband who had betrayed you?

Her gaze landed on the "Save the Date" postcard held to the refrigerator with a magnet. The couple who'd sent the invitation were getting married in the fall. The groom was a friend of Jamie's, or had been. Lily didn't know him or the bride-to-be that well at all. She thought she might give that one a miss.

On the kitchen table, tucked between the salt and pepper shakers, was the statement from the hospital showing the breakdown of costs for Jamie's stay in the ICU. She unfolded the statement, which was several pages long, and scanned through it again. At the end of the running tally was an astronomical figure, but thankfully that had been covered by the health insurance policy they had access to through her employer. She couldn't imagine being burdened with this bill on top of everything else. No longer interested, she tossed it aside. None of it mattered anyway as he'd died in the end, his injuries too catastrophic to recover from.

Married for only five years, Lily had discovered a lot of things about her husband she hadn't known before the wedding. He'd had a gambling problem. During the second year of their marriage, he'd gone into rehab with no success. He went sporadically to Gambler's Anonymous. She'd loved Jamie, he had some great qualities—easygoing, always willing to help people—but the gambling had overshadowed all that and had chipped away at the feelings she'd once held for him. It had gotten to the point where she could only keep the bare minimum in their joint account to cover the household bills. In one day, he'd blown through their savings account on a horse who was a sure bet. That sure bet had stumbled right out of the gate and their money was lost. Jamie had been contrite, promising he'd never do it again. But he had.

It wasn't until after his death that she'd found out the extent of his problem. Apparently, he'd taken out several credit cards in both their names, using their combined incomes to get a higher credit limit. The amount he owed on said cards was staggering. He'd been barely keeping up with the payments himself. And Lily had never known.

It wasn't as if they had anything to show for the credit card debt. No brand-new car or once-in-a-lifetime vacations with beautiful memories or even a swimming pool in the backyard. The credit cards had financed his gambling addiction.

Thus the three televisions to watch various sports games on which he had betted heavily. He was always just one game away from a big win. When he died, one of the first things she'd done was to donate two of those televisions to charity.

Because her name was on the debt as well, she'd become responsible for it after his death. With her own parents gone and desperate for advice, she'd turned to her grandmother, who had talked her out of selling her only remaining asset, her house, to pay off the debts. Her grandmother wanted to gift her some money and when Lily flat-out refused, she offered to make it a loan. But Lily wasn't borrowing any more money.

Hence the scrimp and save and pay-down-the-debt budget. There was no extra money for anything. Her biggest fear was that an appliance would break down or her car would need repairs. But again, her grandmother's wisdom prevailed as she advised her not to borrow trouble.

"Oh, Jamie, what have you done," Lily said, releasing a sigh infused with anger, disappointment, and sadness. She closed her eyes and exhaled deeply. There was no sense in going over this in her head again and again; it changed nothing. She'd been married to a man she loved who'd betrayed her financially and left her in ruin.

Her thoughts were interrupted by the ringing phone. Frowning at the unfamiliar number, she noticed the area code for Hideaway Bay, her hometown back in New York State on the shores of Lake Erie.

"Hello?"

"Is that you, Lily?"

Lily recognized the unmistakable voice of Thelma, her grandmother's lifelong friend.

"Thelma? Is everything all right?" But Lily knew it wasn't. Thelma had never called her before. Lily leaned forward in her chair, bracing herself, her late husband momentarily forgotten.

"Junie's gone," Thelma said.

Something wasn't slotting into place in Lily's mind.

"Gone? Where?" Lily asked, not comprehending what Thelma was trying to tell her about her grandmother.

From the other end came an exasperated sigh, which was pure Thelma.

"She's *gone*," Thelma said, her voice louder, as if increasing the volume of her voice would enlighten Lily. "She died this morning."

"Died?" Lily repeated, trying to make that word fit into the grand scheme of things and failing miserably. She felt like she was in a dark, narrow tunnel and the walls were closing in around her.

"This morning. She went for her usual walk on the beach, and they found her later. I don't know what happened to her. Are you coming home?"

"Of course," Lily said. She blinked hard and stood up from the table, but her legs felt wobbly. Brushing her hair away from her forehead, she asked, "Have you called Alice and Isabelle?"

"No, I tried to call Isabelle first, but it said the number was out of service and I couldn't find an updated one," Thelma said. Of course she'd call Isabelle first; she was the oldest of the three Monroe sisters.

Lily rolled her eyes. How like Isabelle to be incommunicado. God forbid they ever had to get a hold of her, like right now.

"I didn't call Alice yet," Thelma said.

"I'll call her and we'll figure out how to get in touch with Isabelle," Lily said. Alice, their youngest sister, was a corporate attorney in Chicago, and Lily knew that she worked late hours. Besides, she should be the one to call her sisters. She shouldn't leave it up to Thelma; that would hardly be fair. Once she assured Thelma that she'd call back as soon as she had her flight reservations, she went in search of her address book and hoped her sisters' numbers were current.

She paused for a moment. The thought that Junie Reynolds was no longer with them was unimaginable. Lily sucked in a deep breath as the reality began to settle in. Gram not there anymore? She'd been an anchoring force for good in all their lives.

Lily had gone back to the bay to visit Gram from time to time, especially after her mother had passed away from cancer, but now she'd been away longer than she'd lived there. It was no longer home.

She hadn't seen Alice or Isabelle since Jamie's funeral. The middle of the three sisters, Lily had had little contact with the others over the years. They weren't close, and her sisters hadn't really known Jamie, having met him only a handful of times. But despite their somewhat fractious relationship, they'd both flown out for Jamie's funeral. Lily was touched by that, even if they did leave right afterward. Alice had returned to her job in Chicago, and Isabelle, the oldest of the three and the family's confirmed wanderer, had departed for parts unknown.

Lily had left Hideaway Bay as soon as she turned eighteen and had never looked back. She'd gone to college on the west coast for a dual degree in business and English and had stayed after graduation. The thing she remembered most about her final years in Hideaway Bay was how much the three of them had fought before she left.

She pulled open the top drawer of her desk, retrieving the address book covered in pink floral fabric. Her hands shook as she flipped through the book to Alice's address in Chicago and ran her finger down the page until she stopped at her sister's phone number. Hopefully, Alice would have a way to contact Isabelle.

Taking a deep breath, Lily dialed her sister's number. As the phone rang, her chin quivered and tears pooled in her eyes as memories of her grandmother came flooding back.

CHAPTER TWO

1957

Junie

J unie bounced down the staircase, her hand skimming the polished wood of the banister. Raised voices from the kitchen said that it was just as well to get out of the house. Her older sister, Margaret, was kicking up a storm again.

Junie paused at the foot of the stairs, staring through the filter of the aluminum screen door to the outside world.

Her father's voice reached her, his tone implacable. "I don't care if he's the king of England, he's too old for you. What's a guy that age doing with a girl in high school?"

"I'll tell you what he's doing," came her mother's voice, softer in volume though heavier in anxiety. "Nothing good."

Margaret was seventeen and her boyfriend, Bill Jenner, was twenty-eight. Ma and Daddy had had a fit when they found out Margaret was sneaking out late at night to see him. She kept saying he had a job at the steel plant, and Junie had no idea why that should mean anything or serve as some kind of justification.

Above the din, Junie yelled, "Going to meet Thelma and Barb."

Her father poked his head out of the kitchen and called out with no diminishing of his bark, "Be back by ten, Junie."

"Yeah!"

The screen door slammed behind her as she hopped off her porch. Immediately, she scrunched up her nose, assailed by a pungent scent in the air. She glanced at the house next door, at the guilty party. She'd forgotten it was Thursday but there it was; you could set your watch by it. Mrs. Krautwein next door cooked pork and sauerkraut on Thursdays, and everyone on the street had no choice but to deal with it. The smell would dissipate but not very soon in this heat. Brushing her knuckle over her nose, Junie sped up, walking quickly up to the corner of the street.

This summer was one for the record books. It seemed every other day, Junie's dad sat at the kitchen table with the *Courier Express* after work, reading aloud how hot it had actually been the day before. He did so in his undershirt and with the fan blowing on him from where he'd plugged it in beside the table. There was only one fan in the Richards's house, and it went wherever her parents went, which meant that it never ended up in Junie's bedroom.

"Got up to eighty-seven yesterday," her father had said tonight before dinner.

"Warmer than that today, I bet," guessed her mother, hovering over the big pot, her favorite, the one that came out at least four times a week and in which she now mashed the potatoes. It had the letters USN stamped on the handle. Her brother had lifted it during his time in the service. At the time, Junie's dad had quipped to her uncle, "Can you get me a new car?"

"You'd think being so close to the lake would cool things down a bit," her father said, probably for the hundredth time.

"Too much concrete," was her mother's response, as it always was. She wore a light, sleeveless cotton dress. Tight pin curls held in place by metal bobby pins framed her face.

Junie spotted her friends Thelma and Barb standing around the corner, waiting for her. Thelma gestured

with her hand, waving for Junie to hurry up. Thelma
could be so impatient at times.

Thelma and Barb were as opposite as day and night.
Thelma wore dungarees rolled up to her knees with a
pair of scuffed saddle shoes and a red sleeveless blouse
that she had tied in a knot at her navel. Her red
hair was pulled back in a messy ponytail by a rubber
band. Barb on the other hand was tall and willowy,
her shoulder-length blond hair held in place by a
headband that matched her pale blue pedal pushers.
Her cotton shirt had been pressed, and on her feet
were a pair of brand-new white tennis shoes. Junie's
mom said Barb reminded her of Grace Kelly.

"Jeez, Junie, what took you so long?" Thelma
whined. Her red bangs had curled with the humidity
and had receded back to her hairline. "I've got to be
home by nine."

"Nine? It's a Friday night," Junie said with a frown.

"I know, I know. But my father's on the warpath,"
Thelma explained.

That was not surprising. According to Thelma, her
father was often on the warpath. There never seemed to
be any particular reason. Maybe he liked ranting—some
people were happier being grumpy, Junie's mother
had said once. Maybe he was bitter or sad or even
heartbroken that his wife, Thelma's mom, had died two

years earlier, leaving him alone to raise Thelma and her four younger brothers.

Thelma's availability since then had declined dramatically, since she was frequently charged with minding her brothers. Often if Barb or Junie asked her to come out or meet up, Thelma's answering posture would give away her dismay. Her rounded shoulders would slump, seeming to take inches off her height. "I have to babysit," she would say with so much dejection Junie felt sorry for her. Since Junie's mom and Thelma's mom had been good friends, the Kempf family were sometimes guests at Junie's house for dinner. All those boys. One was more annoying than the next. Junie decided a year ago that she was glad she only had to live with Margaret.

"I don't know how you live like that," Barb now commented, her blue eyes wide. Of the three of them, Barb was openly considered the fortunate one. She lived a far different life from either Junie or Thelma. Her father was a doctor and her mother stayed at home. Doing what, Junie had no idea.

"I have no choice," Thelma muttered.

The evening sky was clear except for a few thin clouds off to the west, where the sun was setting, making it look as if someone had brushed strokes in swaths of pink and lavender and blue. Junie inhaled deeply of the heavy air and looped her arms through Barb's and Thelma's. She loved summer. Everything seemed possible.

They paused in front of Ed Konacker's Appliances. The illuminated front window display was full of televisions. The rest of the shop was shrouded in darkness. A repeat of an episode of *I Love Lucy* played on all the screens. Thelma stared, her mouth slightly agape, and laughed when Lucy scowled and pouted.

"Hey, do you guys want to go out to the lake with me next weekend?" Barb asked, twirling a strand of her hair around her finger.

Thelma turned away from the televisions. "Do we want to go out to the lake with you? What kind of question is that? Of course we want to go out to the lake with you."

Barb blushed and Junie patted her friend's arm. Sometimes it seemed as if all the finesse had been given to Barb and none to Thelma.

"When does the car pull away from the curb?" Thelma asked, walking away, continuing up the street. Absentmindedly, she tightened her ponytail.

Barb giggled and said, "I'll let you know."

The Walsh family had a cottage out on Lake Erie, about twenty miles south of the city in a small town called Hideaway Bay. Junie had never been out to the lake or even to the beach. Her mother hated sand. Said it went everywhere and you couldn't get rid of it. But

Barb spoke so much about her cottage at Hideaway Bay that it had left Junie curious. Sometimes Barb and her mother went away for weeks and when they'd return, Barb's skin would be the color of butterscotch and her blond hair would almost be white.

As they walked along, Thelma pushed her hands into her back pockets and said over her shoulder to Junie, "Maybe you'll see Paul Reynolds."

"Maybe I will and maybe I won't," Junie said with a shrug, trying to sound casual. But the mere mention of his name sent her heart rate up a notch. Ever since she'd met up with her friends at the corner, she'd been searching for his car, a 1951 Chevy Bel Air the color of midnight. She'd had a crush on Paul for the last year. A serious crush. If her parents were upset about Margaret, they'd go through the roof at the thought of their fourteen-year-old daughter making cow eyes at a nineteen-year-old. Her father would send her off to live with his sister in Wisconsin so fast her head would spin.

When they reached Cone King, the sun had almost disappeared into the horizon, but the sky remained the color of lavender and pale yellow. There were two long lines in front of the ice cream stand, reaching all the way back to the street. The fluorescent lighting hummed, and the fly zapper buzzed constantly in the background. Junie kept her back to the stand, watching the traffic go by, looking for that Chevy Bel Air.

Thelma slapped her on the arm.

"Ow!" Junie frowned. "What did you do that for?"

Thelma rolled her eyes. "Come on, what do you want?" She gave a pronounced eyebrow lift and nodded toward the board.

Junie stammered, "Oh, lemon sherbet."

"Lemon sherbet is lovely," Barb agreed.

"Lemon sherbet, really?" Thelma said, stepping in front of them. She leaned on the small Formica-topped counter and spoke directly to the ice cream stand attendant. "Give me a banana split, Ralph, with extra chocolate sauce."

Ralph mumbled something, his peaked paper hat beginning to wilt in the humidity.

"Yeah, yeah, I know, it'll be extra." When he stepped away from the counter, Thelma yelled after him, "And don't be stingy with the chocolate sauce, Ralph! I'm paying for it!"

When Junie and Barb stepped up to the counter, grateful that Thelma's mouth was quiet because it was full of ice cream, they said in unison, "Lemon sherbet on a waffle cone."

They burst out laughing. Junie nudged Barb and said, "Jinx, you owe me a Coke."

Ice creams in hand, they headed away, just as the school baseball team pulled up in two cars: one a four-door turquoise-and-white station wagon, the other a dark Buick. Both had all their windows down, and they were packed with teenage boys who hollered and screamed in the back seats.

Someone from the team had his arm out the window of the station wagon and banged on the side door to get the girls' attention, to which the driver yelled, "You dent that door, Stanley, and I'll dent your head!" The three of them looked over to the car to see Stanley Schumacher with his scrawny arm hanging out the window.

"Hey, Thelma, wanna do a little necking later?" Stanley yelled, leaning out the car window.

Thelma swallowed her mouthful of ice cream and shouted back, "The only necking we'll be doing is when I get my hands around your neck and throttle it, Stanley!"

This was met with guffaws from Stanley, who receded into the shadows of the back seat. Junie and Barb giggled as they headed down the sidewalk.

Junie licked around the side of her ice cream to keep it from sliding down the outside of her waffle cone.

For a moment they stood on the corner of South Park and Whitfield, where Twomey's bar was located and had been in operation since the turn of the century. The door of the bar opened, and Johnny Mathis's "Chances Are" floated out into the street. In that brief moment, Junie glimpsed her sister Margaret in her poodle skirt and white blouse, a wide red belt cinched at her waist.

On her wrist was a chunky red bracelet. She had her arm draped around the shoulder of her boyfriend, Bill, and they looked at each other like there was no one else in the world.

A drop of ice cream landed on Junie's blouse, distracting her, and the door to the bar closed.

"Darn, this was a clean blouse," Junie said, rubbing her napkin on the spot on her blouse.

"I'll bring a bib for you next time," Thelma teased, scooping up banana split and shoveling it into her mouth.

Junie looked up. "Ha, ha."

The door to the bar opened again, and Paul Reynolds stepped out.

Junie swallowed hard. *You can keep Rock Hudson and Kirk Douglas*, she thought. Paul wasn't tall but he was solid, and muscles pushed against the fabric of his T-shirt. A pack of Camels was rolled beneath one of the sleeves. His face was beautiful, or at least Junie thought so. Even in the dusk, his eyes were large and glittering.

He stood on the stoop of the bar and looked around, not noticing them. He tugged the pack of cigarettes from beneath his sleeve, tapped one out, and pulled a lighter from the pocket of his pants. Casually, he trotted down the stairs and came to rest on the sidewalk as he cupped his left hand around his cigarette and flicked the lighter open. The blue flame illuminated his face for a quick moment, and the evening shadows played across the planes and angles of his face. After the cigarette was lit and he drew in a lungful of smoke, he glanced at the three of them.

Quickly, Junie ditched her ice cream cone into the grass. She didn't want him to think she was some kind of baby. Out of the corner of her eye, she caught the expressions on her friends' faces: Barb was wide-eyed, and Thelma wore an amused look.

"Hey, Paul," Thelma called.

He turned to face them. Up the street, Junie spotted his car parked against the curb. How had she missed that?

"Hey, girls," he said, taking a step closer to them.

"You know, you'd really make Junie's day if you'd notice her," Thelma cooed.

"Shut up, Thelma," Junie hissed, her cheeks hot and flushed. She couldn't look at Paul Reynolds. She prayed the sidewalk would collapse and she'd be swallowed up by the earth.

"Is that right?" Paul said, causing her to look up and meet his gaze. He reached into his pocket, his lit cigarette dangling from his mouth.

Junie's eyes were glued on him, thinking he was the most handsome man she'd ever seen. His hair looked like silk, and she imagined running her fingers through it.

His eyes narrowed as a stream of bluish smoke floated up in front of his face. He fished something out of his pocket and tossed it to her.

Junie caught it with both hands and opened up her palms to look at it.

It was a dime.

"Call me when you grow up," he said with a wink. He turned and walked away, flicking an ash onto the ground.

Tears stung Junie's eyes and when he was out of earshot, she rounded on Thelma. "What did you go and do that for?"

"I was only trying to help," Thelma said.

"I don't want your help! I'm never going to speak to you again!" Junie said, and she spun on her heel and broke into a run, heading home.

"Junie! Come back," Barb called after her. Thelma grumbled something, but Junie couldn't hear as she was almost a block away.

Everything was ruined. Thelma could be such a jerk sometimes. If Thelma's mother hadn't died, Junie would have dropped Thelma like a bad habit. But her mother kept telling her to be kind, be nice. Thelma was going through a difficult time with the loss of her mother. Maybe she was going through a difficult time because she *was* difficult.

CHAPTER THREE

Lily

Lily agonized over whether to fly or drive. If she flew, she'd get there quicker. But if she drove, she'd have her own car in Hideaway Bay, and she thought the drive might be easier on Charlie. She'd worried over that as well. Initially, she was going to board Charlie, but there were two strikes against that: the cost, and she didn't know how long she'd be gone. She had to be mindful of her money. The decision to take Charlie with her was easier to make than whether to fly or drive.

That had become a problem. Decision-making. Since Jamie's death, Lily had felt inert. And at times, she felt incapable of making a decision, especially if it was about something important. For whatever reason, she didn't trust her judgment. Not anymore. She'd explored this in grief therapy. It turned out that she blamed herself for not noticing how severe Jamie's gambling addiction had become. What kind of wife had she been? Apparently, one with her head stuck in the sand. How had she missed all those red flags? She'd arrived at her own conclusion: she'd been too trusting. It would never have crossed her mind that someone she loved would betray her like that. As a result, she was more conscious of each decision she made, especially if other people were involved. She wanted to trust her own judgment, but she wasn't sure yet. She would have liked to explore that further in therapy, but she'd had to put an end to that due to lack of funds.

In the end, she made the decision to drive across country with Charlie. He was used to the car, and Lily had taken him on road trips to Santa Fe and Lake Tahoe. Granted, he'd never gone on a journey this far, but she knew he'd handle it better than an airplane trip. She didn't like the thought of her dog caged and docked below decks in cargo. Although large, Charlie tended to be fearful. But even though the decision was made, it didn't stop her from second-guessing herself.

Her boss at the solar panel company where she worked had been understanding. Lily worked in the human resources department and had been at the job for the last ten years. Although it was a family-owned company and they were lovely to work for, sometimes Lily felt she could perform the job on autopilot. They'd been gracious when Jamie died and again now, telling her to take all the time she needed to go back east for Gram's funeral.

After talking to Alice, who'd seemed truly stunned and speechless during their five-minute phone call, it was discovered that Isabelle's whereabouts were currently unknown. But then that was Isabelle for you, Lily thought. Alice couldn't leave for two more days because of work commitments, so with Lily's three-day drive, she would arrive only a day after Alice.

Diana and Cheryl dropped everything and came over as soon as they heard Lily's news. She gave them each a copy of her housekeys so they could keep an eye on the place. She knew that each one was busy with their own lives so she made sure her time away wouldn't be too much of a burden on either one of them. The only thing they had to do was bring in the mail and water her two houseplants. She had all the lights on an electric timer, and she'd told her elderly next-door neighbor that she was going away.

She didn't sleep well the night before the trip. There was a lot of tossing and turning. Gram's death inevitably brought up memories of her mother's death. And with both of them now gone, she truly felt adrift.

Their first stop on their long journey was the drive-thru for coffee and a plain glazed donut. Once she had ordered and swiped her card, she set her coffee down in the cupholder in the center console of her SUV. Charlie stuck his head between the two front seats and whined.

"Hold on, buddy," Lily instructed, pulling into a parking space. The dog paced in the confines of the back seat, and Lily tried not to laugh as she pulled the donut out of the brown paper bag, ripping it in half and giving the bigger half to Charlie. He swallowed it whole.

"I've told you several times you need to chew your food," she said, eyeing him in the rearview mirror. Satisfied, Charlie sat back in his seat, looking out the window.

"I know you can hear me, Charlie," she said. She ate her half quickly and took a sip of her coffee, determining it was still too hot to drink. She wiped her hands on a napkin and crumpled it up and tossed it in a small bag she kept for garbage. She headed out onto the highway, heading toward the thruway entrance, heading home to Hideaway Bay.

Gram's death aside, Lily had mixed feelings about returning to the bay. Although the lakeside town had been Gram's home from early on in her marriage, it had not been the same for Lily or her sisters. They couldn't get out of Hideaway Bay fast enough, away from its small-town, provincial feel.

But now here she was returning after all these years for Gram's funeral. A funeral she'd have to plan, now that her own mother was gone. All those years ago, she'd been eager to leave and not look back. Now, hardly a success story, she felt as if she should be waving a white flag upon her return.

Nearing the end of the first day's drive, she decided to keep an open mind about being home. What was there to hurry back to on the west coast? An empty house and a boatload of debt, courtesy of her late husband. Yes, she'd be flexible. There was no reason to rush back and at the very least, it would be good to see her sisters and some of the friends they'd grown up with, like Thelma's granddaughters, who were still in the area. She had become a cliché, she thought: seeing everyone only at weddings and funerals. Except there had been no weddings.

Maybe spending some time in Hideaway Bay would be good for her. She might even stay a week or two after Gram's funeral. There was no return date set in stone. She needed to examine what was left of her life, such as it was. The change of scenery might be just the thing she needed to determine what she wanted to do next. More than anything, she hoped the answers could be found in Hideaway Bay.

CHAPTER FOUR

Junie

Junie carried a paper bag packed with her belongings as she piled into the back seat of Mrs. Walsh's Buick. Barb had carted a small floral suitcase with her and had parked it on the seat between them. Embarrassed at her brown paper bag, Junie stuffed it down onto the floor next to her feet. She was anxious to see this Hideaway Bay that Barb always spoke about. Junie's mother had been nervous and must have called Mrs. Walsh three times, making sure it was all right and asking what kind of things she'd need for the weekend. At the time, Junie had protested, "Stop, Ma, she's going to think we're idiots."

But her mother wouldn't be consoled and fretted until the day of the trip arrived. On the Thursday morning of the departure, her mother pressed folded bills into Junie's hand. Junie looked at the windfall in her palm, wide-eyed.

"Here's a bit of money. Make sure you buy your own things. And treat Barb once in a while. We don't want to take advantage."

"Okay."

Her mother hugged her goodbye and it seemed like she wouldn't let go.

"You're smothering me." When her mother pulled away, Junie noticed her eyes were wet. "Ma, I'm only going for the weekend. I'll be back Sunday night."

Her mother nodded and picked up her handbag from the table. "I've got to get to work. I don't want to be late."

At the front door, she looked back at Junie and said, "Enjoy yourself."

But now, sitting in the back seat of Mrs. Walsh's car, Junie felt unsure. Her stomach was queasy. Barb talked non-stop of all the things she had planned for them. It sounded unlike anything Junie usually did in the summer: bonfires, swimming, maybe some boating. She'd never been on a boat.

She wished Thelma were there. Thelma had been invited, but her father had said she couldn't go. Said someone had to be home to look after the boys. Thelma pretended she didn't care, said she'd prefer the city, but Junie knew she was putting on a brave front.

Mrs. Walsh didn't say too much as they drove away from the city. She wore little white gloves on her hands, and Junie wondered if her hands were sweaty. The radio played but they had the back windows open, and Junie couldn't really hear the music.

As Barb spoke, Junie watched the world pass outside the window. They drove out of the city and past the suburbs until the houses and cars thinned out to fields and pastures. She sat up and leaned against the window, watching it all. The fields were a lush green, and Mrs. Walsh pointed out the start of corn stalks on the left. Junie had never seen cornfields up close. It was quiet out here. She thought it was heaven.

After almost an hour of driving, Mrs. Walsh pulled off onto a narrow road, slowed down at a dip in the road, crossed a set of railroad tracks, and drove into Hideaway Bay. Junie leaned forward and could see a thin blue ribbon of lake in the distance on the horizon. She stared out the window at the passing cottages. They were uniform in that there were towels hanging over porch railings or picket fences. There were lawn chairs out front and sometimes a small pool where a baby in diapers splashed around in the shade.

"Mother, can you go down Star Shine Drive to show Junie the beach and the town?"

Mrs. Walsh was agreeable, and she turned off a side street named Sea Shell Lane, drove to the end of it, made a left onto Lakeview Drive and then finally, another left, turning onto Star Shine Drive. There were more cottages here, all shaded by giant oak trees. But these houses were bigger, grander, set back from the road, and they were directly across from the beach. On one of the big wraparound porches, Junie spied three elderly women wearing floral dresses and sipping something cool from tall glasses. They all laughed about something. Her eyes traveled to the beach. There were people on blankets, everyone was in a swimsuit, and the lake was a sparkling blue color in the mid-afternoon sun. Junie stared with her mouth hanging wide open.

Star Shine Drive led to Main Street, and Junie marveled at all the shops with their striped awnings in various colors. The place was different than the city. There was no litter clogging up the sewers or pushed up against the curb. There were no sirens or honking horns; it was mostly quiet. The only sounds were the cries of seagulls overhead and the water landing at the shore. And the air smelled different. Fresher. Nothing like that acrid smell from the steel plant or, worse, that sour-milk smell that emanated from the cheese factory every afternoon. She looked at every shop as they drove past. There was an ice cream parlor, a five-and-dime, and a little grocery store. People strolled along the sidewalks, no one in any apparent hurry. Women carried shopping bags, and men stopped to talk to acquaintances. It was like they had all the time in the world.

On the other side of town, not that far from Star Shine Drive, was a square plot of land that had a gazebo right in the center of it. As it was July 4th weekend, Barb had told her they would watch the fireworks from the beach.

Mrs. Walsh drove around the town square and pulled into the driveway of a two-story house. Barb had always referred to their house on the lake as a cottage, but Junie was surprised to see it was as big as the house Junie lived in. It was covered in clapboard and had shutters and a deep front porch. There was a wide driveway and at the back of it, Junie spotted a wrought iron table and chairs with an umbrella. The underside of the umbrella sported a floral pattern that matched the cushions on the chairs. Junie had never seen anything like it.

She stepped out of Mrs. Walsh's car and stared at it all, feeling like she was in another world.

They helped Mrs. Walsh carry bags of groceries into the house. The place was large and airy with wood-paneled walls, and easy chairs grouped around a television. The kitchen was old-fashioned, but it was bright, decorated in white and red. Junie didn't know where to look first.

"Can we go to the beach, Mother?" Barb asked.

All the bags had been set on the kitchen table. Mrs. Walsh regarded Junie for a moment and asked, "Junie, do you know how to swim?"

Junie shook her head, and Barb elbowed her and gave her a glare. But there was no way Junie was going to lie to Mrs. Walsh.

Mrs. Walsh wrinkled her nose. "All right. But listen to me, Barbara." Junie's ears perked up at the use of Barb's full name.

"Since Junie doesn't know how to swim, stay at the shore. I mean it, Barbara Jane," Mrs. Walsh warned. She appeared thoughtful. "Go on to the beach and I'll see if Kathy Brennan is around; maybe she can give Junie some swim lessons in the morning."

She was going to learn how to swim too? Wow.

Junie ran up the stairs after Barb, and Barb closed her bedroom door behind them. "Come on, let's get our bathing suits on. Hurry up, Junie."

Junie had never gotten dressed in front of anyone before, other than her mother and her sister, but that was different. Slowly, she turned her back to Barb, but Barb brushed past her. "I'll get changed in the bathroom. Meet me out in the hallway in five minutes. I want to get to the beach."

As soon as the door closed, Junie dug her swimsuit out of the bottom of the brown paper bag, beneath her other change of clothes. Quickly she discarded her clothes and pulled the swimsuit on before anyone could barge in.

She stood in the hall, waiting for Barb, who finally emerged from the bathroom wearing a cute one-piece bathing suit. It was obviously brand new, because the colors were vibrant, not faded from too many washings. Self-conscious, Junie folded her arms over her own one-piece suit, which was baggy around her bum. It had been Margaret's years ago, but it had been handed down to Junie. It was red, Margaret's favorite color.

"Come on, let's go," Barb said, and she flew down the staircase, leaving Junie no option but to follow her.

As they landed on the porch, Mrs. Walsh called after them, "Barbara, you keep your sandals on. No walking around barefoot."

"Yes, Mother," Barb said. She waved for Junie to follow her, and they bounced off the steps of the porch and headed toward the beach on the other side of the town square. When they passed the green space, Barb looked back toward her house, laughed, and pulled her sandals off.

"But your mother—"

"Do you do everything your mother tells you?" Barb asked with a laugh.

Slowly, Junie pulled off her sandals. The street was hot, and she bounced from one foot to the other.

"Come on, pokey," Barb called from the verge of grass in front of the beach. Junie bolted from the street and landed on the prickly grass, which wasn't much better, but at least it didn't burn the bottoms of her feet.

"Do you go barefoot all the time here?" Junie asked.

"Only when my mother isn't looking," Barb said with a giggle.

Junie wasn't convinced, and Barb said, "Your feet will get tough from walking around barefoot, and you'll love it." Somehow, Junie doubted it.

When they reached the sand, that was hot too, and Junie followed Barb to the shore, remembering Mrs. Walsh's instructions.

Her senses were overwhelmed. She stood at the shore and marveled at the way the water rushed in and swirled around her feet. Her toes and feet sank into the waterlogged sand, and it felt squishy. She smiled at it. A slight breeze blew in, giving her relief from the unrelenting sun, and lifted her hair off the back of her neck.

She folded her arms in front of her and pivoted and turned, doing a three-sixty to get a good look at her surroundings. Across the lake was the hazy outline of the Canadian shore. To her left were bluffs covered in trees and shrubs. From where she stood, she could see the Walsh cottage on the other side of the town square. Beyond that were the backs of the buildings of the main town center, and looking north or to her left, she could see Star Shine Drive and the grand houses that lined it.

It was, quite simply, the most amazing place she'd ever been to. And she'd fallen in love.

CHAPTER FIVE

Lily

When she reached the vineyards that lined the highway on both sides in the southern tier of New York State, Lily knew she was almost home. It had been a long three days, but Charlie had been a pretty good travel partner. She was hot and dusty and wanted to take a bath. Her back ached from sitting in the same position for the last three days, and her neck had a crick in it.

She had to force thoughts of Gram and Jamie out of her mind during the journey because they always resulted in an episode of choking and crying. The only time she had to pull over was when she drove out of Erie, Pennsylvania and crossed the New York state line. Realizing she was home, she pulled over on the side of the thruway and had a good cry. Great big sobs. Ugly crying, as Diana called it. Charlie forced his big head between the two front seats, whined, and licked her face.

But she wiped her tears away, pulled off the shoulder, and merged back into traffic. Gram had always said it was the people who were left behind who suffered the most. And that was true with both Gram's and Jamie's deaths. Someday Lily was going to sit down and try to make sense of both losses.

Gram used to say the best part of living on this side of Lake Erie was that the sun set over the lake. Lily remembered those sunsets. They were the best in summertime: the sky slashed with vibrant colors of pink, orange, and lavender, and the lake beneath it a beautiful sapphire color. It was hard to beat.

To Lily's left stood rows and rows of short crops of grapes clustered along low fences. The vineyard industry was heavy in this area. Growing up, there had been only one vineyard, and now it appeared there were many. Big billboards with ads for local wineries splashed out across them were everywhere. Images in warm colors, dot-com addresses, and the promise of wine tours. Granddad always liked one glass of pink Catawba with dinner. She'd forgotten about that. The memory made her smile. She opened her window, and stretched her arm out, letting the breeze tickle her skin. She drew in a deep breath: the scent of home.

It was almost dusk when she spotted the sign for Hideaway Bay, a large wooden sign standing on two posts, painted a dark green with the words "Hideaway Bay, est. 1902" carved in painted gold. The seal depicted a sun setting over the lake, and a cluster of grapes, a nod to all the local vineyards, hung over the words.

Granddad often spoke about the history of the town when she and her sisters were growing up. During the turn of the last century, Buffalo had had more millionaires per capita than any other city in the United States. To escape the heat of the summer, those wealthy people flocked south of the city, anywhere from forty-five minutes to an hour's drive away. They built big homes with wide porches and views of Lake Erie so wives and children could spend the summer at the beach. As those houses went up, so did the smaller cottages for the tradesmen that moved there with their own families to live year-round and service the construction boom. By the 1930s, a supporting town and services had sprung up. By the '40s and '50s, the middle-class were also going out to the lake to escape the humid summer heat Buffalo was noted for. And pretty soon, some of them with their big-industry wages were buying the cheap cottages for their own summer getaways. The community of Hideaway Bay, established by a group of wealthy elites, had gradually become its own vibrant, bustling community over the ensuing decades.

On a map, the town resembled a giant soup ladle, with the shoreline traveling along straight at first and then curving until it resembled a bowl. Hideaway Bay was the town that sprang up around the bowl part of the soup ladle. A natural inlet, the bay was a beautiful piece of real estate. As you traveled away from the beach, there was farmland, followed by the gently undulating hills of the southern tier. The area was profuse with rhododendrons and hydrangeas. Granddad used to say it was because of the sandy, loamy soil.

Before the pull-off to Hideaway Bay, Lily noticed the familiar white-painted produce shack at the side of the road that had been there for as long as she could remember. There was a sign now that read "Anderson Farms." She pulled off, parking her SUV and pushing her sunglasses up to the top of her head. A man in his sixties manned the little shack. Bulk items of spinach, asparagus, and radishes lined the sloping shelf.

"Too early for strawberries, I suppose?" Lily asked.

The man, who wore a name tag that read "Ben," shook his head. "A bit early yet. Another month. But I've got some vegetables."

"Good." In the end, she opted for spinach and asparagus.

"Are you from around here?" he asked.

"I was raised in Hideaway Bay, but I'm only here for a short stay," she said. "I used to come here with my grandparents when I was younger."

"I probably knew them. I've been here since I was a boy, helping my grandfather," he said, putting her fruit into a brown paper bag.

"Junie and Paul Reynolds?" Lily said.

His expression softened. "Sure, I knew Junie and Paul. I met them years ago when they first came out here. My grandfather was alive then." He paused and added another pint basket of raspberries. "Junie always liked the berries."

He took her cash, gave her some change, and handed her the bag.

He seemed to give it some consideration before adding, "I am sorry for your troubles. They were great people."

Lily lifted up the bag and said, "Thanks." Her voice was choked with emotion.

"See you around."

She nodded and kept her head down as she returned to her car.

She pulled back out onto the highway. If you weren't from around here, you'd never know that Hideaway Bay was tucked back in there about half a mile down the road. She coasted over the disused railroad tracks, delighting in the descent in the dip in the road.

Charlie lost his balance in the back and disappeared momentarily from her rearview mirror. But his head soon popped back up and she laughed. The road ran straight to Hideaway Bay. As it was almost dusk, there were barely glimpses of the lake at the end of that road and through the canopy of great oaks. She rolled down the window. It smelled like spring, like wet earth but full of hope. There was mossy green new growth on the trees and shrubs. It all looked so promising.

At the end of the Erie Street, she turned right onto Star Shine Drive and drove to acclimate to being back home. Gram's house was the second house from the end of the road. It wasn't the biggest house on the street but in her opinion, it certainly was the best. Three stories with shuttered windows on the first two floors and dormers on the top floor, which housed a large attic Lily and her sisters always loved to investigate. The front porch ran long and deep. The familiar porch furniture had been brought out in the spring as was always Gram's habit. Over the decades, it had gone from stylish to outdated to vintage. She could almost see Gram sitting there at the one end of the two-seater, a glass of lemonade in her hand, watching the people walk or cycle by, lifting her hand in a friendly wave. But tonight, the porch was empty.

The sky over the lake was sharp shades of red, pink, lavender, and blue. *Red sky at night, sailor's delight*, her grandmother always said.

It's going to be a beautiful day tomorrow, she thought as she sat there, taking the house in. A huge lump formed in her throat, and she pressed her lips together.

In the past when she'd pulled up to the house, the front door would be thrown open and Gram would appear, a kitchen towel in her hand. She'd lean over the railing with a big smile on her face. But not today. The house looked dark and aged. The white paint peeled in some places and the green shutters could use a fresh coat of paint. There were a few shrubs out front, but they looked in desperate need of a trim. She supposed Gram couldn't keep up; she'd been almost eighty.

But still, Lily had spent a lot of time in this house, especially during the summer months and even more so after her mother had died. With death came regret, regret for all the things you didn't do while the people you loved were alive. Things left unsaid. Words not spoken. Hugs not given. After Jamie had died, Gram urged her to come home for a visit, but Lily had promised her she'd come in the summer. As it was May, summer was almost here, but Gram was gone.

Too late.

A soft moan escaped Lily's lips as a lone tear slid down her cheek.

Home.

CHAPTER SIX

Junie

Junie no longer looked for Paul Reynolds when she and her friends walked up and down South Park Avenue in the evenings. She did have some pride. At first it had been hard, as it had become a habit, but she'd remind herself how she felt after he'd tossed that dime to her. Humiliated. And all because Thelma had opened her big fat trap. Junie still fumed over the memory. She didn't speak to Thelma for two weeks after that particular incident.

For reasons unknown even to her, she kept that dime when she should have tossed it away or spent it on penny candy at the corner store. She had tucked it away into the bottom drawer of her jewelry box and from time to time, she'd take it out and turn it around in her hand, studying it, like a talisman.

The first day of August, she woke late in the morning. She didn't bother getting dressed. She pressed her fingers to her eyes, feeling their puffiness. The previous night had been uncomfortable. The air was heavy with humidity, like a hot, wet blanket. She'd only just rolled out of bed, and she could already taste the fine, salty perspiration on her upper lip. Despite this, the day was overcast, and she knew her mother had been praying for rain to ease all their discomfort. She trotted down the stairs to the kitchen for a cup of tea and some breakfast.

As she grabbed the newel post at the bottom of the staircase and swung off the last step, she headed through the living room to the kitchen at the back of the house. She frowned when she saw her parents sitting at the kitchen table. They should have been at work. They never missed work. Her father smoked a cigarette and her mother stared at the inside of her teacup. The morning newspaper sat on one of the chairs, untouched. Her father's gaze was glued to a spot on the wall as if he were lost in thought. The fan blew in the living room, the constant metallic tick the only sound in the house, but there was no one there to avail of its relief.

Junie put the kettle on the stove and turned to her parents. With her hands on her hips she cracked, "Who died?" She took a teacup from the enamel drainboard and dried it with a dishtowel that hung from the rail on the stove.

Neither her mother nor her father answered right away. The ashtray in front of her father was filled with butts. Junie frowned as the kettle began its shrill whistle. The spout huffed as she lifted it off the stovetop and poured water over the teabag in her cup.

Ma spoke first. "Your sister"—her voice was choked, and she cleared her throat—"didn't come home last night."

Junie held the kettle midair on its return to the stove. She narrowed her eyes and tilted her head. "What do you mean? Where is she?"

Her mother shrugged. "We don't know. We've called all her friends. No one has seen her."

"We know where she is, Ceil," her father said grimly. "And who she's with."

Junie sucked in a lungful of air. Her sister was so selfish. So dramatic. She dumped sugar into her cup and topped it up with milk, then brought it to the enamel-topped table with its swirly designs and sat down, the backs of her thighs sticking to the red vinyl seat. There was a bakery box in the middle of the table. Junie immediately recognized the white box with its green print as belonging to Marshall's Bakery, located near the railroad tracks' overpass. Opening the flap, she spied a half dozen glazed donuts, the only kind she and her family ate. She helped herself to one, pulling it apart and dunking it into her tea.

"Junie," her father started, putting out his cigarette in the ashtray.

Junie glanced at her father. His eyes were lined and his face haggard. He looked so old; when had that happened? Even though she herself was only fourteen, the urge to strangle her older sister was strong.

"Promise me, Junie, you'll never run off with a man in the middle of the night." He paused, patting his shirt pocket for his pack of smokes. He tugged it out and tapped out another cigarette. "Once your reputation is ruined, there's no going back."

Junie swallowed hard and whispered, "I promise."

He nodded as if the subject were closed. He lit his cigarette and leaned his head on his hand, Junie forgotten.

Junie was different from Margaret. Always had been. Margaret was boy crazy.

She wasn't sure what to do. Her plans had been to meet Thelma and Barb over at the park. Thelma wanted to play some baseball and although Junie was no longer keen on playing sports with boys as they seemed too rough, she'd go anyway, if only for something to do. But now, she felt she couldn't leave her parents. She decided she'd wait with them. They hadn't asked her to leave so she felt it was okay.

It was while Junie was on her second cup of tea and her second donut that Margaret burst through the front door with Bill Jenner in tow. Even Junie looked at them in disbelief. Both of them acted as if nothing were wrong. In fact, they even appeared to be gloating about it, as if they were on their way to a picnic or something. Her father stood up, his chair scraping against the linoleum. He pulled up his suspenders and Junie watched wide-eyed as her father charged toward the front of the house with her mother on his heels, whispering, "Easy, Joe."

She'd never seen her father this angry.

Junie hung off her seat, craning her neck to see. Margaret was all smiles, her dark hair spilling softly around her shoulders. She wore a white dress with red polka dots and a red belt cinched her waist. Bill had his arm around that waist.

"You've got some nerve walking into my house smiling after you keep my daughter out all night!" her father yelled.

What happened next was so unbelievable that if Junie hadn't seen it for herself, she wouldn't have believed it.

Her father hauled back and punched Bill Jenner right on the chin, and Bill went staggering back, hitting the doorframe.

"Daddy! No!" Margaret shrieked, reaching out for her father. Ma gasped.

Bill regained his balance and massaged his jaw, wincing. Margaret stood in front of him, her arm out as if she could protect him from the rage of her father.

"Daddy, Bill and I got married last night," she said.

Junie's father and mother stood there speechless, gape-jawed, crumbling.

It was her mother who recovered first. "How? You're not eighteen."

Margaret lifted her chin a bit. "We drove to Erie last night."

The age requirement to get married in Pennsylvania was lower than in New York State. Two years ago, their neighbor's daughter had also run away to Erie to get married. A week later, her father dropped dead from a heart attack. Junie narrowed her eyes at her sister and thought if Ma or Daddy died suddenly because of her sister's selfishness, she'd punch her herself.

"You got a certificate?" her father grilled Bill. There was a grim set to his mouth, as if he'd tasted something he didn't care for.

"Yes, sir," Bill said, keeping out of arm's reach. He pulled out his wallet from his back pocket and tugged a folded sheet of paper from it, handing it to Junie's dad.

Daddy appeared to study the certificate, and then he folded it neatly and tucked it into his shirt pocket. He lifted his head. "Right. Ceil, get your handbag. We're going to take a nice drive to Erie and make sure they really did get married."

CHAPTER SEVEN

Lily

Lily sat for a moment, taking in the sight of Gram's house. A red, yellow, and orange-striped beach towel hung over the porch railing. A small faded flag with a sun and flower and the word 'Spring' fluttered from its pole on the porch post.

The front door opened slowly and her sister Alice appeared on the porch.

Charlie whined behind her.

Alice folded her arms and looked at Lily. Slowly, Lily stepped out of her car and opened the back door for Charlie to get out.

Lily approached her sister slowly.

Alice looked well. She'd been favored with an enviable abundance of curly red hair. Lily had been blessed—or not—with pale, thin blonde hair. The slight breeze blowing in off the lake lifted it gently off of Lily's neck.

Charlie reached Alice before she did, and she lavished him with attention.

"Hello, Charlie, how are you?" Alice said.

Hesitantly, Lily climbed the stairs.

In the past, her relationship with her sisters had been fractious, especially as teenagers, and as time went on, Lily always thought it best to keep them at arm's length. But Alice broke into a wide smile and opened her arms and this time, Lily didn't hesitate, stepping into them and wrapping her arms around her younger sister. She squeezed her eyes shut, but heavy tears still escaped.

"Alice," Lily said with a wobble in her voice.

"I know," Alice said with a sigh, her own voice shaky. They hugged each other tightly.

When they pulled apart, Lily kept her hands on Alice's arms and searched her face. There was evidence of crying in the puffy pillows beneath Alice's eyes, but her complexion was clear, and her eyes were as blue as the lake behind them.

"You look well," Lily said truthfully.

"As well as can be expected," Alice said with a shaky laugh.

Lily nodded. "I know. Is Isabelle here?"

"She'll be here later."

"Where was she?"

"She was in Ireland," Alice said.

Lily frowned. "What was she doing there?"

"Backpacking through the United Kingdom and Ireland," Alice explained.

Before Lily could comment, the front door opened and Gram's friend Thelma pushed through. The years had piled up on Thelma. Although not blood relatives, Gram and Thelma practically considered themselves cousins. They'd grown up together and moved out to Hideaway Bay permanently at different times in their lives, for different reasons, but their friendship always remained intact. It had always been the three of them: Gram, Thelma, and their other friend, Barb.

Thelma pulled Lily into a rough embrace, a feature of the older woman's Lily had forgotten about. Thelma had always been rough around the edges, but she had a good heart.

"I can't believe it," Thelma said into Lily's shoulder. Lily breathed in Thelma's perfume, Nina Ricci's L'Air du Temps. Her grandmother claimed Thelma had been wearing that fragrance since 1966.

When Lily pulled away, she searched Thelma's face and asked, "Had Gram been sick?"

Thelma shook her head. "No, not at all. In fact, I thought she was in better shape than me."

Lily supposed at Gram's age—almost eighty—just about anything could happen.

Thelma lowered her head and shook it. "I can't believe she's gone! I've known her all my life. Our mothers were best friends." A loud, pathetic sob emerged from somewhere deep within Thelma that made Lily's heart ache. She pulled the older woman back into her embrace and rubbed her back. Lily cast a glance over Thelma's shoulder at her sister. Alice wore a pained expression on her face and reached out, laying her hand on Thelma's arm. "Come on, let's go inside and have something to eat."

Thelma wiped her eyes with the back of her hand and nodded toward Charlie. "What on earth is that?"

Lily smiled. "That's my dog, Charlie."

Thelma swung her head around to Lily. "Dog? I thought he was a horse or a small pony."

"Nope, he's just a gentle giant."

Thelma looked suspicious. "That's what they all say." And then she muttered, "Until they're jumping on you and tackling you to the ground."

With her arm around Thelma's waist, they followed Alice into the house. Not much had changed in all the years Gram and Granddad had lived here. Looking around, Lily's eyes misted, and a lump formed in her throat. So many memories. An image of her mother flashed before her eyes. She'd died young, here in this house, before the age of fifty from breast cancer. Prior to Jamie's death, that had been the most painful time in

Lily's life. After Mom had died, they had all leaned on Gram, and now Gram wasn't there to lean on anymore. It made her feel adrift and rudderless.

Lily had heard the stories growing up about how Granddad had bought this place for Gram and how they'd planned to retire to Hideaway Bay but ended up out here permanently when Lily's mother was a young girl.

The front room still had its floral and striped wallpaper, and the mantel around the fireplace was painted a robin's egg blue. The shelves that flanked either side of the fireplace were crammed with books. A rocker stood in the corner next to the fireplace, and an afghan of colorful granny squares hung over the back of the red corduroy sofa. Women's magazines were stacked in a wooden rack next to the sofa.

Charlie jumped up on the sofa and stood there. This was a bad habit of his, which Lily was trying to break him of. She gently tugged Charlie's collar to get him down and said firmly, "Off." The dog stumbled to the floor and took off, his nails clicking against the hardwood floor, and he thudded into the end table, causing it to teeter. Lily stretched out her hand and caught the lamp before it fell to the floor.

"You've done this before," Thelma observed with a smile.

"Once or twice," Lily said. Poor Charlie had no spatial perception regarding where he was in relation to his surrounding environment.

Alice led the way to the kitchen at the back of the large house. Charlie, in an effort to be first, raced past Lily and Thelma, causing Thelma to lose her balance, but Lily put her hands out and righted her.

"Gentle giant, huh?"

Lily was apologetic but it fell on deaf ears as Thelma waved it away with a laugh. "Don't worry about it. He's certainly entertaining."

The narrow, white-paneled hallway ran between the living room and the kitchen, and off that hallway there was a dining room. The paneled walls were covered in framed pictures. The center photo was a black-and-white shot of Gram and Granddad on their wedding day. Lily always thought they'd looked so happy. There was a big eight by ten of Lily and her sisters with their mother when they were young. Lily studied it briefly. She guessed it was taken right after their father took off. Isabelle was probably eleven, she'd been nine, and Alice had to be about three. There were pictures of Gram's life, and that included photos of Lily's mother, Nancy, as a baby, and her high school senior portrait. An old black-and-white photo of Gram's older sister, Margaret, also hung on the wall. The walls on both sides were covered. Lily kept moving; she couldn't linger, not in that narrow hallway with all those memories pressing in on her from both sides. Keep moving, that's what she'd always told herself. Just keep moving and don't get stuck in any one place.

The cabinets in the large kitchen at the back of the house had been painted white, and the walls had been painted a bright, sunny yellow. There were fussy, frilly curtains at the window that Lily remembered from her childhood, with a small valance running along the top and a half curtain along the bottom half of the window. Gram had two sets: one for summer and one for winter. The summer ones were white eyelet with strawberries on them, and the winter ones were bright orange.

Lily raised her eyebrows. "Something smells good."

"Your sister has been cooking and baking up a storm since she arrived yesterday," Thelma told her.

Alice reappeared and said, "You know how it is with grief. It's either cooking or cleaning. I chose cooking." She paused, taking small plates out of the cabinet and setting them on the table. "Besides, because I work so much, I never get a chance to bake as much as I'd like to."

"That's how you stay so thin," Thelma remarked.

Lily sat at the old table that had been a wedding present to her grandparents from Granddad's aunt. She'd never seen a table like it before or since. It was round, mother of pearl with a gold leaf design running along the edges. It was a beautiful, unique piece of furniture.

"How long are you back for?" Lily asked.

"I've taken a few weeks' personal time," Alice answered.

Lily didn't know how she felt about that but said nothing. She'd planned on staying a few weeks herself after the funeral. She hoped they wouldn't get in each other's way. Or maybe she would go back home right after the funeral. It wasn't written in stone that she had to stay.

"Are you hungry?" Alice asked.

"I am, actually."

"Great! I've got that cheese dip Gram always used to make," Alice said, heading toward the refrigerator.

"The one with the Velveeta cheese and the Rotel tomatoes?" Lily smiled.

"That's the one." Alice nodded.

"Your grandmother always liked her snacks," Thelma recalled fondly.

Alice pulled a bowl out of the refrigerator and popped it into the microwave. Lily watched as her sister pulled another bowl, a pink Pyrex one, from the upper shelf of the cabinet. She opened a bag of tortilla chips and filled the bowl.

"I haven't had that in years," Lily said about the dip.

Gram had been famous for cutting out recipes from women's magazines and the inside Sunday circulars and trying different recipes. In the summer, they'd sit out on the porch on the wicker furniture with their feet up on the glass-topped coffee table, eating chips and dip. The favorites had been the Rotel dip; bacon, lettuce, and tomato dip; and a spinach dip.

"Can I help?" Lily asked.

"Nah, I got it," Alice replied.

Alice laid a saucer with dipping oil onto the table and brought over a tray with bits and pieces of crusty bread.

"Would you believe there's a gourmet olive oil shop in Hideaway Bay?" Alice asked.

"Get out," Lily said in disbelief.

"It's where Milchmann's grocery store was, right next to the five-and-dime," Thelma said.

"Milchmann's is gone?" Lily asked.

That little mom-and-pop grocery store had been there for as long as she could remember. Mr. Milchmann was lovely, but Mrs. Milchmann always gave the impression that she'd rather be doing anything else than tending the store.

Thelma nodded. "He died ten years ago and Mrs. Milchmann sold the store so fast it would have made your head spin."

"Is she still in town?"

Thelma shook her head. "Nope. Arizona."

Lily took a piece of crusty bread, dipped it into the small saucer of olive oil, and popped it into her mouth. Charlie parked himself next to Lily's chair and looked at the table full of food longingly. But Lily didn't feed him from the table. Besides, he'd eaten not too long ago. But Thelma took some bread and held her hand under the table, and the dog spotted it and relocated next to Thelma. Lily said nothing.

Lily looked around the kitchen and the table, finding all the familiar things both comforting and nostalgic. There was the small mint green sugar bowl at the edge of the table next to the window. She lifted out the spoon and smiled. It had originally been her mother's baby spoon. Her initials, NMR, were carved in the handle. *Nancy Marie Reynolds.*

While the microwave heated the cheese dip, Alice brought over a platter of brownies.

"Brownies?" Lily asked with the lift of an eyebrow.

Alice always did have a sweet tooth, even as a child. She'd always wanted to be taken down to the deli to get candy or ice cream. Granddad used to indulge her. He used to spoil all of them. An image of Granddad walking her and Isabelle up to the corner for ice cream cones flashed through Lily's mind. She could still see her pink and blue sunsuit and her plastic kids' sunglasses and smell the suntan lotion that seemed to be present everywhere.

"Salted caramel ones," Alice said. She returned to the counter when the microwave pinged, and she removed the bowl, giving the cheese dip a good stir with a large spoon. She carried both over to the table.

Alice disappeared to the back hall and returned with three cans of Coke, carrying them over to the table. Lily jumped up, pulled down three glass tumblers, and filled them with ice.

"What happened to Gram?" Lily asked, sitting back down, taking a chip, and scooping up some warm cheese dip. The smell of pimentos was strong. She closed her eyes and inhaled. It was a comforting memory from childhood. She remembered her mother had loved this dip as well.

"Maybe we should wait until Isabelle gets here so I only have to tell the story once," Thelma said, helping herself to a brownie. Lily looked at her, realizing it wasn't Thelma being tough that made her hesitate, but the pain it would cause her in having to relive the event twice.

"Sure, Thelma," Lily said. Alice sat across the table from them, enamored with her brownie.

Lily poured soda into their glasses. When she'd filled Thelma's glass halfway, the older woman put up her hand and said, "That's enough, it gives me gas."

Lily bit her lip, trying not to chuckle. She'd forgotten how blunt—and funny—Thelma could be.

"Did you know Sue Ann Nelson—er, Marchek, is back in Hideaway Bay?" Thelma said, referring to the daughter of hers and Gram's friend Barb.

Both Lily and Alice nodded.

"Gram mentioned it last year when Sue Ann arrived here," Alice said.

"Is she staying in Hideaway Bay?" Lily asked, helping herself to more bread dipped in oil.

Thelma nodded. "She is. Been here almost a year and a half now. She's renovated the whole cottage, got a divorce, and is involved in all sorts of community affairs here in Hideaway Bay."

"Wow," Alice said. "That must have been a big change. Gram said she lived a wealthy lifestyle in Florida."

"She did, but she'll be the first one to tell you she's happier in Hideaway Bay."

"She used to babysit us. A lot," Lily said with a laugh. "We'd walk down to Milchmann's for candy and we were always barefoot, and Mrs. Milchmann wouldn't let us into the store without our shoes."

"We had to go back home, get the shoes, and walk back." Alice finished the story.

"It seemed a lot of effort for a few pieces of candy," Lily said, appearing thoughtful.

"Always worth it, though."

Lily turned to Thelma and asked, "How's Don and the girls?" referring to Thelma's only child, Don, and his two daughters, Maria and Julia, or Jules as everyone had always called her. Lily had spent a lot of time with Thelma's granddaughters growing up.

"They're all well. Don's getting ready to retire. He's got his thirty years in teaching, and he and Elaine are heading off to Arizona."

"Oh, wow." She hadn't realized Don was retirement age. But she supposed he would be. Don had been Thelma's pride and joy and had done well for himself.

"And Maria and Jules are all right. They're still living here in town, which is nice because I get to see them all the time."

"That's great. I'd love to see them," Alice said. She and Jules had gone to school together.

As Lily was helping herself to a brownie and thinking how wonderful it was that if you listened really hard, you could still hear the surf as long as the windows were open. She tilted her head to the side and listened. From the front of the house came the sound of a car door slamming.

Lily looked around. "Someone's here."

"It's probably Isabelle," Alice said, setting her brownie down on her plate.

Both of them stood up at the same time and headed toward the front of the house. Charlie got up from where he had stretched out near Thelma's chair and trotted after them.

Lily stepped out first onto the wide porch, followed by Alice and Thelma. Charlie stood by Lily's side, his head resting on the porch rail. He gave a half-hearted woof.

Their oldest sister, Isabelle, was at the back of her rental SUV, lifting up the back door and pulling out a small suitcase.

She wore a long denim dress with a heavy, oversized cardigan and big, gold hoop earrings. Isabelle still had a marvelous mane of hair, like Alice. But whereas Alice's was red, Isabelle's was dark, almost black, like Gram's hair used to be when she was a young woman. It was now pulled up into a messy bun. The tallest of the three sisters, Isabelle had always had a goddess quality about her, or at least that's what Lily had always thought. Isabelle had looks that had both taken her places and gotten her in trouble. The high cheekbones, the dark almond-shaped eyes, the pouty mouth. For a long time, Lily had felt like the consolation prize compared to Izzy.

But despite being the oldest sister, she had been the rebel, the least traditional of the three. Over the course of her life, she had traveled extensively all over the world, never setting roots down anywhere. There was one Christmas where Isabelle had pulled up on the back of a Harley with a member of a motorcycle club, the two of them decked out in leather. It had practically given Gram a heart attack, and it had caused a lot of friction between Isabelle and their mother. The visit was cut short, and Isabelle left before New Year's Eve the way she came in, roaring out of town on the back of the bike.

At times, Lily thought her selfish. Isabelle always did what pleased Isabelle and she spared no one's feelings. Personally, she was surprised when Isabelle had flown in for Jamie's funeral. She hadn't really expected her to come out to California for that.

Their oldest sister gave a slight wave and pulled her suitcase behind her with her other hand.

Lily and Alice stepped off the porch tentatively.

Isabelle's smile appeared to falter and as she got closer, Lily thought her sister looked tired. But despite fatigue and something else—stress? Worry? Anxiety?—grief was etched on her face.

"Well, here we are," Isabelle said. And then she surprised them all by bursting into tears and pretty soon, all three sisters were locked in an embrace, crying and hanging on to each other.

CHAPTER EIGHT

1958

Junie

"**M**argaret! What do you expect me to do?" Junie said into the phone. She sat on a stool in the short alcove tucked between the kitchen and the living room, staring at the walls. Years ago, on a phone call, her father had had no paper handy and had written a phone number in pencil on the wall. That phone number was still there, as were hundreds of numbers and messages that had been added through the years.

She'd been on the phone for five minutes with Margaret, who begged Junie to come over.

It had been a year since Margaret eloped with Bill. A tumultuous year. The newlyweds weren't content to keep their drama behind closed doors, choosing instead to let it play out all over the south side of the city, much to the chagrin of her parents. It was all too much for Junie.

"Please, Junie," Margaret wailed into the phone. "He's on his way home! I'm afraid . . ."

"What am I going to do?" Junie demanded. "I'm only fifteen!"

"I know, but please."

"Should I get Daddy to come over?" Junie asked. She felt this was definitely a situation where an adult was required, not some teenager in saddle shoes.

"Never mind," Margaret snapped and hung up.

Junie walked back to the kitchen and glanced up at the clock. She was supposed to meet up with Thelma and Barb at the playground. They'd started playing cards there in the afternoons. But she bit her lip, the sound of Margaret's voice echoing in her head. She'd never heard her sister so afraid. Finally, with a big sigh, she gave up and headed out the front door, closing it behind her. She patted her pocket for her house key, jumped off the porch, and walked in the direction of her sister's house.

Margaret and Bill had rented an apartment in a two-family home. They lived in the space upstairs. It was a four-block walk and Junie was in no hurry to step into the middle of her sister's domestic squabble. For the life of her, she couldn't understand how her sister put up with her husband's temper. They'd certainly not been raised like that. Daddy had never shown his temper on a regular basis like Bill Jenner. If that were so, Junie would have hated living at home.

Relief washed over her when she didn't spot Bill's car parked out front on the tree-lined street. Hopefully, he wasn't on his way, either, despite what Margaret said.

Junie went in through the side door, finding herself in the common hallway of the two homes, and she bounded up the staircase. The door to her sister's apartment was wide open, and she stepped inside the kitchen. The apartment was neat and tidy. You could say a lot about Margaret, but one thing you couldn't fault her on was her cleaning. Junie didn't remember her bedroom at home being so neat, recalling an unmade bed and clothes strewn all over the place on more than one occasion. Maybe marriage changed you.

It irritated her that Margaret had called her to come over and then was nowhere to be found. Why did she want her to come over if she hadn't planned on hanging around? Junie had better things to do than get caught up in her sister's melodrama.

"Margaret?" she called out into the silence. When there was no answer, she called out louder, "Margaret?"

"I'm in here," came a muffled voice from the back bedroom.

Tentatively, Junie pivoted and made her way down the short hallway to the bedrooms at the back of the apartment. The first was a spare room that housed only a desk and a chair. It looked as if it was never used. The second was Margaret and Bill's bedroom. There was a suite of maple furniture: bed, dresser, and bureau. Junie noticed that the bed was made and that a perfume tray and a silver hairbrush, comb, and hand mirror were carefully arranged on the dresser, but that was about it.

When she still didn't see her sister, she called out again. "Margaret, where are you?"

"I'm here, under the bed," her sister cried, her voice muffled.

Junie dropped to her knees, lifted the bedspread, and peered beneath the bed. There was Margaret, now a grown woman, all squashed up like a child playing hide-and-seek.

"What are you doing under there?" Junie asked. Gosh but her sister sure was peculiar.

Margaret ignored her. "Is he here?" she hissed.

"No, no one's here but me," Junie said. "Will you come out?"

Before her sister could reply, the air was punctuated by the sound of a door slamming downstairs and heavy footsteps thundering up the back staircase.

"Hurry, get up, Junie. Don't let him know I'm here, he'll kill me," Margaret pleaded. She waved Junie away.

Even in the dim light under the bed, Junie did not miss the expression of fear on her sister's face.

Junie jumped up, lowered the bedspread, and smoothed it out. She turned around and stood, the back of her legs against the bed.

"Margaret!" came the shout from the kitchen.

Junie didn't move. Her mouth went dry, and her heart thudded against her chest. She could hear Bill coming down the hall, shouting her sister's name. His voice was thick and coarse.

Her brother-in-law pulled up short in the doorway of the bedroom. If he was surprised to see her, he didn't show it, but in his current state it would have been hard to tell.

Bill Jenner was considered a neat, well-kept man, but now he appeared anything but. His shirt was unbuttoned, revealing his T-shirt beneath it. There was a stain on one of the knees of his pants. His hair was mussed, and there was a good two days' worth of stubble on his face. Junie stared at him, her mouth hanging open. The yeasty smell of beer was strong on him.

But it was his eyes. They were wild, as if they could see but didn't. For the first time in her life, Junie was scared. She wondered if Bill even knew what he was doing. Or who she was.

"Where's Margaret?" he demanded. There was no hello, no question as to what she was doing there. Nothing.

"I . . . I . . . don't know," Junie stammered. "She's not here."

"Why are you here?" he barked.

She'd never seen him like this. He was usually quiet whenever he showed up at her parents' house. This was a side to him she would have preferred not to witness. "I was walking back from Park Edge when I thought I'd stop and see if Margaret was in," she said hastily. The speed at which she manufactured the lie stunned her. But she supposed in this situation, it was not only necessary but mandated.

His nostrils flared and for a split second, Junie was afraid he might strike her. But instead, he pushed past her to the closet, where he pulled open the doors and pushed the clothes along the rack, hangers rattling. Dissatisfied, he brushed past her again, glancing in the other bedroom, then opening the bathroom door and pulling back the shower curtain. He slammed the bathroom door closed and stomped out of the apartment. Junie held her breath at the sound of his retreating footsteps. Her heart pounded. Once she heard the slam of a car door outside and the turning over of its engine, she let out the breath she was holding and sank down onto the floor next to the bed. "Oh, Margaret, how do you live like this?"

CHAPTER NINE

Lily

Isabelle took her belongings upstairs to her old room, promising she'd be down soon. They'd all settled in their old rooms. The house had five bedrooms. Gram and Granddad had hoped to have a lot of children but after Nancy had been born, there had been no more. Disheartened at first, they got on with life and made the best of things. At least that's what Gram had told Lily.

Lily, Alice, and Thelma moved from the kitchen to the front porch. Lily helped Alice carry out the snacks and a pitcher of sweet iced tea and tall glasses while Isabelle settled in upstairs. When she re-joined them, she collapsed in the white wicker rocker. Thelma had seated herself in the other rocker, while Lily and Alice sat next to each other on the wicker two-seater. Lily poured glasses of iced tea and passed them around. Isabelle helped herself to a brownie, taking a bite. Part of it crumbled and fell off, but she caught it before it fell to the ground.

"I see you're still baking, Alice," Isabelle said.

"I am, and I see you're still traveling," Alice said.

Isabelle nodded. "You know me, loaded with wanderlust."

Lily regarded her older sister. Isabelle was the antithesis of all those books that claimed your birth order affected your personality. She was not oldest-sister material. She did not take charge, boss anyone around, or try to keep the family together. Instead, she traveled all over the world, going where the wind blew her. Lily didn't think she'd ever owned a house or a car. Her limited knowledge of her sister's itinerary made her sad. But she knew some things, like how her sister had spent time in Costa Rica saving the turtles or something like that. And how she'd learned how to make homemade pizza when she worked in a restaurant in Naples, and one summer, she'd climbed Mount Kilimanjaro for a charitable cause.

Isabelle turned her gaze on Thelma and asked, "So what happened to Gram?"

Thelma sighed, leaning back and rocking her chair gently. She sipped from her iced tea before speaking.

"Your grandmother went for her morning walk on the beach, like she did every day."

"Still at the crack of dawn?" Alice asked.

Thelma nodded. "Old habits die hard. Anyway, apparently the guy that owns the gym was out for his morning run and he saw her go down. By the time he reached her, she was unconscious, and he ran for the doctor." Thelma's voice wobbled but she recovered quickly. "We've got a new doctor now, young and with lots of newfangled ideas."

Lily wondered what Thelma considered "newfangled," possibly incorporating holistic methods instead of the usual cut-back-on-the-salt routine.

"Dr. Morrison ran down immediately—he's living in the old Brentwood house—and started CPR, but it was too late. She was gone."

They all went quiet for a moment, each lost in their own thoughts. There was some comfort in the fact that Gram had died on the beach, the place she loved most in the world. Or at least that's what Lily thought. Once Gram had settled in Hideaway Bay, she never traveled outside of it. When Lily had asked her about it once, she had laughed and said, "Why would I leave Hideaway Bay when everything I love is right here?"

"You'll need to call the funeral home to make an appointment to make arrangements," Thelma said.

For a moment, none of the three sisters said anything, until Lily spoke up. "I'll call them when I go inside."

"Is Old Man Reidy still running the funeral home?" Isabelle asked. She leaned back in her chair, crossing one leg over the other. She had kicked her sandals off and her feet were bare. "He was old twenty-five years ago when Granddad died."

"No, he's gone, died. His son took over the business," Thelma informed them.

"Jordan Reidy?" Lily asked. She'd gone to high school with him, but any recollections of him were vague and hazy. Their paths hadn't crossed much, as they moved in different circles.

Thelma nodded.

"Who would pick mortuary science as a career?" Isabelle asked, making a face of distaste.

"It's a good thing somebody does, or we'd be in big trouble," Thelma said.

"Has anyone called Stephen and Peter?" Lily asked, referring to Gram's nephews. They were the sons of Gram's sister, Margaret, who had been dead a long time.

"I'll call them," Alice said. "I'm sure Gram has their numbers around here somewhere."

"Stephen and Peter came out to see your grandmother at Christmas," Thelma said.

"That's right, Gram told me that," Lily said, acutely aware that Gram's own granddaughters hadn't made it out to see her during the holidays, but her nephews had. After her sister's death, Gram had remained close to her nephews.

"You know how they felt about her," Thelma said. "They were so young when their mother died, and Junie insisted they spend their summers out here with her and Paul and Nancy. They always wanted a houseful of kids. And they had it."

Lily swallowed the lump in her throat. That was Gram, looking after everyone. How had it all fallen apart, with her immediate family flung to the far corners of the globe?

The three sisters left the funeral home the following morning, stepping outside into the morning sun and standing there for a moment to collect themselves. All three were quiet, their eyes red.

Initially it had all gone well. But then they'd disagreed on the casket. Alice had wanted the one with the pink satin lining, Isabelle had wanted the blue one, and Lily couldn't decide. Jordan Reidy stepped in and suggested the one with the magnolia-colored satin lining as a compromise. and Lily and her sisters agreed to that. Then they couldn't agree on the type of memorial card: one with a photo of Gram or one with a poem and a neutral photo of a garden or a landscape.

Finally, as Alice and Isabelle went back and forth about it, Lily interrupted and asked, "Can we have both? Half and half? But instead of a garden scene, do you have a beach scene?"

Alice and Isabelle went quiet, then said, "Yes, something like that."

They managed to get things sorted out without ending up at each other's throats.

No matter what, Lily wanted to keep the peace. She didn't want to be fighting with her sisters while they buried Gram. Gram wouldn't have wanted that.

The wake was scheduled for the next day, and the funeral the day after that at the local church with burial following in the local cemetery. Gram would be buried next to Granddad and close to their daughter, who was also buried there. Lily hadn't been to her mother's grave in years. She thought of buying some flowers and taking them over.

"So that's what funeral directors look like these days," Isabelle observed as they headed in the direction of town. She perched her big, floppy sun hat on her head.

There had been a burst of unusually hot weather for May. The mercury had sailed north of eighty degrees and the forecast had showed no end in sight.

Alice burst out laughing, and even Lily had to smile.

Alice wore a long pale-green maxi dress edged in lace. Her abundance of hair was held back loosely with ribbon. Lily always thought she looked like she'd stepped out of a BBC adaptation of a Jane Austen book.

"I don't remember him looking like that in high school," Lily observed. Somewhere along the way, Jordan Reidy had certainly blossomed, if that's what the men of the species did. He was tall and blond and looked like he got the most out of his membership at the local gym. He'd been kind and solicitous to the three of them. If she were someone who was interested in a man, and if she hadn't been recently widowed, and if she hadn't been so badly let down by her late husband, the funeral director would have ticked a lot of boxes.

Isabelle scrunched up her nose. "Too young."

Lily laughed. "Too young? He's my age."

"You know my rule, I never date anyone younger than myself," Isabelle said firmly.

"Why?" Lily didn't admit that she hadn't known that rule about her sister. How could she? She barely saw her or spoke to her. The air felt tinged with sadness. There was so much she didn't know about her sisters.

She wondered if they felt adrift like she did. Gram had been an anchor for the whole family, a beacon in the night. Even though she lived far away, there was comfort in knowing that Gram was always there.

Gram's death affected her differently than Jamie's had. They were hardly comparable, she conceded. She hadn't known Jamie for as long as she'd known Gram, and

Gram hadn't ever let her down the way Jamie had. But still, Jamie was her husband and his unexpected death had shocked her.

"Do you guys want to explore the town a little? Maybe get a coffee and something to eat?" Alice asked. She shielded her eyes against the late-morning sun.

"Please! This place is a little too sleepy for me," Isabelle said. "If I stay here any longer than I have to, I'm going to slip into a coma."

That barbed remark prickled Lily's skin, and her nostrils flared. She stopped walking and stood there in the middle of the sidewalk. Alice's eyes widened, and she looked down at the ground as if there might be coffee and cake to be found down there.

But Isabelle stood with her hands on her hips, looking around, still clueless.

"Look, if you've got more important things to do, Alice and I can handle it from here on out," Lily said, feeling heat in her cheeks that had nothing to do with the increasing warmth of the day.

Isabelle turned to look at her, about to retort, when Lily cut her off. "And you don't go into a coma from a small, quiet town. Car accidents maybe, but not small beach towns."

Isabelle paled. "Oh sh—I'm so sorry, Lily, that was cruel and thoughtless of me." She reached out, but Lily brushed past her.

"Come on, let's get coffee. Or something stronger." Tears pricked the backs of Lily's eyes as she remembered why she didn't speak to her sisters or even bother keeping in touch with them.

She marched down the sidewalk, taking in all the little shops and boutiques of Hideaway Bay. After a few minutes, she settled down and said over her shoulder, "I don't remember all these shops being here."

"Me neither," Isabelle said.

There was even a holiday-themed shop titled *Ye Olde Christmas Shoppe*. It had a solid red awning with a green wreath on it. Lily couldn't imagine it being successful in a beach town. There were three dress shops and an ice cream parlor, and quite a few restaurants.

"Is that a fusion restaurant?" Isabelle asked, pointing down the street.

"Who knew?" Alice said. "Hideaway Bay has become hip and trendy."

There was also a bookstore farther down the street and the seafood restaurants that had been there forever. Lily immediately looked for the Old Red Top, an old building with a red conical roof at the other end of the beach parking lot. It had been run by Stanley Schumacher and had the best Texas hots anywhere. But that had closed down when Stanley died.

"Wow, the place has really had a facelift," Isabelle noted.

"I'll say," Alice agreed. "Look, there's that new café I heard about. Let's go in there."

"Do they serve wine?" Isabelle asked.

"Wine?" Alice snorted. "At eleven o'clock in the morning?"

Isabelle leveled her gaze at her. "Don't knock it till you've tried it."

Alice threw up her hands in mock defense. "Sorry."

"Come on, maybe we'll feel better after some coffee," Lily said.

They were interrupted by someone calling their names.

"Isabelle! Lily! Alice!" called a female voice behind them.

Curious, all three sisters turned around. Lily squinted her eyes to get a better look, and a smile spread across her face when she recognized Sue Ann Marchek, the daughter of Gram's friend Barb.

"Oh my God! Sue Ann!" Isabelle squealed, and she ran to her and hugged her. Lily and Alice followed suit.

A few years younger than she was, they hadn't hung around Sue Ann while they were growing up, but she used to babysit for them a lot during the summers when she was home with her mother.

Sue Ann hugged each one of them in turn and offered her condolences for Gram's death.

"I can't believe Junie is gone," she said, and her eyes filled with tears. "She and Thelma were the first people I called on when I came back to Hideaway Bay. I've seen them regularly since then."

"So, you've settled back in?" Isabelle said.

Sue Ann nodded. "I've been here for almost eighteen months now."

She was an attractive woman, not quite fifty, with highlighted blond hair. She reached out for Lily's hand and said, "I heard that you lost your husband, and I want to say how sorry I am."

A lump formed in Lily's throat, which tended to happen when anyone mentioned Jamie. Although it was no longer fresh or raw, it still hurt and remained just below the surface. All of it. "Thank you, Sue Ann."

Sue Ann studied the three of them. "You've all grown into beautiful women." She wagged a finger at Alice. "I remember changing your diapers!"

The three sisters laughed, happy to be reunited with their old acquaintance.

"Are you here for a while?" she asked them.

"I'm leaving right after the funeral," Isabelle said.

Lily had not known this and by the look on Alice's face, she hadn't either.

But Alice recovered and said, "I can only stay three weeks and then I have to get back to my job in Chicago. But Lily might stay for a bit."

"That would be lovely," Sue Ann said to Lily.

Lily nodded. It was wonderful to see Sue Ann; she was a link to their past and to Gram and her friends. "We're going out for coffee; would you join us?"

"I'd love to, but I've got plans for the afternoon. But if it's okay, I might stop by and visit you at the house."

They all nodded, and Lily hoped she would. "I'll look forward to it. Stop by anytime."

Isabelle told Sue Ann about the funeral arrangements, and Sue Ann replied, "I'll be there."

After the three of them hugged her goodbye, they waited until she had walked down the street, looking after her, smiling.

"Boy, it was good to see her," Isabelle said. "Hard to believe she used to babysit us. I used to think she was so cool and so pretty. All the boys liked her. She used to do my hair. I wanted to wear it like hers, but it was like mission impossible." She lifted her heavy locks.

"Come on, let's get coffee," Lily said.

The three of them stepped off the curb, looking both ways, and trotted across the street. Before they even hit the curb on the other side, they were hit full force with the smell of fresh brewed coffee and baked goods. The café had a green striped awning and a moss green sign in the shape of a teacup with brown lettering that read *Chat and Nibble.*

It seemed almost normal to Lily that she and her sisters would go for a coffee. Wasn't this what most sisters did? Didn't sisters who got along hang out with each other? She thought of all the times she'd gone for coffee with Diana and Cheryl and never given it a second thought. Yet here, back home in Hideaway Bay, it seemed strange and unfamiliar. But maybe her sisters felt the same way. It was a shame that her relationship with her sisters was anything but normal.

CHAPTER TEN

1960

Junie

Junie had to admit to being bored. How many times could they spend their summer evenings walking up and down South Park Avenue, covering the same area, block after block, always waiting for something to happen and nothing ever did? For the past six weeks since they got out of school for the summer, the routine had rarely varied. It was the same scenery, night after night: cars rolling by, the green patina of the great copper dome of the Basilica to the south, and houses and bars around them. The lake was to the west but there were no glimpses of that from where they were. Besides, hulking giants of steel and other industry dominated the waterfront. The highlight of their evenings was a stop to get an ice cream cone, where invariably Stanley Schumacher would show up and shout something suggestive to Thelma, who would put him in his place. She never thought she'd say it, but she didn't think she could eat another ice cream cone. She'd switched over to hot fudge sundaes, but she noticed the waistband on her shorts was getting tight. It might be time to cut back on the trips to the ice cream stand.

The three of them stood on a street corner six blocks from Junie's house. Thelma had her hand fisted and stared at her fingernails as if they were the most fascinating things in the world. Barb had her arms behind her, her hands latched, a position that was individual to her. She'd been spending a lot of time out at their house at Hideaway Bay and as a result, her skin had gone the color of fawn. She wore a pair of mint green shorts and a pink shirt. Junie gazed southward down the street. A Chevy approached them with a bunch of guys hanging out of it. The car idled, the guys yelling things at a group of girls as they walked on the sidewalk. Smartly, the girls slipped into the drugstore and the Chevy sped up, heading in their direction. Not wanting to stand around and become their next target, Junie said, "Come on, let's keep moving."

"We could go to the show and see *From the Terrace*," Barb said. Barb's longstanding crush on Kirk Douglas had been transferred to Paul Newman.

"How many times have you seen that movie now? Five times?" Thelma asked, slapping her hands on her hips.

Barb shrugged. "I don't know. Five or six."

Thelma snorted. "If we're going to go see a movie we've already seen, let's go see *Psycho*."

Barb grimaced.

Thelma rolled her eyes. "Oh, that's right, you don't do horror. Horror to you is when the maid calls off sick and you've got to lay out your own clothes."

"We don't *have* a maid," Barb said loudly, clearly displeased. "We have a housekeeper."

"Is there really a difference?" Thelma asked with a snort. "In my house, I'm the chief cook and bottle washer."

Barb's eyes narrowed with fury, and she went to say something, but Junie laid her hand on her arm.

"Come on, you guys, stop bickering," Junie pleaded. If she had to listen to any more of it, she was going to call it a night and head home and watch television with her parents.

They walked for two blocks, strolling along in silence, Thelma leading the way with Junie and Barb following side by side. They cut down one of the side streets heading east and walked two more blocks.

"Why don't we go to my house and listen to records?" Barb suggested. "I've got the newest Johnny Mathis single."

Thelma looked up from her fingernails. She'd been in a funny mood all evening. Junie had pressed her on it, and she'd only grumbled, "My old man again."

To Barb, Thelma said, "Go inside on a hot summer night and listen to records?"

Barb, who was usually quiet and shy, did not back down. "Well, walking up and down the street every night is getting old."

"Says you," Thelma shot back. "Let's go to the park and play some baseball. We can grab mitts and bats at my house on the way over."

Barb scrunched up her nose and said, "What do you think, Junie?"

"Yeah, let's take a break from our routine," Junie said. "I'll listen to records." She didn't want to go swing a bat around either. That was okay when she was younger, but she felt she'd outgrown it.

Barb's smile was triumphant, and Junie hoped she wouldn't gloat. Sometimes there was friction between Barb and Thelma, with Junie in the unfortunate position of referee. When she'd mentioned it to her mother, her mother's response had been, "Three is never a good number with friends." That hadn't been helpful at all.

Thelma sulked all the way to Barb's house. She lagged behind Junie and Barb.

The truth was, Junie liked going to Barb's house. It was so different from her own. Everything about it. Barb lived on Coolidge, a side street between McKinley Parkway and Abbott Road. This was the nicer part of South Buffalo. Her street even had a grass meridian in the center of it where big, shady trees grew, and one of the street's residents kept the grass cut and edged during the summer months. If they had put a grass meridian on Junie's street, there'd be no place for the cars. And forget about one of her neighbors cutting the grass on the meridian when they could barely take care of their own postage stamp–sized front lawns.

The Walsh house was a neat and tidy two-story redbrick house with black-shuttered windows and a small white portico out front. Against the side of the house, pink, blue, and purple hydrangeas grew in abundance. In the backyard was an arched gate over which wild pink roses grew. Junie remembered once standing at the edge of Barb's driveway out front when a slight breeze had carried the fragrance of roses around them. Her own mother had declared roses too fussy and had opted for pots of non-fragrant red geraniums.

The front porch light was on. Barb lived here with her parents and her older brother, who was home from college for the summer. He was in med school, following in his father's footsteps. Even Barb was heading off to college once they were finished with high school. It was something that the people—men and women alike—in Barb's family did. In Junie and Thelma's families, you went right off to work out of high school, and you were glad to have a job.

Barb approached the front door and Junie stopped, saying, "Maybe we should go in through the back." Going in through the front meant they'd meet Barb's parents. Junie hesitated. Mrs. Walsh always wore a pinched expression when Junie showed up. Like Junie's plain cotton or seersucker gave her migraines. Not that they hadn't always been kind and polite to her, but it was how she felt in their presence. Like somehow she was lacking.

"Go through the back door?" Thelma snorted. "What are we, the hired help?"

"Shh, Thelma, you and your big mouth," Junie said.

"Don't you dare shush me, Junie," Thelma said, her eyes dark and glittering in the evening light.

"Would you two stop bickering and come in?" Barb said with her hand on the doorknob. A large lantern-style light fixture hung suspended from the middle of the portico. There was a light on in an upstairs window.

Before either one of them could answer, Barb pushed through the door, leaving it open for them to follow.

Thelma marched right up the steps and into the house with Junie following.

The foyer opened up onto a front hallway papered in heavy floral wallpaper and trimmed in white woodwork, with black-and-white harlequin tiles on the floor. On the left was Dr. Walsh's study, and to the right was the living room. Junie wondered what it would be like living in a house as grand as this.

The air was lovely and cool. The staircase banister had spindles painted white, while the steps on the staircase were stained dark. There was a floral runner with gold risers going up the stairs.

The thing that fascinated Junie the most was the drinks cart in the corner of the living room. It was a beautiful piece of black lacquerware with an Oriental design. But it was all the crystal on top of it: a decanter filled with amber liquid, a set of tumblers, and an ice bucket. She tried to picture Margaret and Bill with something like this; it wouldn't last five minutes with them. They'd end up throwing it at one another.

Dr. Walsh was in the front room, a heavy textbook in his hand. He wore a cardigan over his shirt and tie, and a pipe rested between his lips. He straightened the thick, heavy glasses on his face and considered the three of them standing in the doorway of the living room. There was a faint smell of cherry coming from his pipe and Junie loved the smell, wanting to inhale it. Mrs.

Walsh sat on the davenport, leafing through a woman's magazine. She wore a dress with a pleated skirt, a pair of slingbacks, and a three-strand pearl necklace. Her lipstick was subtle, the color of apricots.

"Good evening, ladies," Dr. Walsh said.

"Hi, Dr. Walsh," Junie said.

"Hi," grumbled Thelma, still sulking. Junie elbowed her and Thelma shot her a fierce look.

"Hello, Junie and Thelma," Mrs. Walsh said, setting down her magazine.

Barb inherited her looks from her mother. Mrs. Walsh was tall and slim with blond hair she wore in a chignon. Junie wondered if she ever wore it down. Barb had told her once that her mother had been a sorority sister and, curious, Junie had wanted to ask what that entailed but remained silent for fear of looking stupid.

"We're going upstairs to listen to records," Barb said.

"Not too loud, Barbara," Dr. Walsh said, returning to his textbook.

"There's lemonade and ice cream in the kitchen," Mrs. Walsh said.

Without a word, Barb headed up the stairs to her bedroom, followed by Junie and Thelma. As they rounded the top of the staircase, Junie glanced in at the bedroom that belonged to Barb's parents. It reminded her of something from a movie. She'd been in there once, when Barb had gone in to borrow a pearl bracelet of her mother's. Junie had gotten quite an eyeful. It was unlike her parents' bedroom with all the mismatched furniture jammed into a small space. Two things in particular had made Junie's jaw drop. The first was the floral chaise tucked in the corner of the room, looking pretty against the heavy striped wallpaper. On it was a thick book, and Junie could not imagine stretching out on a piece of furniture so divine simply to read a book. The other piece that intrigued her was Mrs. Walsh's vanity table. It was kidney-shaped and had a chair covered in dark pink watered silk. The top of the dressing table was covered in glass, and beneath the glass were lots of black-and-white photos of Mrs. Walsh when she was younger. Perfume bottles and cosmetics lined the top of the table. Junie could only dream of sitting there, brushing her hair or putting on lipstick or dabbing perfume behind her ears and on her wrists like she'd seen Margaret do. Her own mother—usually clad in only a slip—would stand in front of the sink in the upstairs bathroom and lean over it to draw on some eyebrows, smacking her lips together after she applied her lipstick. The worlds of the Walshes and the Richardses were as far apart as they could be.

Barb's bedroom was a wondrous place. All done up in pink, there was a double bed with a canopy that Junie found fascinating. All the furniture was white and gold French provincial and it all matched, unlike the furniture in Junie's room: odds and ends that had been collected from the thrift shop or passed on to her from dead relatives. Barb had a desk built into bookshelves crammed with books, many of which she had let Junie borrow. Barb also had a princess phone on her nightstand. Junie didn't have a phone in her bedroom. She didn't even have a nightstand! There was a long closet in the room, and it was packed with clothes. In the corner was a record player, and there were albums strewn all over the floor. The wall directly above the record player was covered in eight by ten autographed glossies of Paul Newman, Kirk Douglas, Joanne Woodward, Elizabeth Taylor, and Rock Hudson.

The three girls sat on the floor, grouped around the record player, while Barb pulled a record out of its sleeve and set it on the turntable, laying the arm down on the record.

Thelma remained quiet, and Junie hoped she wouldn't sulk all night. She and Barb got into a discussion about Johnny Mathis and whether they thought he was more handsome than Elvis. Jokingly, they disagreed. Thelma didn't partake in the conversation, choosing instead to play with the rug, pulling at a thread. Junie hoped she didn't end up unraveling the whole thing.

Junie pulled a book from the pile on Barb's nightstand.

Victoria Holt.

"That's a good one," Barb said. "Really romantic. The hero is so debonair."

Thelma crossed her arms over her chest and burst out laughing. "Romantic? Would you get off cloud nine. Wait until you're washing their dirty underwear. There's nothing romantic about men."

Barb's cheeks went bright red, and she rolled her lips inward and glared at Thelma.

Junie ignored Thelma, put the book down, and pulled another off the shelf. *Seventeenth Summer* by Maureen Daly. She'd read this one before. She leafed through it, settling down on the floor.

Junie rolled over onto her stomach, her knees bent with her feet up in the air. She flipped the book open to the first page and began to read.

Suddenly, Thelma jumped up. "Look, I gotta go."

"Where are you going?" Barb asked.

"Home. This is boring," Thelma said. Thelma wasn't known for sedentary activities; she always needed to be on the go. Always needed to be moving. Or talking.

"All right, talk to you later," Barb said. She was reading the album's jacket cover and did not look up.

"Yeah," Thelma said tightly, "I'll talk to you tomorrow."

Before Junie could say anything, Thelma slipped through the door, closing it behind her.

Barb sighed. "I don't know what's up with her lately. She's so cranky."

Junie made no comment. When Thelma would gripe to her about Barb sometimes, she'd remain quiet then too. Both of them were her best friends, and she wasn't going to be caught in the middle.

CHAPTER ELEVEN

Lily

The morning after the funeral, Lily woke early, right at daybreak, after a restless night. Despite the cool night air, she'd tossed and turned. The previous day had been long and draining. It had been hard to say goodbye to Gram, almost as hard as it had been when they buried their mother.

There had been a church service followed by a graveside service. The day was shiny and bright, too nice for a funeral, Lily thought. Rain or a gray sky would have seemed more appropriate. Lakeside Cemetery was situated on a small parcel of land on a gently rolling slope overlooking the lake. It was a beautiful final resting place. It was a relatively new cemetery in that the land had been hastily acquired in 1919 as the town sprung up.

Lily turned over in her bed and sighed. Charlie lifted his head from his dog bed on the floor, watching her. The day before hadn't been a good day for Charlie either. After the burial, everyone had come back to the house for something to eat and Charlie, overwhelmed by the sheer number of people—and strangers at that—kept bumping into things. Only one vase had been lost but fortunately, none of their guests had been knocked over.

Residents of Hideaway Bay who had known Gram for a long time had brought dishes, and Lily and her sisters had extended the dining room table and put the two leaves in it. They set up all the food on the table and placed chairs throughout the main level of the house. Some guests chose to sit on the front porch. There were so many people that she hadn't seen in years, and she met so many new people she didn't remember half their names. All had a kind word to say about Gram. Later, when she crawled into bed, she was exhausted.

With a yawn, Lily pulled the blankets up to her chin and looked around the room that her grandparents had designated hers. Its windows overlooked the side and back of the house, but from the side window she could still hear the surf. The walls were covered in a floral chintz wallpaper with flowers in varying shades of violet, lavender, and purple. All the woodwork had been painted cream by Granddad at her request, and the old lavender-colored chenille bedspread was still on the bed. Her mother had stripped down and restored the reclaimed furniture, giving it a distressed look.

Early morning sun filtered into the room through the sheer curtains, casting the room in an opaque, gauzy light. There was a slight breeze that gently lifted the curtains away from the sill. Lily tilted her head on the pillow and listened to the sound of the water at the beach across the street. A quick glance at the bedside clock told her it was only six-thirty. But she knew there was no going back to sleep. With another sigh, she flipped the blankets back and swung her legs out of the bed. She felt around for her slippers with her feet, slipped them on, and padded off to the bathroom to wash her face and brush her teeth. The house was quiet, and the doors to her sisters' bedrooms were firmly shut. When she finished, she headed back to her room, where she found Charlie standing, waiting, and wagging his tail.

He gave a little whine when she closed the door behind her.

"Give me five minutes, bud, I've got to get dressed." Hurriedly, she threw on a hoodie over her T-shirt and pulled on a pair of khaki pants. She gave her hair a quick brush before she pulled on a pair of sandals.

"Come on, Charlie, let's go," she whispered. She didn't want to wake her sisters.

Quietly, she slipped out of the room, tiptoeing across the hardwood floor, followed by Charlie, whose nails made a *tap-tap* sound on the floor. She made her way down the staircase, pocketed a house key from the crystal bowl on the console table, and opened the front door. Charlie bounded out, flew across the porch, stumbled down the steps, and landed in the grass. Lily rolled her eyes. What a klutz, she thought.

She grabbed a plastic bag and stuffed it into the pocket of her pants in case Charlie should drop a package somewhere along the way. She stood on the front porch and took in a deep lungful of fresh air. Although the air was still cool, the emerging sun was warm. It was going to be another warm May day.

She stepped off the porch and headed up Star Shine Drive, glad that there was no one out yet. It was quiet, as if the whole town were still asleep. The dog loped ahead of her, his head turning left and right, stopping every once in a while to sniff the road or something else that caught his attention.

Lily walked the length of the road and turned around right before it reached the main center of town, although she was dying for some coffee. Rather than return to Gram's house, she detoured in the direction of the beach, heading toward the wooden boardwalk.

When she reached the boardwalk, she pulled off her sandals and stepped into the thick, cool sand, her feet sinking down into it. It felt good. Sandals in her one hand, she headed toward the shore. Charlie headed off in the other direction at a canter.

"Stay close," she advised. He never went too far. He was too lazy. And too afraid.

Her gaze traveled up and down the beach, but it was empty. It was nice to have the whole place to herself. She waded in the water at the edge, staring down as the foamy surf washed over her feet, curling around her ankles. The water was cool but not cold. During the hottest summers, the water could be as warm as bathwater.

She'd learned how to swim at this beach. Granddad had taught all three of them. He'd said it was important to learn how to swim. With her hands on her hips and her sandals dangling from one hand, she stared out at the horizon. The sun rising in the east behind her warmed her back. What was it about water and the beach that somehow recalibrated her? She could easily understand why Gram loved it here and had chosen to make it her home for the rest of her life. Gram never spoke about it but from what Lily had gathered, there was a lot of drama between Gram and her older sister, Margaret. Margaret had died young, and Gram never spoke about that either. Lily wondered if

Margaret's death had been the catalyst for their move out to Hideaway Bay from the city.

She stepped out of the surf and walked along the beach. Something caught her eye and she stopped, spotting a piece of beach glass half embedded in the sand. With a smile, she bent down and picked it up. The shard was smooth, its edges dull, the pH of the lake a perfect buffer. It was bottle green in color. As she always did, she wondered about its history.

She walked farther up the beach running parallel with Star Shine Drive until Gram's house was directly in front of her. Along her way, she picked up several more pieces of beach glass in green, brown, and white, and one a shade of blue that reminded her of lapis lazuli. Carefully, she deposited her handful into her pocket. With a quick glance over her shoulder, she called Charlie, and he picked up his pace until he was at her side.

Full of affection for her canine companion, she reached down and buried her head against his neck. "You're a great dog, Charlie."

They walked side by side away from the shore, heading up the beach. Lily sat down in the sand and hugged her legs to her. Charlie sat next to her and stared out at the lake as if he found it interesting.

Lily stared out at the navy blue water, spotting some fishing boats on the horizon. Serious fishermen were out at the crack of dawn. Granddad had done a bit of fishing from time to time with friends but had never owned a boat of his own.

With everything going on with Gram and her funeral, Lily hadn't had time to think about Jamie and the huge debt he'd left behind. Now was as good a time as any to think about her predicament. There was no sense in putting it off. She didn't even know what her options were. If she had any, she suspected they were few.

In the months following his death, Lily had made arrangements with the lenders with a payment amount that would strangle her if she wasn't careful. Thus no extras in her life. She'd be saddled with that bill for a long time, and at the end there'd be nothing to show for it. Her mind raced. The only assets she had were her house and a paltry savings account.

She squeezed her arms around her legs, thinking she was going to have to get a second job. At least a part-time one. Or, if she sold her house, she could pay the bulk of that debt. Not all of it, but most of it. But then she'd have to find an apartment, and rent in California wasn't cheap. On further contemplation, selling the house seemed more like a lateral move. She bit her lip and exhaled a loud breath. She wasn't sure what she should do.

From behind her, she heard, "There you are!"

Lily turned and caught sight of Alice walking toward her. She wore a pale cornflower-blue dress with an ivory-colored sweater. Her red hair framed her face. Her sister was very pretty, and Lily couldn't understand why she was still single.

Alice plopped down on the sand next to her and crossed her legs. Her perfume was light, and Lily thought it suited her.

"You're up early."

"I couldn't sleep," Lily said, staring off toward the boats on the lake.

"Me neither."

Charlie stood and walked around Lily to Alice and sat down in front of her, excited by a new face and attention from someone other than Lily. He licked Alice's face.

"Yuck!" Alice said, laughing, but she gave in and lavished the dog with affection. Within minutes, the dog plopped down, putting his head in Alice's lap. Alice stroked the top of his head.

"Is Izzy still asleep?"

Alice snorted. "I think she may have had a late night with a bottle of wine."

Lily smiled. Isabelle had always been a night owl. During summer vacation when they were young, Isabelle stayed up until dawn playing CDs. Sometimes they'd play board games, and Izzy always tried to coax Lily into staying up late with her. But Lily could never last past two or three in the morning. She smiled at the memory of it.

There were a few moments of silence.

"You've had a horrible year, Lily," Alice said softly. A breeze came along and loosened her hair, sending a thick strand across her face. She tucked it behind her ear.

"I guess so."

"I'm sorry I've been such a terrible sister," Alice said.

Lily tilted her head toward her, brushed her hair off her face, and narrowed her eyes in confusion. "What do you mean?"

"I should have kept in touch after Jamie's funeral, should have checked on you."

"You're so busy with your job, I didn't expect you to call," Lily said, trying to let her sister off the hook.

"That's no excuse. I should have made the effort," Alice said.

"We are not that kind of family," Lily said, her voice full of regret.

"No, we're not. Though Mom and Gram always wanted us to stay close."

"I don't even know if that's possible."

"Don't say that, Lily."

Lily didn't know if she had the energy to round up her sisters. She couldn't keep looking after everyone, making sure they were doing what they were supposed to be doing. She'd done that with Jamie, and it hadn't worked out. He still managed to rack up a lot of debt behind her back so apparently, she shouldn't be taking charge of anything.

"How are you doing?" Alice asked.

"Okay," Lily said with a shrug.

"It must be hard to lose your husband so young."

Lily snorted. "You don't know the half of it."

Alice continued to rub the top of Charlie's head absentmindedly. After a moment, she said, "Why don't you tell me the half of it I don't know."

Lily contemplated this. Should she share her burden? If she spoke it out loud would that make it seem more real? Could she trust her sister? When they were younger, Alice couldn't keep a secret to save her life. But surely that wasn't the case anymore, right? She was older, established in her job. She could be discreet, couldn't she? It would be a relief not to have to hide it from her sisters.

"Remember what Gram used to say?" Alice prompted. "Joy shared is doubled, and sorrow shared is halved."

Lily smiled. "Yes, she did say that, didn't she." Gram had certainly seen her share of sorrow in her life. Lily buried her head in her arms for a bit, overwhelmed.

When she lifted her head, she poured out her story about Jamie's gambling problem. And about the debt he'd left behind. When she was finished, she felt empty. She continued to hug her knees and stare at the sand.

"Jeez, Lily, I am sorry. You must be full of conflicted emotions," Alice said aptly.

"To say the least. I feel as if this debt has marred my grief. Jamie was a good guy and yet I'm angry at him about the debt," she said. "And maybe for dying so young and leaving me alone."

"That's probably natural. Stages of grief and all that."

When Lily didn't comment, Alice asked, "What are you going to do about the debt?"

"I've got payment arrangements made, but they've really put me behind the eight ball." Lily tried to keep the whine out of her voice, but she couldn't help it. There was a lot to whine about in her life right now. "I'm still thinking about my options."

"Do you have anything you could sell?"

"Only the house, but then I'd have to find an apartment so that doesn't seem like the best solution at the moment. I was thinking of getting a part-time job."

Alice paled. "In addition to your full-time one? That's a lot to take on."

"I know," Lily cried, burying her head in her arms again. She felt as if she were at the bottom of a hole with no way to get out.

"Boy, he seemed like a nice guy from the few times I met him," Alice said.

"He was a nice guy, but he had problems," Lily said. She certainly didn't want to speak ill of the dead, but facts were facts. Jamie had left her a huge mess to clean up.

"On your way back home, why don't you stop in Chicago and stay with me for a bit," Alice suggested, her expression bright.

"Thank you so much, I will keep that in mind. My plan is to stay for a while but it may be more prudent to go home and go back to work. I only get a certain number of days for bereavement and then it starts dipping into my personal time." She didn't miss her job. Although the people she worked for were nice, her heart wasn't in it any longer. Before Jamie's death, she had thought about looking for another job but had felt disloyal to her boss for doing so. But then Jamie died and there was relief that she hadn't taken a new job, that she could settle into her comfortable groove at work amidst the turbulence of heartache.

"You don't have to go right away, do you?" Alice asked.

"I don't want to, but I should," Lily admitted. Despite her grief, there was a lot of comfort being back in Gram's home. It was familiar and felt like a soft place to land.

Alice stood, brushing sand off her bottom. Charlie jumped up and looked back and forth from Lily to Alice.

"Come on, let's go back and have breakfast," Alice said. "I've made my famous French toast and all it needs is to be heated up."

"I love French toast," Lily said, getting to her feet. As they walked through the sand toward the street that separated the beach from the houses, Lily asked. "Don't you have to get back to work yourself?"

"Not for a few weeks. I've taken my bereavement days plus some vacation," Alice said.

"When was the last time you took a vacation?"

Alice shrugged. "It's been so long that I don't remember. What does it say about me that it took Gram's death for me to take a break?"

"Don't judge yourself, Alice," Lily said quietly. She shifted gears and asked, "How's your job going?"

"It's going great," Alice said. But her expression and her tone made Lily think otherwise. Her sister didn't say any more, and Lily didn't press her. She was sorry they didn't have the kind of relationship where Lily could challenge her on her statement.

Behind them, a jogger ran past, running parallel with the shore.

"I'm sorry I went and dumped my problems into your lap."

"Lily, it's okay. Your problems are serious. I'm glad you confided in me. Things will get better, you know. You won't always feel this way."

Lily couldn't imagine feeling any other way. She didn't know if the term embracing widowhood was a thing, but she was determined to make the best of it, get on with her life, and most of all, clean up Jamie's mess and try to mourn her husband properly. The debt had made her angry but other than that, they had been happy together. She'd thought she would be with Jamie for the rest of her life.

She changed the subject, tired of talking about her predicament. It depressed her. "When's the last time you spoke to Gram?"

"Actually, I spoke to Gram a few weeks ago. I was planning on taking two weeks' vacation in August and coming to stay with her. To put my feet up."

"I bet she was looking forward to it. And you deserve it, I know you work those crazy hours."

Alice nodded, smiling. "She seemed excited, started making plans about all the things we could do together. She even said she was going to ask you and Isabelle to come out as well so we could all be together." Her voice wobbled and broke on the last few words.

"Oh, Alice," Lily said. It warmed her heart to think that Gram had had something to look forward to, knowing that at least one of them was on their way home. But it felt like a lost opportunity that the three of them hadn't met up with Gram and spent some time together. It wasn't meant to be, she told herself.

Alice swiped away some errant tears, looped her arm around Lily, and said, "Come on, I think there's some stuffed French toast waiting for us."

"When did you make that?"

"Last night, after you went to bed. I wasn't sleepy and baking helps me to relax," Alice said with a shrug as they made their way across Star Shine Drive toward their grandmother's house.

CHAPTER TWELVE

1962

Paul

Paul Reynolds drove out to Hideaway Bay after work. He was alone, as most of his buddies had already headed out to the lake earlier in the afternoon. Going to the lake on the weekend was more out of habit than anything; it seemed to be where everyone from the city went. It had been a long week and he was tired, but he didn't want to spend a Friday night inside sitting with his parents watching a repeat of *Rawhide*. But still, it would have to be an early night as he had a side job in the morning, and that meant he'd have to leave the lake shortly after sunrise.

He'd gotten his union card the previous year which also meant a union wage, and there was money to spend. Not that he was careless with it. Like his father had taught him, the first thing he did with his paycheck was deposit a percentage into his savings account. He worked Monday through Friday at his union job and worked side jobs on Saturday for the extra cash. He had some vague plans for the future. He didn't know exactly what yet, he was only sure that he was going to need some cash to do it. Buying a house was a goal. His father had talked to him about buying a two-family home; that way he'd have a tenant helping pay the mortgage. It was an idea that appealed to him. But for the time being, he continued to live with his parents, saving money.

The late afternoon sky was a dull white. No bright-orange fireball heading for the horizon. The summer had been a bust. The weather was unusually cool for July and instead of watching girls in shorts and two-pieces, he'd been looking at them all summer wrapped up in cardigans and long pants.

During the hour-long drive out to the lake, Paul debated several times doing a U-turn in the middle of the road and returning to the city. This was going to be a waste of time, he told himself. It was always the same crew doing the same thing, and he was starting to get tired of it. Biting his lip, he pulled in front of the cottage where his friend Eric lived with his family for the summer.

It was a small summer-rental cottage that ran off the main street of Star Shine Drive. Eric's parents rented it every July and August. Paul had been coming out here with them for as long as he could remember.

Paul said hello to Eric's parents and at the invitation from Eric's dad, he grabbed a cold bottle of beer from the icebox. He shot the breeze with Eric's parents for a few minutes and then pushed through the wooden screen door, wincing when it slammed behind him. Taking a slug from his beer bottle, he headed out in search of his friends. He walked along the sandy drive until he hit Star Shine Drive. Instead of turning and heading toward town and taking the boardwalk to the beach, he cut across at that point, the dry sand kicking up behind him as he walked.

The night air was cool, and Paul could hear the lake water lapping against the shore. There were bonfires all along the beach, and Paul kept an eye out for Eric. At six six, he was hard to miss.

But it wasn't Eric he spotted first. He heard the high-pitched laugh of Eric's girlfriend, Sheila, and turned his head in the direction of the sound just as Eric scooped her up and tossed her into the shallow waters of the surf.

"Eric!" she wailed.

Paul sighed. It was the same thing, the same antics every weekend. Plus, everyone seemed paired up and on more than one occasion, he'd felt like the odd man out.

Eric spotted him and waved. With a nod, Paul parked himself on one of the logs that had been placed around the bonfire.

He looked over and caught Eric pulling Sheila out of the water and pulling her to him. Paul laughed. He was going to be best man at their wedding. He envied Eric: a college graduate who was getting ready to settle down.

Paul crossed his legs at the ankles and stared at the bonfire in front of him. The orange flames leapt into the air and the dry kindling and timber crackled. He looked over his shoulder again at Eric and Sheila as Eric placed his hands on either side of Sheila's face and leaned in to kiss her. Embarrassed at witnessing such a private moment, Paul looked away, feeling around in his pockets for a pack of cigarettes. *I really should quit*, he thought. He didn't like the way they made him feel.

He was distracted by the arrival of Stanley Schumacher, a kid who usually got on people's nerves. Not Paul's, though. He didn't mind him. Stanley had to be about nineteen or twenty now; he'd been a few years behind Paul in high school.

"Hey, Paulie," Stanley said.

Stanley was the only one who called him Paulie. How old were they, ten?

"Have you seen Thelma around?" Stanley asked.

"Thelma who?" Paul asked. Holding his beer bottle between his legs, he turned his head to face Stanley.

Stanley used too much Brylcreem in his hair, and still had the on-fire acne that had plagued him for years. But Paul had to give the kid a lot of credit; he certainly didn't let it hold him back.

"I'm thinking of asking Thelma out on a date," Stanley said with a dreamy expression on his face, pushing his glasses up on his nose.

Paul eyed him. He knew vaguely of this Thelma. She was a tough-talking girl with a lot of brothers. *Love makes the world go round*, he thought.

"Jeez, I'm starving!" Stanley said. "You'd think you'd be able to get a hot dog around here."

A guy—someone Paul didn't recognize—came up behind them, surprising them. He ran his hands through Stanley's hair until it was sticking up and knocked his glasses off his face.

Paul laughed, and Stanley straightened his glasses and called after the offender, "Why don't you go take a long walk on a short pier!"

The other guy laughed and gave Stanley a two-finger salute, hopping over the log they sat on, running off, kicking sand in his wake.

"Jeez! Kids these days," Stanley said, shaking his head. He smoothed his hair down with both hands, seemingly unperturbed. Paul suspected Stanley was used to that kind of behavior.

Paul took a gulp of his beer, and his gaze circled around the vicinity of the bonfire. He half listened to Stanley next to him. Most of Stanley's conversation revolved around his plans for the summer and how hungry he was. People were starting to gather around the fire, but these were new faces, no one he recognized. Eric called out to him, and Paul turned his head toward his friend's voice when something caught his eye, and his gaze was arrested directly across the bonfire.

Three girls had approached the circle, but two of them he didn't even see. His eyes had landed on the one in the middle. She was a brunette with dark, arched eyebrows. She was dressed modestly in a sleeveless cotton floral shirt with buttons up the front, a pair of yellow capris, and sandals. The flames of the bonfire highlighted her face. The girl at her right ribbed her and the dark-haired one laughed, revealing beautiful teeth. How had he never seen her before? Taking another gulp of his beer, Paul stood up from the driftwood log, brushing off the seat of his pants, and made his way over to the girls.

"Hey, Paulie, want to go find something to eat? Maybe we could round up a hot dog or burger somewhere . . ." Stanley's voice trailed off behind him.

As he rounded the bonfire, he immediately recognized the girl at the brunette's side as Thelma Kempf, the girl

Stanley had spoken of earlier. And the cool blonde was Dr. Walsh's daughter, everyone knew that. Paul's gaze landed on the shapely brunette, and he narrowed his eyes and thought, *No way, that can't be Junie Richards.* The last time he'd seen her, she'd been a kid. He glanced at her again. Whoa.

She stood huddled with her friends, laughing and giggling, holding a bottle of beer but not drinking from it. As soon as they spotted Paul, the three of them stopped laughing and broke their huddle, reforming into a line.

Paul kept his gaze on Junie's face. She regarded him over her bottle of beer, her expression unreadable.

"Junie?" he asked. He nodded to Thelma and Barbara.

"Yes?" she asked.

"Do you remember me? Paul Reynolds?" No wonder he was still single. He needed a better opening line.

Standing next to Junie, Thelma snorted, and Paul cast a frozen glance at her. She shut up but she still smirked. The other friend, the doctor's daughter, seemed to regard him with curious disinterest.

"Of course I remember you, Paul," Junie said softly. She took a delicate sip from the beer bottle but didn't make eye contact with him.

"Hey, Thelma, come here," Stanley called from the other side of the bonfire.

Thelma rolled her eyes. "Come on, Barb, let's see what Stanley wants now. He's been pestering me since the third grade."

And suddenly Paul was alone with Junie. Up close, her beauty was luminescent. There was a slight scattering of freckles across the bridge of her nose and in the firelight, her eyes appeared more gray than blue. The last time he'd seen her she'd been just a kid in saddle shoes.

"I've never seen you out here before," he said.

She looked up at him. "Oh, I come out here from time to time. Barb's family has a cottage near the green."

She was referring to the green space directly across from the beach at the end of town. There was a gazebo and a war memorial there and some giant oak trees.

"Are you working?" he asked.

She nodded. "At McAllister's."

He knew it. It wasn't far from where he lived. A family-owned drugstore that still operated a soda fountain. He smiled to himself, thinking he was about to become a frequent customer of the place.

He went to say something, but Junie had started digging through her purse, which hung over her arm. Patiently, he waited. In the distance, a tinny radio played, and he heard people talking but he only had eyes for her.

"Are you here for the weekend?" he asked.

"No," she said, pulling out a small pink change purse.

"Do you need a ride home tonight?" he asked, hopeful. He'd planned on staying but he'd change those plans in a heartbeat.

She smiled warmly at him but shook her head. "No, we're heading back to the city later." She returned her attention to her change purse.

Frowning, he watched her, wondering what she so desperately needed. She opened her change purse and pulled a dime from it, handing it to him.

"As it turns out, I didn't need your dime after all," she said coolly with a slight lift of her chin, and she turned on her heel and walked away.

Paul was left staring at the dime as a distant memory came back to him. He groaned and muttered, "Paul Reynolds, you idiot."

CHAPTER THIRTEEN

Lily

Lily helped herself to a second serving of Alice's amazing stuffed French toast. It was filled with cream cheese and blueberries and there was a lovely, sweet syrup from the blueberries. It reminded her of when they were younger and Alice's favorite toy had been her Easy-Bake Oven.

She popped another decadent forkful into her mouth as Isabelle breezed into the kitchen, a vision of soft blue in a gauzy kaftan with matching headband that seemed to be able to hold Isabelle's mane in place. It appeared to defy gravity. Isabelle eyed the casserole dish on the table.

"What do we have here?" she asked.

"Alice made stuffed French toast and it is simply divine," Lily said. "You must try it."

Isabelle pulled up a chair and said, "I plan on it." She glanced over to the counter. "Is there any coffee?"

Alice nodded. "There's some left, but I can make a fresh pot if you want."

"No, don't bother, I can drink this," Isabelle said easily.

Why couldn't it always be like this, Lily wondered. Why couldn't they sit down together without sniping at each other? Why couldn't the camaraderie be easy amongst them? Wasn't that how it was supposed to be with sisters?

Isabelle stood up from the table and headed toward the counter, pulling the coffee pot off its stand and grabbing a mug from the cabinet above. "Oh look, there's Granddad's old coffee cup!" She broke into a smile and rearranged the mugs on the shelf to get at it. She pulled it out and Lily had to smile at the familiarity of it: it was an old mug with the New York Yankees logo on it. Granddad used to drink coffee and tea out of it all the time.

Isabelle poured herself some coffee and carried her mug over to the table, sitting down again. She helped herself to a generous portion of the stuffed French toast and laid it on a plate. She took a sip of her coffee before picking up her fork.

"Don't you put any cream or sugar into your coffee?" Lily asked, trying not to wince. She was trying to eat the last bites on her plate, but she felt full. She normally ate fresh fruit, granola, and yogurt for breakfast. But this was too tempting to resist.

Isabelle shook her head. "Nope. I like it black."

"I prefer tea myself," Alice said.

Lily hadn't missed the selection box of teas on the counter that Alice must have brought with her. There'd been rooibos, chai, ginger pear, and others. Funny how she didn't know these little details about her sisters and sad at the same time, too.

"Alice, this is wonderful," Isabelle said, taking a second mouthful. A dab of blueberry syrup remained on her lips and she took her pinkie, wiped it off, and licked her little finger. "You missed your calling."

Alice smiled at the compliment.

"I spoke to Thelma after the funeral yesterday to see if she knew who Gram's attorney was," Isabelle said as she speared another portion of French toast with her fork. Lily frowned, thinking it was unseemly that Gram wasn't even in the ground for a day and her older sister was making inquiries as to who the attorney was.

"What's the hurry?" Lily asked.

Isabelle looked up from her plate. "I want to get out of here."

Lily bristled, and Alice shifted uncomfortably in her chair. Lily pushed her half-empty plate away and picked up her cup of coffee, holding it with both hands. She reminded herself that now wasn't the time to get into a fight with her sister, no matter how much she annoyed her.

"Is it that bad?" Lily asked with a forced laugh so her sister wouldn't think she was attacking her.

"It's time for me to move on," Isabelle said. She popped another forkful into her mouth and rolled her eyes in pleasure. "Alice, you should think about giving up law and doing stuff like this instead."

"You've only just arrived," Lily said.

Isabelle cut up more French toast on her plate. "You know I don't stay long in one place."

Why did Lily feel there was a disconnect between her and Isabelle? Growing up, they'd been as opposite as chalk and cheese. Isabelle was always the rebel, staying out past her curfew, raising hell in school while Lily had been concerned with getting good grades and joining various after-school clubs. At their high school, Isabelle had been voted "most popular" of her class and Alice had been voted "most likely to succeed." Lily hadn't been voted anything.

"I was hoping we could spend some time together," Alice said.

"Not all the memories here are good," Isabelle said in a tone that indicated that the topic was closed to further discussion.

Lily decided she'd say no more and exchanged a look with Alice, hoping Alice would follow her lead. She didn't have the energy for a confrontation. She didn't have much energy left for anything.

"Anyway, I rang the attorney before I came downstairs and we have an appointment with him this afternoon," Isabelle informed them.

Lily got that Isabelle was in a hurry to get out of Hideaway Bay and get back to her life, wherever she led it. But as for herself, she was in no hurry to get back to her life on the west coast. There wasn't much left of it. It wasn't like she had a lot of plans while she was in Hideaway Bay—she supposed she could look up some high school friends, but she didn't know if she felt like doing that. Could she stand to see how successful they were, how many children they'd had, how they had settled down and created lives for themselves when all she had to show for things was a big, clumsy dog whom she loved dearly and a huge debt she doubted she would ever crawl out from under? She didn't think she could bear their looks of pity. Reuniting with old friends was put on the back burner for the time being.

"What time?" Alice asked.

"Two." Isabelle lifted her head, her breakfast almost finished. "Is that all right?"

"Fine."

"No problem."

Isabelle leaned back, clasping her hands and laying them over her belly, full. She glanced at the kitchen clock and Lily wondered why her sister seemed so restless, agitated almost. Was Hideaway Bay really that bad? But she didn't think her sister would stick around long enough for her to get to the bottom of it. Other people's problems were a nice distraction from her own bag of trouble. She eyed Alice, wondering what was going on in Chicago. If they'd been close, she'd know the intimate details of their lives. But they weren't those kinds of sisters. She didn't think it was possible to feel any sadder than she already did, but sadness set in, took hold, and settled over her like a blanket.

CHAPTER FOURTEEN

1963

Spring

Junie

"Hey, Barb," Junie said when they crossed paths on McKinley Parkway. She was on her way home from her afternoon shift at the drugstore.

Her friend carried a pile of books in her hands. Even in the mid-afternoon heat, Barb barely broke out in a sweat. She was all decked out in a pair of mint green pedal pushers and a sleeveless white cotton blouse that had tiny daisies embroidered on it. A matching green headband kept her blond hair in place.

Junie, on the other hand, felt tired and in need of a cool bath. She hadn't seen Barb in a while. Barb was home for her annual spring break from college.

"Where's Thelma?" Barb asked.

Junie shrugged. "I don't know. I think she had to babysit her brothers today." After a pause, Junie nodded toward the books in Barb's arms and asked, "Where are you going with those?"

"Returning them to the library so I can take out more," Barb said with a laugh.

"Do you mind if I come?" Junie asked.

"Sure, come on."

The traffic was heavy, and Junie waited until a car with a noisy muffler passed before she spoke, admitting to her friend that she'd never been to the public library. From time to time, she'd used the one at their high school. Barb stopped in her tracks and looked at Junie. "Are you serious?"

It was true; she'd never been, and she'd like to see it. Her family didn't really read books. Her parents read the newspaper every day, and Margaret used to read movie magazines when she lived at home, but Junie had only read books given to her by Barb when they went to high school together.

Junie laughed nervously. "Yes, I'm serious. How does it work?"

Barb explained to her about the process of using a library card, how long you could take a book out for, the fine if you returned it late. When she finished, she announced, "Don't worry, Junie, I'll help you."

"How was your first year of college?" Junie asked as they walked on.

"It was good, but I was terribly homesick for the first term," Barb said, looking down at the sidewalk. When they were kids, they avoided stepping on the cracks but now that they were older, they didn't seem to care.

"Really? You never said."

Barb had written to Junie from time to time, but sometimes to Junie it felt as if Barb were on another planet. She knew that Barb had also written to Thelma once, but Thelma never wrote back, and Barb had never sent her another letter. When Junie had pressed Thelma on it, Thelma shrugged and said, "We have nothing in common. She's off to college, in a sorority house, and I'm trying to figure out a new way to cook ground beef and keep my brothers out of jail."

The library was located in an old two-story brown brick house, and Junie approached it with quite a bit of curiosity. The building was set way back on its lot. At Barb's side, she climbed the steps and went inside.

"Am I allowed in? I mean, I don't have a library card," Junie said, panicking, hating that she didn't know about something as simple as getting a library card. Barb must think her stupid.

Barb tilted her head and regarded her. "Of course you are, come on."

Junie noticed two things when she first stepped inside—well, actually three, if you counted the hushed silence. It was cool, and the place smelled like paper and wood. She looked around in awe at the rows and rows of wooden shelves housing all sorts of books. Barb had been a frequent visitor to the library and for a brief moment, Junie wondered if her friend had read every book there.

"Come on, Junie, let's get you a card," Barb said.

Junie followed her to the desk, where Barb set her books down for return and made conversation with the librarian, whom Junie didn't recognize. When Barb informed the woman that Junie would like to get a library card, the woman turned her friendly smile on Junie, went over a few things with her, and handed her some paperwork to fill out. The librarian's wood-grain desk was very neat, Junie thought. There was an ink pad with a stamper lying next to it. In a leather cup there was a varied assortment of pencils and pens. On her blotter was a calendar of the month with all sorts of notes scribbled around it.

The librarian looked to be in her mid-forties with a beehive of red hair, and she wore a dress the color of a tangerine. Junie remembered Mrs. Walsh saying once that women with red hair should avoid wearing any color resembling red. Junie looked her over, deciding that the orange dress looked well on the woman.

Junie nodded, signed the paperwork, and followed Barb around. Barb pointed out the various sections, showed her how to use the catalog, and took her to a shelf to show her the books. Then they separated, Barb heading off to the section marked romance, and Junie torn between general fiction and mystery. Finally, she decided to give general fiction a try. Fascinated, Junie pulled books off the shelf and studied them, reading a page or two before returning them to the shelf. She wasn't quite sure what she wanted to read, but she thought she'd know it when she saw it. She was a little overwhelmed with all the choices.

"Have you read this book?" came a decidedly male voice from behind her. Startled, Junie turned and came face to face with Paul Reynolds. Her lips parted slightly and the hair on her arms stood up.

She hadn't seen him since that night at the bonfire last summer out at the lake. Not that she hadn't thought about him, because she had, but it seemed there had never been an opportunity to run into him. She had played it cool then. At the time, she'd been pleased with herself.

His hair was as dark as ink. His eyes were such a bright, translucent blue she wanted to get lost in them.

He held a heavy tome toward her. She tilted her head and scanned the binding.

"*To Kill a Mockingbird*," she read. "I saw the movie."

"The book is always better than the movie," he said with a grin. That grin of his did all sorts of things to her. Her stomach somersaulted and her knees felt like jelly.

She was at a loss for words. Paul Reynolds talking to her in the stacks of the library. If she'd ever guessed in a million years that he'd be hanging out here, she would have gotten a library card sooner.

"Have you read it?" she asked, taking it from him.

He nodded and sidled closer to her until their arms were practically touching. His nearness was not unpleasant, and he smelled nice—some soft cologne, not something he had gone swimming in.

Paul leaned in toward her and Junie was aware of a myriad of sensations. Her heart thudded against her chest and despite the heat, goosebumps broke out along her arms. Up close, she noticed his blue eyes were flecked with gold and ringed in sapphire. She had to resist the urge to reach out and touch the stubble on his jaw.

"Say you'll go out with me, Junie Richards," he whispered.

Junie swallowed hard, the book in her hand forgotten. When she didn't say anything, he pressed, "Wherever you want to go, whatever you want to do."

She arched an eyebrow, wondering about his sincerity.

He continued. "The drive-in? A movie? A burger?"

Junie didn't know why, but she decided to test him, to see how sincere he was or if he was teasing her again. Making fun of her as he had done all those years ago. The memory of it still made her cheeks burn. She stared down at her shoes and swung her gaze back up at him, summoning her courage.

"Anything?" she asked with a slight tilt of her head, feeling a bit braver.

"Anything," he repeated. He leaned his elbow on a bookshelf and ran his finger along his lips.

"I'd like to drive out to Hideaway Bay," she said, her eyes never leaving his face, watching his reaction.

He didn't hesitate or show any sign of surprise. He simply said, "Fine. Friday night? After I finish work?"

Junie found herself nodding, surprised that he'd been so agreeable and hadn't tried to talk her into doing something closer to the city.

"I'll pick you up at six," he said, and he turned to walk away as if afraid she might change her mind if he hung around any longer.

"Wait, don't you want my address?" she asked.

Paul turned his head on his fine set of shoulders and grinned. "I know where you live, Junie Richards."

Oh.

Junie didn't move for a few moments, standing there against the bookshelves with a book in her hand, trying to process all that had happened in the space of a few short minutes.

Barb appeared, a stack of books in her arms, and asked, "Did you find something?"

Junie stared at the space Paul had recently vacated. "As a matter of fact, I did."

CHAPTER FIFTEEN

Lily

Lily and her sisters decided to walk to the attorney's office in town. It was another gorgeous sunny day in Hideaway Bay. The previous night during the weather forecast, it had been mentioned how the warm temperatures were breaking records for May. Lily wished Gram were alive to see it, but then she comforted herself with the thought that Gram most likely had seen many such days during her lifetime.

They headed south on Star Shine Drive toward Main Street. As they walked along, Lily noticed that the beach was packed. People had decided to take advantage of the unusually hot May weather. Blankets covered almost every square inch of sand. Bright beach umbrellas in vibrant shades of orange, red, and blue staked their claims. Seagulls circled overhead, and some people opted to ignore the "do not feed the birds" signs posted everywhere, which led to the birds dive-bombing the beachgoers. A volleyball net had been set up and currently two teams comprised of twenty-somethings in swim trunks and cute bikinis competed, with the ball being swatted back and forth over the net. The familiar lifeguard towers, with a fresh coat of red paint, were placed at intervals along the shore. Out on the lake, all kinds of boats were anchored offshore, forming a ring around the bay. Lily suspected that this was going to be the scene until Labor Day.

It was amazing to her how life carried on in the midst of death. It was almost insulting that they could all be enjoying themselves on the beach when Junie Reynolds had died. It tore at her heart. But she had felt the same way when Jamie had died.

She recognized no one and felt a little sad. There'd been a time when she knew everyone in the bay, knew who the year-round residents were and who the families were who were there only for the summer. And they had all known her and her sisters. But not anymore. She'd been gone too long.

"Is it me or is the place full of strangers?" Isabelle asked, echoing her thoughts.

"I was thinking the same thing," Alice added.

The town was as busy as the beach, with people lining the sidewalks and going in and out of shops along the main thoroughfare. The main street still had its red brick road, which Lily used to find fascinating as a child as she'd never seen a road like that anywhere else. It reminded her of *The Wizard of Oz*.

The attorney's office was situated right on Main Street, tucked next to the vacant Old Red Top and across the street from the Hideaway Bay Olive Oil Company.

When they swept through the front door of the law office of Stodges and Hindermarsh, they were hit with a blast of arctic air from the air conditioning that made the goose bumps rise on Lily's arms. She was sorry she hadn't brought a cardigan or a shawl with her.

"It's freezing in here," Alice said.

Lily and Isabelle agreed.

They were asked to wait in the front reception room, and Lily and Alice plopped down together on the sofa while Isabelle opted for the club chair. They didn't have to wait long before they were ushered into the office of the senior partner, Arthur Stodges. He was elderly, almost as old as Gram, and the girls knew him from when they grew up in Hideaway Bay.

Three leather club chairs had been placed in front of his desk, and Lily and her sisters situated themselves in the chairs with Isabelle taking the middle.

Arthur Stodges shook each of their hands and then spoke a few words about Gram, saying he'd known her since she and Granddad bought the house on Star Shine Drive. In fact, he told them, he'd been a recent law school graduate then, and had been the closing attorney when they'd purchased the property.

These revelations caused Lily's eyes to mist over. Beside her, Isabelle cleared her throat. And Alice stared straight ahead as if unseeing.

When he was finished, he smiled and said, "I suppose we should get on with the business of the day." He donned a pair of reading glasses and leafed through the two-page will that had been updated five years ago by Gram.

The three of them sat quietly, listening to Gram's last wishes. There was nothing shocking; it was pretty straightforward except for one part. The house and its contents had been left equally to all three of them to "do with whatever they saw fit." There was also some money and investments that were to be liquidated and divided equally between the three of them. The only stipulation in the will was that they had to wait a year before they sold the house.

Mr. Stodges told them what would happen next: how the will would have to go through probate before they could get their inheritance. As long as no one contested the will, the process should only take three to six months.

It seemed as if the meeting was nearly over, but Mr. Stodges appeared to hesitate. From his desk blotter he pulled a white business-sized envelope and handed it to Isabelle. From where she sat, Lily recognized the familiar scrawl of Gram's writing and saw that all three of their names were on the outside of the envelope. Lily and Alice stared at the envelope as did Isabelle.

"Your grandmother asked me to give you that letter in the event of her death."

The three of them shook his hand, thanked him, and left their forwarding addresses and phone numbers with his assistant. Isabelle led the way out, tucking the envelope into her purse.

All in all, they were only in the attorney's office for three quarters of an hour and when they stepped out into the blistering heat of the mid-afternoon sun, it was Lily who suggested they stop at the ice cream parlor for a cone.

The Pink Parlor was noted for its homemade ice cream. It used to be Lily's favorite place when she was a kid. Delicious ice cream aside, she always thought the place was cute. It was all done up in various shades of pink, with white bistro tables and matching chairs. The walls were painted a pale pink and there were gray faux-marble countertops and floor tiles. In the corner was a pink-and-white striped barbershop pole. Big front windows faced west and let in a lot of light in the afternoon. The ceiling was high, giving the whole place an airy effect. In the summer, when the days were hot and bright, there'd be bistro tables outside beneath a pink-and-white striped awning. The staff wore either pink-and-white striped aprons or solid yellow ones that reminded Lily of lemonade.

They approached the counter and looked through the glass at the big vats of ice cream. With flavors such as rhubarb pie, pancake and syrup, cotton candy, and sea salt, Lily had a hard time deciding.

"Look, they have lemon sherbet," Alice enthused.

They all knew it was Gram's favorite; she never indulged in any other kind.

"Well, that settles it. I'm getting a lemon sherbet on a waffle cone," Alice said.

Lily waffled between that and an ice cream sundae. "Oh jeez, I don't know, I can't make up my mind."

Isabelle sighed. "It's only ice cream, Lily, not a major life decision."

Lily felt her cheeks go hot. "Lemon sherbet for me too, then."

When they stepped up to the counter, Isabelle said, "Three large lemon sherbets on waffle cones."

They were still working on their cones when they reached the house. Lily could feel the sun beating down on her scalp and back, and she was anxious to get out of the heat and put her feet up on the porch, watching the goings-on across the street at the beach.

The three of them stood in the driveway, looking at the old house. Lily wondered if her sisters were thinking the same thing she was: that Gram's house was now their own. But to Lily, it would always be Gram's house.

Charlie stood at the screen door, watching the three of them make their way up the driveway. He barked and whined, but they paid no attention to him as Isabelle had pointed to the old martin house high up on a pole in the backyard. Granddad had built it to attract the birds, which supposedly were populous in the area at one time. Lily didn't know if any martins had ever nested in there, but the birdhouse had been up there for as long as she could remember. She wondered if it should be taken down or left alone, or maybe taken down, painted, and put back up. She told herself it was a decision that didn't have to be made today.

Tired of waiting and having spotted their ice cream cones, Charlie jumped through the screen portion of the door and ran toward them. Lily and her sisters stared at him, stunned.

"Did he just jump through the screen?" Isabelle asked.

Alice laughed. "I guess the first order of business will be to replace the screen door."

Lily went to scold him, but Isabelle interrupted her. "Aw, leave him alone. I think it's kind of nice that he wants to be with us. If only we could get that reaction from a decent man."

Alice snorted and Lily chuckled.

Charlie looked longingly at what was left of Lily's cone. Feeling guilty, she tossed it to him and he wolfed it down.

"Doesn't he ever chew his food?" Isabelle asked.

They climbed up onto the porch, and Isabelle sat in the wicker rocker and gently rocked back and forth. She held her hand out for Charlie to come to her and obediently, he trotted over so she could pet him. But when he eyed the rest of her cone, she laughed and gave it to him. He licked the palm of her hand.

"Next time we should remember to bring something back for Charlie," Alice said.

"He likes vanilla ice cream. No chocolate."

"Noted."

"What do we think of Gram's will?" Lily asked. She was curious about her sisters' thoughts regarding their inheritance.

Isabelle spoke first. "As for me, I think it's perfect. It will give me a nice chunk of change to go traveling. I'm thinking Tibet or Nepal or India."

As for Lily, the inheritance came at the right time. Once they sold the house, she could use part of her portion to pay off her debts. The thought of selling the place made her a little sick, but she needed the money. It also made her resentful to have to use her inheritance to pay off Jamie's debt.

"I suppose we'll have to decide what to do with the place," Alice said. "The only thing I know is I don't want to sell it."

Lily's heart sank. She didn't want to sell it either, but she felt she had no choice. She did not need two homes. And her life was in California. She also knew that she didn't want to get into a big fight with Alice.

"Why don't we read the letter Gram left us," Isabelle said, pulling the envelope out of her purse and waving it around.

"Let's hear what Gram has to say," Lily said.

The three of them got comfortable, and Charlie stretched out by Isabelle's chair and closed his eyes.

Using her fingernail, Isabelle sliced open the envelope and pulled out the contents. When she unfolded the letter, Lily could see that it was only one sheet.

Isabelle leaned back in her chair and began to read:

Dear Isabelle, Lily, and Alice,
If you're reading this letter, then I am no longer with you.

As you know, I've left everything to you, as was always my wish since your mother died.

The house on Star Shine Drive is full of memories, mostly happy ones. I understand that you all have your own lives in places that are far away from Hideaway Bay. You have my blessing to sell the house as I don't want anyone to feel obligated or tied down to the house or to the past. But I ask that you wait for one year after my death before you decide. People should never make major decisions in the first twelve months after a death. And once the house on Star Shine Drive is sold, that will cut all your ties to Hideaway Bay. But I leave the decision to the three of you.

On a final note, my greatest desire has always been for the three of you to put your differences aside and patch things up. Your siblings are the people in your life who will know you the longest. I ask that each one of you do your part to mend the fence. I promise you that if you do, you will be richly rewarded and you will not regret it.

Be happy.
Love,
Gram

They sat there in silence for a while, a silence punctuated by Charlie's snores, the muted conversations of beachgoers, and the low whine of a lawn mower in the distance.

It was Alice who spoke first.

"You know, Lily, you could sell your place and live here in Gram's house. You could move back to Hideaway Bay."

Lily's eyes widened in alarm as she looked at her sister. That was the problem with Alice: She wore rose-colored glasses and tended to view things optimistically. She had a fairy-tale outlook on life, making things sound simple when they were anything but.

When Lily said nothing, Alice continued. "If you sold your house, you could put the proceeds toward that massive debt Jamie left you with."

Isabelle stopped rocking. "What debt?" A frown furrowed the skin between her dark eyebrows.

Lily sighed. She supposed she could tell Isabelle. After all, she was her sister; that would mean something, wouldn't it? And hadn't Gram wanted them to "mend the fence"? But she reminded herself to pull Alice aside later and ask her not to blab her business all over town.

Lily told Isabelle the condensed version of her sorry tale.

"What are you going to do?" Isabelle asked. "You can't live the rest of your life under the shackles of that kind of debt. It will wear you down."

"I know that. I've been stuck in a bit of a rut since Jamie's death."

"That's understandable, Lily," Alice said reassuringly.

"Alice is right. You could live here for the year, or you could come traveling with me," Isabelle said.

Lily blinked. She couldn't imagine globetrotting with Isabelle and living a bohemian life. But at least they gave her some options. She did appreciate her sister's offer.

Isabelle shifted the conversation. "Do you have any savings?"

"Not like that," Lily replied.

"It makes the most sense for you to sell your house and move in here for the year," Alice chirped again. "Who knows, maybe I'll sell my place in Chicago and move in with you."

Lily stared at her, not sure if she was joking or not. She couldn't tell.

"I don't know. I have a job back home and friends."

"You could have all that here," Isabelle pointed out. She crossed one leg over the other and rocked gently.

They went quiet for another moment, and Lily's head spun from all the possibilities that had been presented to her.

"I definitely don't want to sell Gram's house," Alice repeated. Alice was the most sentimental of the three, so this statement did not surprise Lily and by the look on Isabelle's face, it didn't surprise her either.

"You can buy out my share," Lily said.

"We'll see. We'd have to wait the year per Gram's instructions," Alice said.

"Of course," Lily said. She wondered what was prompting Alice's thoughts about moving back to Hideaway Bay. Just because she didn't want to sell Gram's house didn't mean she had to permanently move back. But it was true what both her sisters said: Gram's will gave Lily some options she hadn't had that morning. It made breathing a little bit easier.

"You can buy out my portion as well," Isabelle chimed in. "There's no way I'm staying in Hideaway Bay."

Lily and Alice exchanged a glance between them. They knew Isabelle loved traveling, but they hadn't known she felt so strongly about not returning to Hideaway Bay.

"I have no interest in keeping the house. Or anything that ties me to this place. When the year is up, I'm all for selling. If you want to keep it, Alice, be my guest, but you'll have to buy me out."

Alice flinched. Isabelle's delivery could be harsh sometimes. And with Alice, you had to proceed with caution. She was the sensitive sort. Lily supposed they were all sensitive in their own way, or maybe only with each other.

Alice's chin wobbled, and Lily immediately recognized her sister's imminent breakdown. She reached forward and patted Alice's hand. She glanced over at Isabelle and said pointedly, "We don't have to make any decisions today. Let's see how the year plays out before we go putting the for sale sign up in the front yard." There was no sense in bursting Alice's balloon.

Alice leaned back in her chair, lifting her leg to rest her foot on the seat of it. She rested her elbow on the armrest, biting her finger, her head turning toward the lake across the street.

The tears that had threatened only moments earlier disappeared, and Lily let go of her hand and leaned back against the wicker lounge. Charlie, sensing tension, got up and paced along the porch, traveling from Lily to Alice to Isabelle then back again.

Lily leaned forward, kissed the top of his head, and whispered, "It's all right, Charlie, settle down."

Chapter Sixteen

1963

Junie

Junie waited at the front door for Paul. They'd been dating for two months now. She wanted to intercept him before he came into the house. Behind her, in the kitchen, was the sound of both Margaret and the baby, Stephen, crying.

"Not yet, Bill!" Margaret wailed. Stephen fussed in her lap. Junie had heard her say the baby was teething.

"I said it's time to go home, Margaret," Bill said.

Junie rolled her eyes, listening to them bicker. It was always the same old thing. Bill liked to tell Margaret what to do, and her sister didn't like being told what to do.

"What's the rush?" her father asked sharply. "It's early yet. Margaret might want to sit outside on the porch with the baby." Bill said something Junie couldn't hear, but his tone was churlish.

Everyone went quiet except the baby, who continued to fuss.

By the time Paul pulled up in front of the house, the argument had picked up again and the voices had raised to shouting. Junie didn't bother saying goodbye. She exited the house, the door slamming behind her. She carried her purse in one hand and pulled on her jacket because the autumn nights had been cool. There was a bushel basket of apples on the front porch whose sweet, crisp smell drifted up to her. She grabbed two, buffed them on her coat, and slipped them into her pockets.

She looked up and down the street as she trotted down the steps. When she spotted Paul getting out of his car, her features softened, and she broke into a smile. But she immediately cringed, her smile fading and her neck disappearing into her hunched shoulders as more shouting emerged from the house. Their raised voices were like nails on a chalkboard to her.

As Paul walked up the driveway, twirling his car keys in his hand, he glanced toward the house and his expression darkened.

"What's going on?" he asked, nodding toward her house. He stood next to her, placing his hand on her arm. She liked when he did things like that.

She didn't look at him. Instead, she looked down, kicking a stone with the toe of her shoe. "The usual. Margie and Bill are at it again."

"They fight like this all the time?" Paul asked, incredulous.

Junie nodded. "They decided to bring their fighting over here." She still didn't look at him. She couldn't. Her stomach roiled and she felt the heat in her cheeks.

He took her hand in his, rubbing her knuckles with his fingers. She always loved how her hand felt in his: safe and connected.

He lowered his voice to a whisper. "Come on, let's get out of here. Twomey's for a beer?"

"That's the last thing I want. Drink is the cause of a lot of grief." She didn't know what she wanted to do. Suddenly, she was tired and not in the mood for anything.

"For someone so young, you sure are loaded with a lot of wisdom," he said thoughtfully.

Junie glanced up at him, loving the look of him. The thick, dark hair, those beautiful blue eyes. She couldn't help reaching up and stroking the side of his cheek. He took her hand and kissed the inside of her wrist. Her stomach calmed down and the tension seeped out of her body.

"Come on, then, we'll drive out to the lake."

"Paul, it's almost seven. It's an hour's drive. It'll be almost dark by the time we get there."

"So what?" he said. "It's not too cold. We'll pick up burgers or hot dogs on the way."

"It's a long way to go for a burger or a hot dog," she said.

"Not too long if you're in good company," he said, and he winked at her.

The smile that emerged on her face was slow but generous. He always knew what she needed. He was good that way.

He opened the car door for her, and she stopped before she slid in. "Are you sure you don't mind? It's a drive."

"Not at all, it'll be fun," he said easily.

She smiled, all her fears and worries evaporating. She leaned into him and pressed her lips to his. "Paul Reynolds, you know, you could make a girl fall in love with you."

"That's the plan."

CHAPTER SEVENTEEN

Lily

Lily was up early and decided to head down to the beach. As she made her way down the stairs followed by Charlie, she smelled something delicious and heard the sound of the oven on. She followed the aroma to the kitchen and spied Alice at the sink, washing up dishes.

"What are you making?" Lily asked. "It smells divine."

"Egg strata."

Lily leaned over and peeked through the oven window at the scrambled egg mixture. She spotted ham, melted cheese, and tomatoes.

"It needs another half hour," Alice said. She rinsed the dishes under the tap and laid them in the dish rack to dry.

"I never realized how much you like being in the kitchen," Lily noted.

"I find it therapeutic."

Lily couldn't help but wonder what else was going on in Alice's life that she was baking and cooking up a storm. Her sister hadn't been out of the kitchen since she'd arrived.

"Why are you up so early?" Alice asked. The dishes done, she emptied the dish bowl of soapy water and placed it upside down, leaning it against one wall of the sink, just like Gram used to do.

Lily made a face. "Couldn't sleep. Thought I'd go for a walk on the beach."

Charlie whined at her side, anxious to go.

"Do you mind if I tag along?" Alice asked, peeling off her yellow rubber gloves. She glanced at the clock on the wall. "I've got time."

When they were growing up, their mother used to say—quite often—"take Alice with you." That was always met by groans and protests from Lily and Isabelle. There had been such an age difference between them; Lily was six years older than Alice, and Isabelle was eight.

"Yeah, sure, come on," Lily said.

At the front door, Charlie whined and pranced around. Lily kicked off her slippers and slipped into a pair of cheap flip-flops. When she opened the front door, Charlie brushed past her, knocking her off-balance and into the wall with an "oomph." He leapt off the porch and lumbered toward the beach.

"Stop!" she called after him, and he did as he was told, sitting on the lawn and looking back at her expectantly. She didn't want him darting across the street. Even though it was the crack of dawn, there could still be the odd car going by. Besides, he needed to wait for her. What he needed was some manners, she thought.

"He's kind of clumsy, isn't he?" Alice observed, pulling a hoodie on over her T-shirt and jeans.

"Very."

Once they crossed the street, Alice kicked off her sandals and carried them along as they walked across the sand.

"I forgot how much I love the beach," Alice said.

"But you've got a beach in Chicago."

Alice shrugged. "I know, but I rarely go. I'm always working. By the time I get home at night, it's dark."

Lily bent over to retrieve three pieces of beach glass. A blue, a green, and a brown. Over the last few days, she'd been carrying a small plastic container with her to the beach every morning, and it filled up fairly quickly. She liked collecting the glass, but she didn't know what she was going to do with it yet. Maybe nothing.

"I forgot about all the beach glass around here," Alice said. She bent down and retrieved a piece that was half buried in the sand. It was cobalt blue in color. Every day, the tide brought in a new batch, washing it ashore and depositing it on the sand.

Charlie trotted off, stopping every once in a while to stick his snout in the sand and investigate something, but he remained within earshot.

When they were younger, they used to take their pails to the beach in the mornings and fill them with beach glass. Green, brown, and white were the prominent colors. Sometimes Lily would find a lavender-colored piece or a shard of pottery or china. Red and orange were rare finds, and she always felt lucky when she found one.

Alice handed the piece to Lily, who turned it around in her hand and then looked out on the horizon. Many years ago, the Great Lakes had been the route from the Atlantic to the interior of the country. Granddad had said the lake at one time had been filled with trawlers and other types of boats. Looking out at the empty horizon, it was hard to imagine. The boats used to dump their garbage overboard, and the glass bottles sank and broke and over time—many decades—the water would dull the edges.

She handed it back to Alice, who shook her head and said, "No, you keep it."

Lily added it to her collection in the plastic container.

She stared out at the lake, thinking of everything hidden beneath the surface of the water. The shallowest of the Great Lakes, Lake Erie was some two hundred and fifty feet at its deepest point.

Granddad had regaled them with tales of shipwrecks off Lake Erie, which he never seemed to be in short supply of. Once in a while he'd pepper his stories with tales of the other Great Lakes. He told them about the battles on Lake Erie and Lake Ontario between the United States and the British during the War of 1812. He'd even shown them a small cannonball he'd found on the beach back in the 1970s. After he died, Gram had donated it to the Buffalo Historical Society.

The lake reminded Lily of the way people were in general: appearing one way on the outside, but one never really knew what was lurking beneath the surface.

The walk was short, only twenty minutes, as Alice reminded her of the strata in the oven waiting for them back home. Despite the early hour, there were a few people on the beach. Lily called Charlie and with a wave beckoned him back to her. As they hit the sidewalk before crossing the street back to the house, they ran into Thelma talking to a man Lily didn't recognize.

The sun was climbing in the sky behind the houses across the street. It was going to be another scorcher. And although Lily knew she should start making plans to head back to California, she felt as if there was no hurry. She asked herself again, as she had several times, what was she returning to? For reasons she couldn't explain, she liked being back at Gram's house with her sisters. Given their history, it defied logic.

Thelma waved them over with a hearty "Hello, girls!"

Lily and Alice walked over and hugged Thelma in turn. Thelma seemed to be getting along all right in the aftermath of Gram's death. She was dressed in a light fleece jacket and a pair of jeans and sneakers. She still wore her wedding set on her left hand, although she'd been a widow for years. On her right wrist she wore a silver cuff bracelet with a turquoise stone set as its centerpiece.

"How are you holding up?" Thelma asked, stepping back and placing her hands on her hips.

Alice shuffled and looked down at her feet. Lily nodded and murmured, "All right."

"Let me introduce you to Simon Bishop," Thelma said with a nod toward the man who stood at her side. The name sounded vaguely familiar, but Lily couldn't place it. Maybe Gram had mentioned it once or twice? She couldn't be sure.

Lily eyed him, gathering her assessment. He was tall and broad-shouldered with dark wavy hair and dark eyes that reminded her of rich chocolate. He wore a navy blue polo shirt and a pair of khaki shorts that showed off his tanned legs, and he had deck shoes on his feet.

"Simon, these are two of Junie's granddaughters, Lily and Alice."

"I'm sorry for your loss," Simon said. He eyed Charlie. "That's a big dog."

"They'll tell you he's a gentle giant but don't believe them. He's as clumsy as they come."

Simon laughed and reached out and petted the dog on the top of his head. Charlie stepped closer to Simon and sniffed at his legs.

"Did you know Gram?" Alice asked.

He smiled. "Sure, everyone knew Junie. She was the salt of the earth."

Lily smiled. That was an expression Gram used to use to describe good people. It warmed her inside to have it said about her grandmother.

"I'm sorry I couldn't be here for the wake and funeral. I was in the southwest doing a series of book signings," he explained.

"Don't worry about it, Gram would have understood," Lily said.

"When I first arrived in Hideaway Bay, your grandmother and Thelma were quite welcoming."

"Where's Isabelle?" Thelma asked. With a turn toward Simon, she added, "Isabelle is their older sister."

"How long are you girls in town for?" Thelma asked.

Alice scrunched up her nose. "I go back in two weeks."

Alice's tone indicated that she wasn't looking forward to that, or at least that's how Lily read it.

"And you, Lily?"

"My plans are up in the air," Lily said truthfully. "But I should be making moves to head home. Probably in the next week or two."

"It's a shame none of you can stay," Thelma said.

"Do you live in Hideaway Bay full-time or only for the summer?" Lily asked Simon, not wanting to leave him out of the conversation.

"I live here all year."

"He's currently looking for an assistant," Thelma said. "Part-time. He's writing his next book."

That's where Lily knew him from. He was a fairly well-known horror writer. Jamie had read a book or two by him. All she remembered was the one night he had to sleep with the bedroom light on.

"So, if you know of anyone . . ." Simon said.

"Lily could do it," Alice volunteered.

Lily stared straight ahead, not blinking. Her impulsive sister had volunteered her for a part-time job.

"I couldn't—"

Alice cut her off. "How long is it for?"

"Only for the summer, maybe a little longer. Three or four months," Simon said.

"I should be heading back to California," Lily said. Her voice sounded weak. She hadn't thought about getting a job in Hideaway Bay. Her plans were up in the air, and she didn't know what she wanted to do.

Thelma ignored her, apparently having joined Team Alice, and asked, "Didn't you used to work for a publishing company?"

"Well, yes, I did, out of college, but it was only an internship," Lily stammered. "I haven't worked in that field since then."

Simon smiled. His smile was breathtaking: broad and generous. It could quite possibly power the whole area of Hideaway Bay. "I understand if you have to get back to California. But if you change your mind about that, the job is nothing too formal; you'd be working out of my home office."

"Oh, I don't know," she said, wracking her brain for something definite. Why did she feel as if she were being swept up in a current and pulled out to sea?

"Why don't you think about it and come out to my house some day? I'll give you the particulars of the job and you can decide if it's for you or not," he said easily. "No pressure."

If it was no pressure, why did she feel obligated? A little voice in her head told her to pack up her car and drive back to California immediately.

Inspiration hit her. "Oh, you know, it probably wouldn't be a good idea. As you can see, I've got my dog with me, and I can't leave him alone at the house."

Simon eyed the dog, petted him on his head, and smiled. "That's fine. You can bring him with you to work."

Foiled. She sighed.

"I live in a house on the bluff," he said. He turned and pointed to the multimillion-dollar houses lining the cliffs. He pulled his cell phone from his pocket. "Give me your number and I'll send you my address."

Lily found herself rattling off her phone number despite her misgivings. Again, she felt swept up in a tide.

"Thanks for that. I look forward to hearing from you," he said.

"Sure," she said, her voice faint. Beside her, Alice and Thelma smiled encouragingly.

"Nice meeting you both," he said. He put up his hand in a wave and turned and headed up the sidewalk toward town.

"He must be in a hurry for an assistant," Lily said. Surely there must be someone else in town who could do this? Why had she been singled out? Were Thelma and Alice being helpful? Did they think she needed a distraction?

"He sure is," Thelma said. "His last two books were flops. It's make-or-break with this one. His career could be over if he doesn't get it right." That was Thelma, noted for her characteristic unbridled honesty. Tell it like it is, she herself would say.

"Thelma, would you join us for breakfast?" Alice asked. When Thelma hesitated, Alice added, "I've made strata. There's plenty."

"Well, all right, as long as it's not too much trouble," Thelma said.

"Not at all," Lily said. "There's more than enough."

Thelma inserted herself between the two of them and they headed back to Gram's house. Behind the house, the morning sun had just cleared the roofline.

As they stepped into the front room with its wide-planked floor, Thelma's eyes misted. "It's not the same without Junie here," she said, her voice shaky.

Lily wrapped her arm around Thelma. "It's never going to be the same."

Thelma shook her head and cleared her throat. "Well, come on, where's that breakfast I was promised?"

Lily and Alice exchanged a smile. Thelma had never been known as the touchy-feely type. Gruff and unsentimental was more like it. Lily could never understand how Thelma and her Gram had become such good friends, lifelong friends. But then didn't Gram always say that? That old friends were the best friends.

They tramped through to the kitchen, the morning sun filtering through the curtains at the window. Alice laid a quick table with three settings, and Thelma took the seat closest to the window.

While Alice served up the plates, Lily toasted rye bread and put the kettle on for tea.

"Would you prefer tea or coffee?"

"Coffee is fine," Thelma said. "Instant. None of that coffeemaker stuff."

Lily pulled down the jar of instant coffee from the cabinet that she knew Gram had kept on hand for her friend. She didn't feel like coffee herself and went through the variety of teabags in the cupboard before settling on a mint one.

The toast popped up and Lily buttered the slices quickly and laid them on a plate, carrying them over to the table. She grabbed two jars of jam from the refrigerator, one apricot, the other raspberry.

"You girls eat like this every day?" Thelma asked. Although her voice sounded judgmental, Lily knew it was not. It was Thelma's default tone. Lily and her sisters had been around Thelma since they'd been born so they knew not to be offended.

"No," Lily said.

"No, I just feel like baking and cooking," Alice said. "In Chicago, I only have a bowl of cereal in the morning and a glass of juice."

"I like Raisin Bran myself," Thelma added. "It keeps me regular."

Lily wanted to laugh but held back. She saw a slight tug at the corner of her sister's mouth.

Once they were all seated, they dug in. Despite her age, Thelma had a good appetite. She had two servings of the strata and three slices of toast.

"I imagine you've been to see the attorney about Junie's will," Thelma said.

"We have," Lily said.

"Gram left us the house"—Alice's gaze circled around the kitchen—"but we have to wait a year before we can sell it."

Thelma nodded. "Junie told me as much. That's a smart move on your grandmother's part, making you wait a year. I know it might seem like an inconvenience, but you don't want to do something rash or something you might regret later."

"I suppose you're right," Lily said truthfully.

"And what are your plans for the house? Probably sell it?" Thelma pressed.

"We haven't decided anything yet," Lily said, noncommittal. There was truth in that. She didn't know what was going to happen. It was another instance of uncertainty in her life.

"I'd like to keep it," Alice piped in. "I think we should open an inn." She cast a side glance at Lily. "Lily and I."

"An inn? Why?" Lily asked, stunned. She didn't know where to begin with her protests, so she started with the obvious. "Neither one of us has any experience in the hospitality sector."

"How hard can it be?" Alice asked.

It was always harder than you thought it would be.

"You've got a great idea," Thelma said, slathering apricot jam onto another slice of toast. "This is a great location, right across the street from the beach and great views. Plus, you've got that big front porch where people could sit outside and watch the sunset."

Lily glared at the older woman, wishing she wouldn't play it up so much.

"That's what I thought!" Alice said. "This place is ideal for an inn. There are plenty of bedrooms and—"

"That's a problem," Lily interrupted. "Most people these days would prefer their own bathroom. They're not going to want to share with strangers." She didn't want to burst Alice's balloon, but she did need to pull her back down to earth.

"Those rooms upstairs are pretty big. We can easily add a bathroom to each one," Alice said.

Lily's eyes widened and she looked at her sister, her mouth dropping open but no words coming out.

"You should have a contractor come out and see if it's doable," Thelma suggested.

"That's a great idea," Alice said. "Do you know of anyone?"

"I do, I'll drop his number by later," Thelma said. "Hideaway Bay Home Improvement. The guy that owns that, Dylan Satler, lives next door to Sue Ann Marchek."

Lily nodded and said, "I think we're getting ahead of ourselves here. We don't know what Isabelle wants to do."

"Isabelle will want to sell it," Alice said, pouting. "I'd hate to think of strangers living here."

Lily wanted to put the brakes on her sister's ideas, but the thought of people other than Gram living here gave her pause. She hadn't even thought about that. She pushed her half-empty plate away, her appetite gone.

"Didn't you like it?" Alice asked, a frown creasing her forehead.

"It was delicious. But I've lost my appetite."

Charlie nudged her hand, and she smiled at him and scratched his fur beneath his collar. No matter what happened, at least she had her dog, she thought.

Thelma drained her mug and stood up from the table, pushing back her chair. "Well thanks, girls, for the breakfast, but I've got to run. There's a meeting in an hour about the Labor Day Festival and I'm on the committee."

"Is that thing still going on?"

"Yep, and it gets bigger every year." Thelma regarded Lily for a moment. "Would you like a stall? Junie said you used to do a lot of crafts."

Lily shook her head. "I haven't done any crafts since Jamie died. Besides, I'll be back in California by Labor Day."

"That's a shame, it's the biggest festival in Hideaway Bay. Kind of ends the summer and things."

"I wish I could stay; I'd love to help out," Alice said.

"You wouldn't be able to come back then?" Thelma asked. "For the long weekend?"

Alice shook her head. "The three weeks I took off to come here for Gram's funeral will be all the time I'll be able to take."

Thelma scowled. "What kind of company is that?"

Alice sighed. "I'm sorry, I worded that wrong. I've got all kinds of PTO accumulated in my bank, but I'm too busy at work to take any time off."

"Let me give you one piece of advice—unsolicited, of course," Thelma said. "No one on their deathbed ever wished they had worked more." Thelma started to move toward the front of the house. "Life is all about family and friends and the people you love."

Alice appeared thoughtful and said softly, "Thank you, Thelma, for the reminder."

Thelma said goodbye and Alice walked her to the front door. Lily overheard her sister say, "Don't be such a stranger. You're welcome any time."

Lily grumbled into her cup as she sipped her tea. She hated being the bad guy, but the house was going to have to be sold eventually.

CHAPTER EIGHTEEN

1963

Junie

Junie sat on her front porch during the afternoon. Thelma had called and was on her way over. The house was quiet as Ma and Daddy were at work, but from next door, she could hear Mrs. Krautwein's television blaring. *Guiding Light* again—it was all the woman could talk about. When she went on about what was happening on the soap opera, Junie's eyes had a tendency to glaze over.

Paul would be there later, after work. Ma had invited him and his parents over for dinner to discuss wedding plans. Ma was excited to be planning a wedding; she felt she'd been cheated out of one when Margaret ran off and got married down in Erie.

Thelma rounded the corner. She had on dungarees, which she'd rolled up, a sleeveless red-and-blue plaid blouse, and a pair of saddle shoes. Junie smiled at the sight of her. She was so unassuming. From a distance, Junie could see from the way Thelma's bangs curled up close to her hairline that she had trimmed them again. But as she approached the house, her face bore a darkened, distracted expression. Junie's smile wobbled at the thought of something bothering her friend. Since Barb left for college, their trio felt like a two-legged stool. She wondered if Bobby had broken up with Thelma. They had been dating for six months and Junie wondered what she saw in him; they seemed so ill-suited to each other. But when Junie brought it up once, Thelma had replied, "He's better than nothing."

"Hey," Thelma said, walking up the short driveway and sitting on the step below Junie.

"Hi, Thelm," Junie said. Tension rolled off of Thelma's body and Junie frowned, wondering again what had happened.

Thelma leaned forward, resting her elbows on her knees.

"What's wrong?" Junie asked.

"Who said anything's wrong?" Thelma snapped.

"Now I know something's wrong." They'd been friends too long for Junie not to be able to read Thelma. She scooched down one step until she sat next to her friend, arm to arm, elbow to elbow, thigh to thigh.

Thelma sighed, then burst into tears. Quickly, she wiped them away with the back of her hand.

Junie felt a bit sick to her stomach. She had never seen Thelma so distressed. She'd never even seen her cry before; she was usually so tough. "What is it? Has something happened?"

When Thelma spoke, her voice wobbled, but she managed to get the words out. "I guess Bobby and I are getting married."

Although this surprised Junie as Thelma had said more than once that Bobby was all right "for now," she threw her arm around her friend and squeezed her.

"Congratulations! We can plan our weddings together. Wait until Barb finds out."

This resulted in Thelma breaking down into sobs, and her shoulders shook beneath Junie's arm. Junie looked at her friend in alarm. Shouldn't she be happy? Junie was. She couldn't wait until she married Paul and started their new life together. Paul had got down on one knee on Christmas Eve, right before they were to go to midnight Mass, and proposed. She'd been hopeful, half expecting it, but she was still surprised. All during Mass, her cheeks hurt from smiling, and she kept looking down at the diamond solitaire Paul had slid on her finger. Later she'd heard her mother on the phone with her aunt in Wisconsin: "You should see the ring, it's a real knuckle dragger." It had been a wonderfully happy Christmas.

Thelma's distress pulled Junie back to the present.

"What is it?" Junie asked, her own voice shaking.

Thelma stopped crying long enough to whisper, "We have to get married."

Oh.

Junie had heard of girls being in the family way before marriage. But she'd never known one personally. There'd been that one girl in school—Brenda was her name. She disappeared for most of the year only to return in April, looking a bit heavier and haggard. There were rumors that she'd gone away, had a baby, and given it up for adoption. Junie couldn't imagine anything worse.

Her heart broke for her friend. Thelma was tough, but then her life had been difficult. Junie often wondered if, had things been different—had her mother not died so young, had her father not been such an oaf—Thelma might have turned out different. Still, she was her best friend. Tears stung the backs of Junie's eyes and she swallowed hard.

"Everything's going to be all right," she announced with more conviction than she felt.

"Is it?" Thelma asked, looking at her friend for the first time since she arrived. Her eyes were red and swollen and there were dark circles beneath her eyes, suggesting there'd been a lot of crying and perhaps some sleepless nights. Although a baby before marriage would keep anyone up at night. "I'm afraid Bobby might back out and not marry me."

Junie's head reared back in shock. "Why would you think that?"

Thelma's tears slowed and she appeared thoughtful. "Because he's got that weak chin, and he can't make a decision to save his life. Every time we go out to eat, he can't decide between a hot dog or a hamburger."

Junie thought Thelma being pregnant was a different situation but said nothing. She was also dying to ask her about the sex, but she didn't want to annoy her friend. She already had enough on her plate.

"What are you afraid of?" Junie asked, lowering her voice.

"Honestly? That Bobby won't marry me, and I'll have to give up my baby," she said. Immediately, her eyes welled up again until her tears spilled over. "I know what it's like to grow up without your mother, and that isn't going to happen to my kid."

For the first time since she'd known Thelma, Junie realized that she had a mother-sized hole in her heart that might possibly never heal.

"Could you keep the baby and raise it yourself?" Junie asked, thinking out loud.

Thelma snorted. "With my father? In that house? I wouldn't raise a bird in that house."

Junie nodded. "All right. But Bobby has said he'll marry you?"

Thelma nodded. "That's what he said last night."

"When?"

"As soon as possible. Within the next week or two."

"That soon?"

"I'm going to be having a baby in five months."

There was bound to be speculation when Thelma had her baby. Junie thought of what her mother sometimes said, about how the first baby comes any time, but the second one takes nine months. She hadn't understood that growing up, but she did now.

"Well, on the bright side, I hope it's a boy. I've got lots of experience raising boys," Thelma said with a forced laugh.

Until that moment, Junie realized, she'd never appreciated Thelma's situation. It couldn't have been easy to be forced into raising your brothers after your mother's death. There had been no female relative to step in and help, and therefore it had fallen to Thelma. More times than not, Thelma had had to cancel plans with her and Barb because she had to take care of her brothers. There had been no help and there had been no thanks.

Junie gave her friend a reassuring smile and decided it was her job to cheer her up. "Just think, next summer, we'll have a baby with us down at the lake." And hopefully by next summer, she'd be pregnant as well. She'd warned Paul that she wanted a lot of kids.

"I don't know about that," Thelma said. "I don't know how we're going to do this. How will we live on his wages working at the factory?"

"He'll have to get a better job," Junie said. "Does your dad know?"

Thelma shook her head. "No way. I'm not telling him until after we're married. Don't want to get kicked out of my house. I have nowhere to go."

"Nowhere to go? You'd come here, of course!" Junie said.

Thelma looked at her, shocked. "You'd take me in?" Her expression was one of incredulity.

"Of course I would," Junie said with a laugh. "Do you think I'd let you be thrown out to the wolves?"

A smile broke out on Thelma's face. The first true one since she'd arrived.

Junie threw her arm around her once more and smiled. "That's what friends are for."

"I guess so," Thelma agreed.

"What's wrong?" Paul asked as he pulled away from the curb. They were going for a drive.

It had been two days since Thelma had appeared at her house with her news and Junie had been unable to think of anything else. Her own wedding plans had served as a pleasant distraction from Thelma's troubles. For her, things were coming along nicely.

Dinner had gone well with Paul's parents. Ma had made her famous pot roast and she and Paul's mother had got on well, which was a relief. Mrs. Reynolds had brought a pineapple upside-down cake, and Junie had thought when she bit into the golden sugar crunch that there were definitely going to be perks to joining Paul's family. And miracle of miracles, there had been no phone call or unexpected visit from Margaret. Her sister was now pregnant with her second child after multiple miscarriages. She continued to fight all over the south side with her husband, much to the dismay of Junie's parents.

It had been decided that it was to be a fall wedding, at the end of September. The church and reception hall had been booked. Her parents had wanted the firehall—as it was significantly cheaper, and thus within their budget—but Paul's father had suggested some hotel. It was the only uncomfortable moment of the evening, when her mother's eyes widened and her father squirmed uncomfortably in his chair, not saying anything. But then Paul's father and her father stepped outside on the porch, had a chat, and when they stepped back inside, both were smiling and laughing. The hotel it was, then.

Junie and Paul had booked a honeymoon in New York City. Junie had never been outside of Buffalo, other than Hideaway Bay, so she was more excited about this than the actual wedding itself. But despite her excitement, at the back of her mind was Thelma and the situation in which she found herself. Church weddings in the fall, receptions at fancy hotels, and honeymoons were not in Thelma's immediate future. It was going to be a trip downtown to the justice of the peace and then right back to work at the cardboard-box factory after the ceremony.

As she sat in the passenger seat of Paul's car, she leaned against the window, twisting her engagement ring around her finger, debating about whether she should tell him or not. After some thought, she decided she didn't want to go into the marriage keeping secrets from him. Besides, she knew he wouldn't blab the news all over town. Paul could be counted on to be discreet. How many times had she talked to him about Margaret and her husband? He was a good listener.

Sometimes, on the warm summer evenings, they liked to go for drives. Paul would drive by the sites he was working at to show her, proudly. Or sometimes they drove north, south, east, or west with no particular destination in mind. More than once, they'd ended up out at Hideaway Bay. She liked the window rolled down so she could feel the warm summer breeze against her arm and neck and lifting her hair off her collar.

"Junie? Why so quiet?" Paul asked.

"It's Thelma," she finally said.

"She break up with Bobby?" he asked, looking over at her, one hand rested casually on the top of the steering wheel. It was one of the first things she'd thought, as well, when Thelma arrived two days ago, upset. It made her wonder if the marriage was doomed before it had even started.

Junie sighed and rested her chin on her hand, looking out her window. "They're getting married soon because Thelma's pregnant."

Paul's head snapped in her direction. "You're kidding me, right?"

Junie shook her head. "I wish I were."

Paul went quiet, and Junie could see the muscle twitching along his jaw.

At the back of her mind, she couldn't help but think about her and Paul's relationship. Her mother had once told her to never let the boys get "frisky" because that's how trouble started. Paul was a gentleman through and through. They hadn't gone all the way, as she'd told him she wanted to wait for their wedding night, and he'd been agreeable. But she couldn't help but wonder if he'd been too agreeable. When he kissed her, she felt all kinds of things. Deep in her belly was the most wonderful fluttering sensation that felt like if the kissing continued, it could build. She was anxious to explore that. But it would have to wait.

Paul turned onto Ithaca Street, a shady, tree-lined street where couples parked for a little bit of necking. She smiled to herself.

He pulled up along the curb in front of a darkened house. "I can hear you worrying over on my side of the car."

"Just thinking."

"Tell me."

Junie wondered if she would sound foolish. Maybe she was being ridiculous. She put her hands in her lap and stared at them.

Paul turned the knob on the radio, lowering the volume.

"Thelma and Bobby haven't been going out that long," she started.

"So?"

"Well, they didn't wait very long before they . . ." Her voice trailed off.

Paul chuckled. "Basic math says they didn't wait at all!"

Junie lifted her head and laughed. Playfully, she hit him on the arm. "No, I don't mean that."

Paul leaned into her. She could smell his aftershave, something subtle. His shirt was pressed, and his pants had a crease in them. But those blue eyes of his . . . He was so lovely, sometimes she couldn't believe how lucky she was.

"Are you jealous"—Paul's eyes twinkled with mischief—"that Thelma knows about sex, and you don't?"

Junie felt her cheeks go hot. "Well, no, I—" she stammered. "Okay, maybe a bit."

"You'll get your turn," he said with a devilish grin.

She sighed and went back to staring at her hands. "It's just that . . ."

"What?" Paul pressed.

"Their relationship seems to be full of passion," Junie said.

Paul scoffed at her suggestion. "Their relationship is a lot of things, but I doubt it's passionate."

When she didn't say anything, he studied her by the dashboard light. "You think because she ended up pregnant they have a lot of passion? You think maybe we're not passionate people because we've decided to wait?"

Junie shrugged her slim shoulders. She didn't really know. She certainly hoped that wasn't the case. How sad would that be?

Paul reached over and laid his hand on her thigh. That touch stirred something within her. Something so deep and primitive that she bit her lip.

Paul lowered his voice to a whisper that felt like a caress. "Don't confuse passion with lack of self-control. What goes on between Thelma and Bobby is none of our business. I'll tell you what my father once told me: no one—and I mean no one—knows what goes on between a couple except the couple themselves."

Junie found herself nodding. There was some truth to what he said. Margaret was a prime example. To everyone outside her marriage, the whole situation looked disastrous and untenable, yet Margaret would be the first one to defend Bill, or "my Bill," as she referred to him.

Paul edged closer to her, reaching his arm across the back of the seat, and faced her. "You think because I haven't tried to have sex with you, that I'm not interested?"

Junie slowly turned her head to look at him. His magnificent face was all chiseled planes and angles in the shadows cast by the dashboard lights. He really was beautiful.

He slid across the bench seat, putting his arm around her and pulling her close.

"I have wanted to make love to you since I first saw you," he whispered.

A warm, pleasant blush fanned out across her chest, up her neck, and over her face.

"When you gave me that dime?" she teased softly.

He looked startled, and then a bark of laughter escaped his lips. "No, when I first *saw* you. When I first noticed you. Two summers ago, at the beach, at the bonfire, when you gave me my dime back."

"So, you do want me?" she asked.

"Of course!"

"Your self-control is admirable," she said.

"I know. I should get some kind of prize," he muttered.

They were quiet for a few moments. Junie enjoyed being in his arms. Paul picked up her hand and held it in his, rubbing along her knuckles, caressing the back of her hand.

"The truth is, I respect you, Junie. I would never want to put you in a position like the one Thelma finds herself in today. I couldn't do that to you. We have the rest of our lives to discover each other in the bedroom."

She liked the sound of that. She couldn't help it that she reached up for him, wanting to kiss him, wanting to feel his lips on hers. Sometimes, even in the midst of his embrace, she felt as if she couldn't get close enough to him.

A week later, Junie was on her way to her shift at the drugstore. Her thoughts were preoccupied with bridesmaids' dresses. She couldn't decide between lavender or a soft blush color. They were going for a fitting on Saturday, she and her bridesmaids. Thelma had to bow out because of her burgeoning pregnancy. But Junie was distracted by the appearance of Stanley Schumacher crossing her path.

Stanley hadn't changed much since their school days. He was still pimply, his hair was too slicked down, and his glasses were like the bottoms of Coke bottles. But his clothes were always clean. Junie couldn't help but like him. He always seemed to be in a good mood. And despite the constant bullying in grade school, he had risen above it. It turned out he had a mouth on him and although he couldn't fight with his fists, he had a penchant for cutting his tormentor down to size with a wicked quip. He was scrappy, she thought. Besides, he'd always been nice to her, and there was no reason to be unkind to him.

He stopped when he spotted her. He was dressed in dungarees and a green-and-orange plaid shirt.

"Hey, Junie, how's it going?"

"Great, Stanley, how are you?"

"Couldn't be better. Listen, is Thelma still seeing that loser, Bobby?" he asked. He rocked on his heels, watching her expression.

Oh no, thought Junie. She knew Stanley had carried a torch for Thelma since grade school.

"Oh, jeez, Stanley," Junie started, fumbling for words.

Stanley paled. "Is she all right? Nothing has happened to her, has it?"

"No, she's fine," Junie said. She figured it would be best to tell him the truth. He'd find out anyway. And someone else might not be as kind. "I'm so sorry, Stanley, but Thelma and Bobby got married yesterday."

His face crumpled, and he looked as if someone had punched him in the gut. Junie felt for him; she'd had no idea his feelings for Thelma ran so deep. Her heart ached for his obvious distress.

"That idiot isn't good enough for her," Stanley said, his voice full of emotion. Junie had to agree with him on this point, but Thelma was married to him now with a baby on the way, so she kept her opinion to herself.

"Again, I'm sorry," she stammered.

"Thanks for letting me know, Junie, you've done me a solid," Stanley said, and before she could respond, he walked away.

She watched him until he disappeared around the corner, hoping that someday he would find someone worthy of that fierce, loyal love of his.

CHAPTER NINETEEN

Lily

It was almost midnight and Lily was curled up on the wicker sofa on the front porch, listening to the surf roll in across the street. The night air was warm for May. Charlie lay at her feet, snoring and farting. As she sat there, she filed her nails, not thinking of anything in particular.

After an evening of baking, Alice had gone to bed, declaring that she was beat. The house retained the aroma of vanilla from the cake she had made. Fortunately, there had been no more talk of turning Gram's house into an inn, and Lily was grateful for that.

Isabelle appeared in the doorway, wearing an orange-colored shift that fell to her ankles. Lily could see the straps of her bathing suit around her neck. Her wild mane of dark hair was pulled on top of her head into a messy bun.

"Oh, I thought you had gone to bed," Isabelle said. She grabbed a beach towel off the porch railing, rolled it up, and tucked it under her arm.

"Too warm to sleep," Lily said. "Where are you going?"

"I'm going for a swim."

"Now? It's dark out! And wouldn't the water be a little cold?"

Isabelle shrugged. Even at the best of times, her cavalier attitude got on Lily's nerves. She acted like she didn't care. Like she'd rather be anywhere else but there. Like she had better things to do. It was an insult to their mother and to their grandparents. But Lily bit her tongue and kept her thoughts to herself.

When Isabelle didn't respond, Lily asked, "Have you ever gone swimming at night before?"

Isabelle chortled. "I've been going out swimming every night since I got here. You and Alice are usually in bed."

Lily felt herself go pale. "Isabelle, you shouldn't swim alone at night. Or ever."

The current was unseen and could be powerful. There hadn't been a lot of drownings at Hideaway Bay, but there had been some. They'd grown up on the beach and all three of them were good swimmers, but

Lily remained respectful of the water. Granddad had pounded into their heads that if they got caught up in a rip current, they needed to start swimming parallel to the beach. She never forgot that, and she hoped she'd never have to find out if it worked or not.

"Okay, Mom," Isabelle said, rolling her eyes.

Lily clamped her lips shut, deciding it wasn't worth the fight. If Isabelle wanted to do something stupid and careless then that was on her. It was foolish to even try and argue with her. Isabelle had a fierce stubborn streak, but Lily hadn't realized that some of her ideas bordered on the downright dangerous. It made her wonder what else she'd gotten up to during her world travels.

Isabelle sighed. "Why don't you come with me and then I won't have to swim alone."

"In the dark?"

"Well, yes, it would be dark," Isabelle said. "But I don't go out too far."

"That's a relief," Lily said, her voice full of sarcasm.

Isabelle stepped off the porch and looked over her shoulder. "Make up your mind. Are you coming or not?"

With a sigh of exasperation, Lily uncrossed her legs and stood. "All right, give me five minutes to put my suit on."

"What about Clumsy?" Isabelle asked with a nod toward Charlie.

"He'll go too." *That way he can sound the alarm if we go missing,* Lily thought sourly.

She dashed upstairs and when she reached the landing, the floor creaked loudly, causing her to pause and wince. There was no light coming from beneath Alice's bedroom door, and Lily tiptoed to her room, careful not to wake her.

In her room, she hurriedly stripped off her clothes and pulled on her bathing suit, grabbing her cover-up from the closet and zipping it up as she tiptoed back down the stairs.

Isabelle waited at the curb with Charlie by her side. She appeared to be talking to the dog, but Lily couldn't hear what she said. She pulled the door closed behind her, twisting the knob to make sure it was locked, then patted her pocket for her house key. She took another towel from the railing and folded it up quickly. Satisfied, she joined her sister at the curb.

They walked across the street to the beach. The street was quiet, the streetlamps illuminating the houses along Star Shine Drive. Some were darkened and others had lights on in the windows, but for the most part, all was quiet in Hideaway Bay. The only sound was the water lapping at the shore.

The sand was still warm, having retained some of the heat from the day. But when Lily dug her feet in, it was much cooler below the surface. Charlie loped alongside them, apparently game for anything.

Near the water's edge, Isabelle threw her towel on the sand and kicked off her sandals. Then she pulled her shift over her head and tossed it on top of her beach towel. She removed the clip from her hair and her hair tumbled down around her shoulders. Lily did the same, except she folded her cover-up and placed it neatly on top of the beach towel.

Tall and lean, Isabelle had a toned, athletic body, whereas Lily was shorter with more curves. In high school, Isabelle had played basketball and volleyball while Lily had been more interested in art club and French club.

The two of them stood at the water's edge, letting the gentle surf wash over their feet. It was cold and Lily shivered. Although it was dark, the moon shone bright on the water, making the inky black surface shine in places. Isabelle trudged forward into the water and once she was in deeper, she dove in. Lily went at a slower pace, getting acclimated to being in the lake in the dark. It had been a long time since she'd gone night-time swimming. Although the water was chilly, it was refreshing, and she traveled further out until she was waist-deep. She turned and beckoned Charlie, who paced along the shoreline, whining.

"Come on, Charlie," she encouraged, but the dog didn't budge from his position at the water's edge.

Isabelle's head popped up and she blew out a long, gasping breath. "That feels great!" Her dark hair was plastered against her head, and she treaded water, straightening the straps of her bathing suit. Lily cupped her hands, pushing the water away from her, the water sluicing through her fingers. It was actually quite enjoyable. Away on the horizon, she could see some lights from a handful of boats bobbing up and down on the current. Along the bluff, the multimillion-dollar houses were lit up, beacons along the shore, bright, shining lights piercing through the trees of the bluffs. Turning around, she could see the warm glow of the living room light at Gram's house, bathing the porch in a triangular shaft of amber light. Looking toward the town, she could see the twinkle of lights from the old-fashioned streetlamps.

"It's lovely out here," Lily finally admitted, her breath coming in a gasp.

"I know, right?" Isabelle smiled.

Her sister seemed so relaxed, a different person from the one she'd spent time with. It dawned on her that wherever her sister traveled to—or at least the places Lily knew about—there was always a body of water nearby. Ireland, England, the west coast, the east coast. On further contemplation, Lily couldn't picture her sister in a landlocked place. The more she thought about it, the more she realized that all of them had ended up in places where there was water nearby. Whether consciously or unconsciously, she couldn't say. Maybe the beach was in their blood; it wasn't much of a stretch to arrive at that conclusion. This enlightening thought buoyed her.

After half an hour, they made their way out of the water, dripping wet and laughing. Lily couldn't remember the last time there had been such camaraderie between the two of them.

She picked up her towel off the sand and wrapped it around her shoulders. Charlie pranced around her, looking for attention. She gave him a reassuring pat. Isabelle tilted her head to one side and shook her hair loose.

They were surprised by a man walking by at this late hour. He was dressed semi-casually in a short-sleeved business shirt and khaki shorts. She guessed him to be five ten, maybe five eleven with thick, close-cropped dark hair. Lily could see the glow of his Fitbit on his wrist. Isabelle straightened up and the man gave her an appreciative glance.

"Evening," Isabelle said softly.

He nodded in acknowledgment to her and kept walking.

Lily smiled to herself, watching the appreciation unfold between the two. Isabelle's gaze did not follow him. Instead, she busied herself collecting her belongings off the beach.

"He liked what he saw," Lily teased.

"Too short and too young," Isabelle said, folding up her beach towel.

"How could you tell?"

"I had at least an inch on him, and I'm almost forty and he hasn't seen forty yet. He's close, though. And that is my cardinal rule: never date anyone shorter or younger than me."

"Wow, you've given this a lot of thought."

"It's not that I've given it any thought, it's what I've learned from experience."

For a few moments, Lily wondered about her sister's romantic life. Isabelle didn't advertise her love life; she kept that private. Lily was pretty sure she'd had some boyfriends, but she didn't know how serious they were.

They walked across the sand, heading toward Gram's house. Isabelle cast a glance down the beach where the man had disappeared. Lily wondered if her rule was a little shaky.

She felt compelled to ask, "Izzy, has anyone ever asked you to marry them?"

A grin spread out across Isabelle's face. "Maybe once or twice."

"But you said no?"

Isabelle shrugged. "I'm not a long-term person for anyone. I don't want to be tied down like that. When I get bored, that's when I move on to the next place."

Lily thought that was kind of sad; it definitely wasn't the lifestyle for her. But then Jamie came to mind, and her marriage had such mixed results that she wondered if Isabelle might be onto something.

"How about a glass of wine when we get back?" Isabelle suggested as they reached the sidewalk.

"Sounds perfect." Lily thought she could use a glass of wine.

With a nod over her shoulder, Isabelle asked, "What about Clumsy? What does he drink?"

"Strictly water. Neat."

Isabelle burst out laughing.

***

They'd only just poured the wine and made themselves comfortable on the porch when Alice appeared in the doorway. Her hair was flat against one side of her face, and she wore a sleeveless cotton nightgown that grazed her knees. Her face had a sleepy look and her hair—a mass of red curls—spilled around her shoulders.

"Have you guys been swimming?" she asked. On her face was the familiar moue of hurt, like when she was a child and she'd been left out of one of their activities.

"It was a spur-of-the-moment thing," Lily said to reassure her.

Isabelle jumped up from her seat. "Have some wine with us. I'll get you a glass. Sit down over there."

Alice took the other chair and sat down in it, drawing her legs up. Charlie walked over to her, his tail thumping so hard against the small wicker coffee table that it slid to one side. Lily leaned over to grab hers and Isabelle's wine glasses before they got knocked over. He settled next to Alice's chair, his head as high as the armrest. Alice was able to hang her hand off the chair and pet him. It wasn't long before his eyes were at half-mast.

Isabelle returned with a glass, poured a liberal amount of wine into it, and handed it to Alice.

"I should tell you that I'm leaving the day after tomorrow," Isabelle announced as she sat down.

"Already?" Alice said. A look of disappointment flashed across her face. "I thought we'd spend more time together."

Lily didn't understand why Alice was making a fuss as she herself had to get back to Chicago within the next week.

"Yep, time to move on."

"But this is where your roots are," Alice said.

"You know me, sis, I don't put roots down anywhere," Isabelle said. The streetlight out front cast them all in silver shadows, and her eyes were dark and glittering.

"Maybe it's time," Alice said, sipping her wine delicately.

"You seem like you don't want to be here," Lily said cautiously to Isabelle. The last thing she wanted to do was pick a fight with her sister. Don't poke the bear, as Granddad used to say. They'd had a companionable swim together and she didn't want to ruin it.

Isabelle shrugged and shifted in her chair until her legs were hanging over the arm and she faced the beach. There was nothing to see in that direction as the beach was blanketed in darkness.

"When I was eighteen, I couldn't get out of here fast enough," Isabelle said softly, still staring in the direction of the darkened beach.

"I think we all felt like that," Lily said. She herself had wanted to see the world beyond Hideaway Bay. "I'm sure most teenagers feel like that."

"But I felt like that as soon as Dad left us," Isabelle said, fingering the rim of her glass.

Silence descended among them; the only noise was the snoring of Charlie at Alice's feet.

Their father had upped and left when Isabelle was eleven, Lily was nine, and Alice had just turned three. It had been at the start of summer. One day he'd been there and then one day he wasn't. Went on a milk run but left a note on the table saying he couldn't do it anymore. Lily had often wondered what it was that he couldn't "do." She wished he could have been more specific. Did he mean fatherhood? Or the marriage? Or Hideaway Bay or his job? That one line had left her wondering most of her life.

"When he left, I often thought that if I left too, I could find him and bring him back home to us," Isabelle said softly. "I don't know if this constant wanderlust is some form of subconscious searching. Looking for him."

"It wasn't your job to bring him back. He should have wanted to stay," Lily said.

"I never even knew him. I thought it was something I did," Alice said.

"Alice, you were still a baby, how could you have done anything wrong?" Lily said.

"Actually, Alice, Dad left once before you were born and then came back. You were a post-reconciliation baby," Isabelle informed her.

"I don't remember that," Lily said.

Isabelle nodded. "He did. I remember. I was about seven, and I drove Mom nuts asking when he was coming home. When he left the second time, I thought for sure he'd come back as he had the first time. I think there's still a part of me that thinks he might yet come home."

"Well, goodbye and good riddance," Lily pronounced. There was no sense in shedding tears over a man who obviously didn't care for them.

"Hasn't it affected your life that Dad left us?" Isabelle cried.

Lily shrugged. "I chose not to let it. It was a reflection on him, not me."

The lines in Alice's forehead furrowed even deeper as she stared at Lily slack-mouthed and said, "That sounds so healthy."

"Maybe, maybe not," Lily said with a shrug, taking a sip from her glass.

"More wine?" Isabelle asked. Before they could respond, she was out of her chair, refilling their glasses.

They were quiet for a moment, each lost in their own thoughts.

It was Isabelle who spoke first. "It's not that I don't want to be here in Hideaway Bay, it's that everywhere I look, I see reminders of Dad. And it's painful."

"Everywhere I look, I choose to see reminders of Mom, Gram and Granddad," Lily countered.

Isabelle let out an aggravated sigh, but Lily thought that was her problem. Their father left them. But it had been Mom who stayed and Gram and Granddad who had provided a stable influence in their lives. And she chose to focus on that.

"Maybe some of us were more wounded by his departure," Isabelle said. Lily didn't have to see her sister's face to hear the pain in her voice. Obviously, their father's leaving had greatly affected Isabelle. Lily had not known this.

"What was he like?" Alice asked.

"He was marvelous," Isabelle said immediately.

"Well, he was until he left, then he wasn't so great," Lily said. She couldn't help herself. She wasn't going to gold-plate memories of a man who had abandoned them.

Isabelle ignored her and looked at Alice. "He was human. He had flaws and was complicated, but when he was here, I never once doubted he loved me. That didn't happen until after he left."

"Have you tried therapy?" Lily asked.

"Are you being smart?" Isabelle snapped.

"No, of course not," Lily said defensively. "I didn't know it affected you so much."

"Well, it did," Isabelle said tightly.

"I don't know why his leaving didn't affect me the same way it did you," Lily said, trying to find some common ground so her sister didn't bite her head off.

"Because we're not the same people," Isabelle said sharply.

"Is that why you never married?" Alice asked Isabelle.

"Maybe," Isabelle said, setting her empty wine glass down on the table. "Do you know I've never been dumped? I always do the dumping."

Lily stared at her sister in disbelief. "Oh, Isabelle."

"You're afraid of getting left, so you head them off at the pass," Alice said, her voice barely above a whisper. "Is that any way to live, Isabelle? You might have let go of the love of your life."

Isabelle snorted. "I can assure you, there was no one who would have qualified for that title."

"How would you know if you never gave anyone a chance?"

Isabelle shifted in her chair and said, "Enough about me. What about you, Lily? Didn't know Prince Charming was an inveterate gambler who'd sell the shirt off your back to place a bet?"

Lily's eyes widened. She felt personally attacked. She decided no answer was the best answer. She stood up, wobbled a bit, and steadied herself. She grabbed the empty wine glasses off the table. "I'll say good night now, while we're all still talking to one another."

"Oh, come on, Lily, I thought we were having a heartfelt chat," Isabelle protested.

Lily scoffed. "Heartfelt! You've got such a big wall built up around your heart that you can't get anywhere near it."

She opened the screen door and called, "Charlie, come on, bedtime." Obediently, the dog opened his eyes, stood, and trotted into the house after her.

After the screen door closed, she heard Alice say to Isabelle, "Why do you always have to be like that? So spiky."

Lily didn't stick around to hear Isabelle's response. She was beyond caring.

CHAPTER TWENTY

1965

Junie

Junie arrived home from her shift at the drugstore. Outside her apartment, she stamped off her boots, the snow falling in clumps on the mat. Once her boots were off, she placed them on the rubber mat next to the door. She juggled a pile of mail in one hand and a bag of groceries in the other as she unlocked the door to hers and Paul's apartment. Shortly after they married, they'd purchased a two-family home, occupying the downstairs unit.

The apartment was cold, as she turned the thermostat down while they were at work. With a glance at the clock, she realized she had time before she got dinner ready. Once the groceries and the pile of mail were laid on the kitchen table, she shuffled in her stockinged feet to the thermostat and turned it up. She rubbed her hands together and headed toward the bedroom, her hand on the small of her back. In the bedroom, she sat on the edge of the bed and sighed, staring at her ankles. She had to stretch her feet out to see past the blooming bump of her belly. Only four more weeks. She wanted it to be over with. Her ankles were swollen, and she was uncomfortable. More than anything, she'd like to take a nap. She was always so tired but if she dared lie on the bed, she'd go out like a light, and what kind of wife would she be if her husband came home and there was no dinner?

Finally, she forced herself up and stripped off her dress and slip. She sat back down on the edge of the bed, unhooked her stockings from their garters, and peeled them off. Shivering, she dressed quickly in heavy pants and a maternity blouse with a pair of thick wool socks. From the closet, she pulled one of Paul's heavy cardigans and pulled it on. After she hung up her dress, she headed back to the kitchen and turned on the kettle. While she waited for it to boil, she put the groceries away, except the chuck roast. Pot roast was on the menu for dinner that night. Paul was working outside at a job site, and he'd come home frozen. Junie liked to have a hot dinner for him. But she had a few minutes before she needed to start browning the piece of meat in the pan.

Tea made, she sat down in one of the two chairs at their small kitchen table. She nibbled on a cookie and sipped her tea, sorting through the mail. On top of the pile was a letter from Barb. Ignoring the rest of the mail, Junie picked up the letter opener from the table and slit the envelope across the top. She pulled out the letter, anxious to hear the news from her friend, who was out on the west coast.

Once Barb had graduated from college, she'd taken a job with a firm in New York City and then transferred out to San Diego when the opportunity arose, which had surprised both Junie and Thelma. Thelma had wondered more than once why Barb would want to go to California. Junie supposed it was glamorous and exciting. And having to walk home in the middle of winter being eight months pregnant, Junie supposed she couldn't blame her.

She took another sip of her tea and unfolded the letter.

Dear Junie,
Hope you are well.
It won't be much longer until you have your baby. I'm so excited for you. I wish I could be there. How's Paul?
How are Thelma, Billy, and little Donny? I sent her a Christmas card last month with a letter in it, and

Thelma did send me a card but no letter. You know how she is. I'm dying for news!

I have news of my own. Jim has asked me to marry him, and we hope to have a June wedding back home. I hope you'll be my matron of honor! I've sent a letter to Thelma asking her to be a bridesmaid. Two of my sorority sisters and my cousin, Louise, will be bridesmaids as well. I know it means I'll have to live out here in California because of Jim's career with the Army, but I really love him and cannot imagine living without him. I'm sure you felt the same way when you were about to marry Paul.

Mother and Father are really excited to be planning a wedding in June. I'll be home in April to go over dress fittings and such. I can't wait to see you and Thelma and to meet your new baby! Gosh, we've come a long way, haven't we? Marriage and kids!

Love,
Barb

Junie set the letter down, smiling to herself. She was happy for Barb. Barb had brought Jim home last summer to meet everyone, and Junie couldn't help but like him. He was kind and polite, and she thought he and Barb were well suited for each other. When she'd said as much to Thelma, Thelma had groused, "He's all right. But what's up with all that 'yes, sir' and 'no, sir,' and 'yes, ma'am,' and 'no, ma'am' nonsense? Is that how he talks to Barb when they're alone?" Junie had laughed at the time, but she thought there was nothing wrong with having some manners. After dinner, she'd call Thelma and see if she got her letter from Barb today as well.

Junie finished her tea and quickly leafed through the rest of the mail. It was nearly time to start the dinner. There was the electric bill, a letter from her aunt who lived in Wisconsin, and—

Her heart froze when she arrived at the last letter. It was official-looking and it was addressed to Paul. In the left-hand corner, she noticed the return address.

The draft board.

Junie swallowed hard. She knew this day would come sometime. Practically every male she knew had been getting their draft notices. Boys she went to school with. Thelma's brother Frank. Vietnam was a place she barely knew anything about but now that it might affect her life, she watched the news and tried to learn as much as she could. She didn't understand it all. Despite her fear that Paul would be next, she'd pushed thoughts of war to the back of her mind and gotten on with her life.

A quick glance at the clock told her that Thelma would be home from work by now. She waddled over to the phone on the wall and dialed her number.

"Hello?"

"Thelma, it's Junie."

"Hey, how are you? Oh my God, are you in labor?"

"No, no, nothing like that. I think Paul got his draft notice," Junie said. Her voice shook and she suppressed the urge to cry.

"Think?"

"Well, there's an envelope with a return address that looks suspiciously like the draft board."

"Why don't you open it up?" Thelma asked.

"I can't do that. It's not addressed to me."

"So what? I open all of Bobby's mail." Junie could practically see Thelma rolling her eyes.

It would never occur to Junie to open Paul's mail any more than he'd open hers. But then, her marriage was different than Thelma's.

"I wish Bobby would get drafted," Thelma said with a sigh. "Just to get him out of my hair for a bit."

Junie was glad her friend couldn't see her horrified expression. It was a bit much to want your husband drafted and going off to a foreign land just because you were sick of him. The thought of Paul being drafted made her want to throw up.

Thelma changed the subject, but Junie was only half-listening. Finally, she told her she had to go get Paul's dinner. She forgot to ask Thelma if she'd received a letter from Barb. Thelma hadn't mentioned it, so hers must not have arrived yet.

After she hung up, she went through the motions of searing the chuck roast and peeling potatoes and carrots. Every once in a while, she'd pick up that envelope and study it as if she could glean some answer from it.

Once the pot roast was put in the oven, Junie took the envelope and put it in her bedside drawer. She'd give it to him after he ate his dinner. No sense in ruining his appetite. There'd be plenty of time for the letter.

The dinner was set and there was nothing more for her to do. Exhaustion—most of it mental and emotional—washed over her, and she took a few minutes to stretch out on the bed and get off her feet.

She rubbed her belly as she stared at the ceiling. She and Paul were so excited about this baby. They were finally starting the family they'd dreamed of. On Saturday nights, they stayed up late, talking about their future and their plans.

The sound of Paul coming in the door roused her from her reverie and she swung her legs around and sat on the edge of the bed, dangling her feet for a minute.

Paul appeared in the doorway. He'd hung up his coat and hat, and he wore a plaid flannel shirt over a white thermal top. Both were tucked into his work pants. His hair was plastered to his head from wearing his hat all day, and his cheeks and the tip of his nose were red.

He strolled in and kissed her hello. "Are you all right?"

She nodded, smiling. "I'm fine. Putting my feet up for a minute."

Paul nodded, appearing happy with her answer. "What's for dinner? It smells wonderful."

"Pot roast," she answered. She let him help her off the bed.

Paul rubbed his hands together. "Great. I'm starving and I'm cold."

Reflexively, Junie reached out with both her hands to briskly rub his upper arms and warm him up.

"Come on, go wash up, I'll serve up the dinner." She smiled.

Before he headed off to the bathroom, he kissed her again. As she walked down the narrow hallway to the kitchen, she could hear the water running in the sink and pictured Paul lathering up his hands with Lifebuoy and vigorously washing them. She smiled to herself, thinking how she'd gotten used to that in their short married life and realizing she'd be hearing that sound for the rest of their married life.

Paul ended up having two servings of the pot roast and declared it delicious. Vinegar was the secret. Her mother had shown her how to put a couple of tablespoons into the roasting pan to keep the meat tender. During dinner, she didn't mention anything about the draft notice, if that's what it was. Instead, she let him talk, telling her all about the job and some funny story about one of the guys he worked with.

When she cleared the plates, Paul leaned back in his chair and sipped from a cup of coffee. Junie made her way to the bedroom, retrieved the envelope from her bedside table, returned to the kitchen, and laid it on the table in front of Paul.

"What's this?" he asked, setting his coffee cup down.

"It came today." Junie sat in the chair next to Paul, watching his expression. But his face revealed nothing. Meanwhile, she was falling apart on the inside.

Without a word, Paul tore open the envelope and scanned the letter, his lips moving silently. When he finally spoke, he was quiet. "It's an order to report for induction."

Junie pressed her lips together and asked, "When?"

"February third," he said. His eyes scanned the letter again.

"That's only three weeks away!" Junie said. "Where do you have to go?"

"The local board and from there, if I qualify, I'll be inducted into the armed forces."

"But you won't have to go to Vietnam, will you? I mean, you're married and you're going to be a father," she said. When Paul didn't answer right away, she began to panic. She brushed her hair out of her eyes. "Paul, talk to me. I'm scared."

Paul folded the notice and slid it gently back into the envelope. "Junie, I can't say that."

Her eyes widened; his tone indicated something other than what his words were telling her. "But you don't want to go, do you?" She couldn't be hearing this.

"How can I look at myself in the mirror every morning if I don't answer my country's call?"

He'd never mentioned this before. Junie tried to process it. He wanted to go to Vietnam? What about her and the baby? Thoughts swirled in her mind, and she didn't know what to say or what to ask first.

"My dad fought in World War II as did his brothers and cousins. The men in my family serve, Junie, it's as simple as that."

"But we're going to be having a baby in a few weeks," she said. Had he forgotten that? She couldn't believe Paul would leave her with a new baby and run off to a country they'd never heard of until recently. Her head swam.

"It would only be for a year," he said.

She felt sick. She rested her head in her hand. "A lot can happen in a year."

"I'd be home before you know it."

"What about me? What about the baby?" she asked. "Don't we matter?"

"Of course you do! You're the most important thing to me," he said, raising his voice.

"And yet you'd run off to war," she said. Weariness filled her.

"I wouldn't exactly be running away from you!"

"Then why does it feel that way?" she cried. When he didn't say anything, she stood up from the table. He reached for her wrist, but she pulled it sharply away from him, her eyes filling up with tears.

When she reached the bedroom, she slammed the door behind her.

CHAPTER TWENTY-ONE

Lily

The following morning, Lily was the first one up. She had no idea how late Alice and Isabelle had stayed up. She threw on a sundress and padded barefoot down the stairs. In the kitchen, she fed Charlie and filled his bowl with fresh water. She buttered a piece of toast and made herself a cup of tea and carried both out onto the front porch.

The town was just coming to life and Lily was getting used to sitting on the front porch and watching the world go by. It was a pastime she was beginning to enjoy. Once she finished her toast and tea, she set her dishes on the low glass-topped wicker table and leaned back. Charlie was off the porch, walking around the front lawn and sniffing at things. Once in a while, he'd lift his head and stare at something that had caught his eye: a cyclist going by, kids playing at the beach, or a car passing in front of the house.

Lily had brought the large container of beach glass downstairs, thinking she might sort it by color. Her daily walks over the past week had resulted in a growing collection. And no matter how much she removed from the beach, it seemed that more washed in the next day.

The day before, she'd stopped at Lime's Five-and-Dime in town and purchased open-topped containers to sort the various colors of beach glass. She'd been delighted when she spotted them, thinking they were perfect for her purposes. If she were honest with herself, she wondered if she was only using this as a distraction from making a decision about returning home.

She palmed a piece of bottle green beach glass and turned it around in her hand, examining it. It was the same color as Jamie's eyes: a clear, translucent, bright green. His eyes were the first thing that had attracted her to him. The memory of it made her smile. Her heart ached at the thought that she would never see him again. Her smile remained on her face as she got lost in memories of happier times with her husband. But doubt crept in and thoughts of 'how could he have done this to me? To us?' pushed their way front and center. Sighing, she swept all thoughts of her late husband out of her mind and tossed the piece of glass into one of the open-topped containers.

Sorting beach glass seemed the answer.

Once the containers were lined up on the table, she scooped up a handful of beach glass and sorted through the colors in her hand, putting each color into its own separate container.

The screen door opened, and Isabelle appeared with a mug of coffee in her hands. Lily looked up at her sister and gave her a tentative smile. From the lawn, Charlie spotted Isabelle and ran toward the porch, tripping on the first step and falling onto the sidewalk.

Isabelle laughed but bent down and patted his head when he finally made it up on the porch. "I've never seen a dog like this before. He's amazing in his own way."

"That he is," Lily agreed, continuing with her sorting.

Isabelle sat down next to her and sipped her coffee.

"What time did you and Alice go to bed?" Lily asked, looking at her. There was no sense in remaining mad at Isabelle. Pretty soon she'd be leaving, and Alice was set to leave next week, and who knew when she'd see them again.

Isabelle brushed back her hair with her hand, and Lily thought she looked tired.

"It was almost four when we made it upstairs."

"You're up early then."

"Couldn't sleep," she said. She nodded toward the containers of beach glass. "What are you doing there?"

Lily thought it was obvious but said, "I'm sorting them by color. I keep looking at them, thinking I might craft with them."

"That's right, Gram told me you like crafts," Isabelle said.

"I love doing crafts. I find it relaxing. I sew, knit, crochet, paint," Lily said, rattling off a list. With a laugh, she added, "But Alice got the baking gene."

"I suppose it would be relaxing," Isabelle said.

"I haven't been able to do anything, though, since Jamie died," Lily admitted.

Isabelle nodded. "Grief is a funny thing. But you'll go back to it, I'm sure. It looks like you're heading in the right direction with your interest in the beach glass."

"Hopefully."

She continued to sort the glass as Isabelle sat next to her, drinking coffee and staring at the lake. Isabelle continued to use Granddad's old New York Yankees mug, which indicated to Lily that maybe not all of her sister's memories of Hideaway Bay were bad.

Lily held up a piece of beach glass, unable to decide if it was blue or green. She would have said blue but in a certain light, it appeared dark green.

As if reading her mind, Isabelle said, "Just toss it into the blue container, Lily."

Lily sighed and said, "I'm having trouble making decisions."

"What do you mean?"

"Since Jamie died, I find myself second-guessing myself. About every decision, big and small." She tossed a handful of brown beach glass into a container.

"Did you know about the debt before he died?" Isabelle asked.

It wasn't the question Lily had expected Isabelle to ask. Lily shook her head. "No." Quickly, she added, "But I knew about his gambling problems."

"That's probably why. On top of the shock and the grief, your confidence has taken a hit as well."

"And that's why I can't make a decision?"

"Give me an example of what decisions you can't make." Isabelle shifted in her chair and leaned forward, setting her mug on the table.

"First, when to return to California. I mean, it's my home and yet here I am, sitting here in Hideaway Bay sorting beach glass."

"Do you want to go back?"

"I really don't know. I have a home there, a job, and friends."

"You can have that anywhere."

"I can't decide whether to sell my house and pay off the debt. I don't know what to do," Lily said.

"Sometimes, not making a decision is a decision," Isabelle said pointedly. "The fact that you're dragging your feet about returning to California tells me that your heart isn't there. Because if it was, you'd be anxious to return."

Lily hadn't thought of it that way. There was some truth to what Isabelle said. Was living in California another one of those things where she was only going through the motions?

"No one is saying you have to make any decisions today. But I'm going to put on my big sister hat—only for a moment—and say that you should give yourself a timeline. Be gentle on yourself. Say in one week, you must decide how long you'll stay in Hideaway Bay. And then stick to that decision."

Lily thought that might be doable.

"You can stay as long as you like. We don't have to sell the house for a year."

"You wouldn't mind?" Lily asked.

"No, of course not. Why would I?" Isabelle asked.

The opportunity certainly gave Lily more options, and it felt as if the chokehold around her neck was loosening.

She was about to say as much when they heard Thelma call out. Both of them looked up and spotted their grandmother's friend coming up the walkway.

"Hello, girls!"

"Hi, Thelma," Lily and Isabelle said in unison.

Thelma walked up the steps, slightly breathless, and plopped down in the rocker. She had on shorts that went to her knee. Her legs were covered in thick, ropey veins, and she wore a pair of white ankle socks with her sandals.

"Would you like some coffee?" Lily asked. "Or there are some raisin scones that Alice made the other day."

Thelma put up a hand. "No thanks. If I keep eating Alice's baked goods, I'm going to have to go back to Weight Watchers." To illustrate, Thelma patted the waistband of her shorts.

"You won't be the only one," Lily said.

"I won't stay long. I'm looking for a favor," Thelma said.

"Sure, what can we do?" Lily asked. She stopped sorting beach glass for a moment.

"You know I have that group for widows and widowers?"

Lily nodded. Gram had told her as much. After Thelma's husband died, she'd started a club for people who'd lost their spouses, sort of a companionship group for people who were in the same boat. Gram had wanted to join from the beginning to support her friend, but Thelma had said no, it was only for widowers and widows. But then when Granddad had died, she was able to join. A thought occurred to Lily.

"Oh, thank you, Thelma, but I don't need therapy," Lily said quickly. She knew Thelma meant well though. "I went to therapy for three months after Jamie died." The last thing she wanted to do was bare her soul to all her old friends and neighbors in Hideaway Bay.

Thelma rolled her eyes. "Do I look like a therapist, Lily?"

Beside her, Isabelle snorted.

"Exactly," Thelma said, smiling at Isabelle.

Thelma continued. "When I first became a widow, I was lost. And bored. We did everything together. So, I put up a notice on the bulletin board at the parish hall, looking for widows and widowers to form a group. Just to hang out, eat, play cards, and watch movies, that sort of thing."

"Kind of like a gang," Isabelle added with a grin.

Thelma rolled her eyes again. "Not a gang! Although I had a gang when I was ten. Did your grandmother ever tell you?"

Both Lily and Isabelle shook their heads and leaned forward, curious about Thelma's childhood gang.

Thelma continued. "I formed a gang of neighborhood kids. To get into the gang, you had to let me push you off my garage roof."

Lily and her sister looked horrified.

"Did Gram let you push her off the roof?" Isabelle asked.

Thelma nodded. "She sure did, but only on one condition."

Lily lifted an eyebrow in an unspoken question.

"She wanted to push me off the garage roof as well. That's when I knew she was solid," Thelma said with a knowing look.

Lily and Isabelle exchanged a look and a smile. Gram was apparently quite fearless back in the day.

"Anyway, where was I? Oh yeah, Simon Bishop is giving a talk to the group tonight on writing, as some of us want to write our memoirs," Thelma informed them.

Lily thought that those memoirs would be quite interesting to read. She'd love to read Thelma's.

"Anyway, the talk is tonight, and I could use some help running things. Usually, Della from the olive oil shop lends a hand, but she's gone to Boston for a family wedding," Thelma said.

"Like what sorts of things?" Lily asked.

"Anything to do with technology. If Simon has a point power presentation or whatever you call it, our ship is sunk." She paused then added, "After the talk, we'll play cards and then there's refreshments."

"I'd love to help out, but I'm packing and getting ready to go," Isabelle said.

So much for their sisterly moment, Lily thought wryly.

With this, Thelma turned toward Lily, looking at her like she was her last hope.

"What time do you need me there?" Lily asked, realizing she'd been roped into it.

"If you could get there a few minutes before seven, that would be great."

"All right. It's at the parish hall, right?"

"It is," Thelma said.

The parish hall was only a name; there was no parish or church attached to it, and it was away from the main part of town, located out toward the highway, just before the railroad tracks.

Lily made a mental note to be there before seven.

"Did you go see Simon about that job?" Thelma asked.

Lily shook her head. "No, it seemed pointless. I may be heading back to California soon."

"It'd only be for a few months," Thelma said.

Lily shrugged.

But Isabelle interrupted and said, "She'll think about it."

Lily snapped her head in her sister's direction, wondering why she was sticking her nose in.

"Yes, please think about it. He's desperate for help."

"There's no one else in Hideaway Bay that could do it?" she asked.

"As it's only short-term, no one seems to be interested," Thelma said. "Plus, with summer coming, people want to be at the beach."

"I suppose so."

"Where are you headed off to, Isabelle?" Thelma asked.

"I'm going to Taos, New Mexico. I'm doing an article about an artist who lives out there."

"Better you than me," Thelma said, and she stood.

Lily and Isabelle laughed.

Thelma bid them goodbye, reminding Lily that she'd see her later.

Once Thelma was out of earshot, Lily turned to Isabelle. "Why did you tell Thelma I'd think about the job with Simon Bishop?"

"Because I think it might be a good idea."

"You do?"

Isabelle nodded. "It's only for a few months, and it might help you make a decision."

"But I have a job back in California that I need to get back to or I'm going to be fired."

"If it was a job you loved, you'd be making plans to go back already. The fact that you're dragging your feet tells me that you might be unhappy in that job."

"It's not that I'm unhappy," Lily muttered. She looked over at her older sister. "What about you? Are you happy in your job?"

Isabelle didn't hesitate. "I am. I like the freedom my job gives me to travel all over the world and see different places."

"You don't ever get tired of all that?" Lily questioned. "Living out of a suitcase? No home base?"

Isabelle shrugged and stood up, making to leave. "I tired of living out of a suitcase a long time ago, but I don't mind not having a permanent home address. I like to be able to pick up at a moment's notice and take off somewhere."

"It would seem after all these years, you would have seen everything there is to see," Lily observed.

"Not even close," Isabelle said. "I've only scratched the surface."

Lily didn't know how that could be but said nothing. "Do you think you'll ever settle down?"

"You mean get married and have kids?"

"Something like that," Lily said.

Isabelle looked away. "I don't know. I haven't found the right man or situation yet. And besides, I've left it too late. I'll be forty, and having children won't be an option for much longer."

"Does it bother you?"

Isabelle shook her head. "Not really. I was always of the mind that if it happened, it happened and if not, that was okay too."

Lily took all this into consideration. She'd assumed she and Jamie would have children eventually, but that option was obviously off the table.

"Before I leave, I want you to make some decisions," Isabelle said, swinging the conversation back to Lily.

Lily smirked. "Oh, now you're going to be the bossy sister?"

"Maybe, maybe not. But it might help you to be accountable to yourself," Isabelle said. She picked up her empty coffee mug, patted Lily on the knee, and headed into the house.

CHAPTER TWENTY-TWO

1965

Junie

Junie sat with her arms outstretched as the nurse walked in with her newborn wrapped in a white receiving blanket with pink and blue stripes. With a big smile, she welcomed her little Nancy into her arms. The nurse asked if she needed anything, but Junie shook her head, unable to take her eyes off of her baby.

She was in a ward at the hospital with five other women. She was in the middle of three beds on one side of the room, and there were three more on the opposite side. To her left was Jeannie, who'd had her fifth child—another boy—and who vowed to keep trying until she got her girl. On her right was Pam, who'd had a girl, her second child, and who kept an ashtray on her over-the-bed table and smoked nonstop, even while holding her new infant. When her husband arrived to visit, the first thing she'd said to him was "Did you bring me a pack of cigarettes?"

Paul had gone to work that morning, but there was a large bouquet of long-stemmed roses in a glass vase on the windowsill. Although things had been tense between them since the conversation about his draft notice, they'd put that aside when Nancy was born. For the moment, Junie decided not to think about it. For now, she wanted to focus on her new baby and enjoy her.

Thelma walked in, all smiles. Her own little boy, Donny, was almost one.

"Congratulations, mama," Thelma said with a smile.

Junie returned the smile. "Thank you!"

"Let me see her," Thelma said, setting her handbag down on the chair. She lifted Nancy gently from Junie's arms and smiled at the infant. "Welcome to the world, Nancy! I'm your Aunt Thelma. You've got a little friend waiting for you and his name is Donny."

Thelma had surprised everyone, including Junie, with how well she took to motherhood. She was fearless, and Junie admired her for that.

"I'm a little scared to take her home," Junie admitted.

"Nah, you're going to be fine," Thelma said. "You'll take to it like a champ."

"My mother is staying with me tomorrow night when we go home," Junie told her.

Thelma nodded and sat down in the chair with Nancy in her arms. She nodded to the roses on the windowsill. "Did you get those from Paul?"

Junie nodded.

"Boy, you sure have to do a lot to get a bunch of flowers," Thelma said.

Junie burst out laughing.

Thelma kept right on talking. "That would never have occurred to Bobby to send me flowers when I had Donny. He was down at the corner bar, celebrating that he had a son. Haven't seen him since."

Junie knew Thelma was joking, but she also knew that her friend was not happy in her marriage. She'd said as much on different occasions. She wished she could help her but didn't know how. Paul had advised her not to interfere.

Half an hour into Thelma's visit in which she had all the women in the ward laughing on her views of motherhood, pregnancy and marriage, Junie's sister, Margaret arrived, all smiles despite the black eye she sported. Thelma's eyes widened in surprise at the sight of her.

Margaret leaned over and kissed Junie on the forehead. "Congratulations, sis. How are you feeling?"

Thelma snorted. "How do you think she feels? Childbirth is like trying to push a grand piano out a tiny basement window."

Junie and Margaret laughed. Leave it to Thelma to lighten the mood.

Margaret went over to Thelma and took a look at her niece. Her features softened. "Oh, Junie, she's beautiful."

Thelma handed the baby to Margaret, who appeared besotted with the infant.

"I better go," Thelma said. "I left Donny with one of my brothers. After looking after them for all those years, I had to practically strong-arm them into watching little Donny for an hour. I left him in the playpen and gave them strict instructions not to touch him or remove him from it." She shook her head, gave them both a wave and exited the ward.

Margaret looked over at Junie. "You're lucky to have such a good friend."

"I am. But you've got Carol, you and she have been friends since you were little girls."

Margaret shrugged, not taking her eyes off the infant. "I haven't seen Carol in a long time."

Junie frowned. "You haven't? Why? You only live three blocks apart."

"We're busy with our families," Margaret said.

"What happened to your eye?" Junie asked.

"Oh, nothing. You know how klutzy I am. I walked into the corner of the door," she said quickly.

"That must have been some door."

Margaret ignored her and said, "I would so love a little girl."

Margaret had never been klutzy in her life. It was only when she got married that she suddenly became so. Junie pressed her lips together, debating whether to question her more. But they were surrounded by other new mothers and their company, and she didn't want to broadcast Margaret's business all over the place.

Junie stood at the stove, putting glass bottles in a big pot to sterilize them. Her eyes wanted to close but she forced them open. She'd had no idea how exhausting a newborn could be. For an infant five days old and barely weighing seven pounds, little Nancy had certainly turned the house upside-down.

There was the sound of the doorway in the hall opening and Paul coming up the staircase. She sighed. No one had told her that she'd be tired and weepy after having a baby. The draft notice had not been discussed since Nancy was born, but it wasn't something that could be ignored. They'd have to talk about it, as it was getting closer to the day he was supposed to report.

Margaret had sent over a large pan of goulash, at least two nights' worth, and Junie had the leftovers in the oven, keeping the food warm.

Paul came in, removed his coat, and hung it in the closet. He kissed her on her cheek.

"How's Nancy?"

"Good," Junie said with a smile.

She couldn't complain about her new baby. Thankfully, she'd not gotten her days and nights mixed up like Donny had when he was born. Thelma had walked around in a fog for the first three months of Donny's life.

"How was your day?" she asked.

"The usual," he said quietly.

Junie frowned. Paul looked tired. Maybe her getting up with the baby in the night was keeping him up as well. She hoped not.

"What's for dinner?" he asked. He set his lunchbox on the counter.

"Margaret's goulash."

He didn't say anything, just gave a small nod and headed into the next room. From the bathroom came the sound of running water as he washed up. He came back within minutes holding Nancy, all wrapped up in a receiving blanket. Junie's mother had come over the first night and showed them how to bathe Nancy and swaddle her in a blanket. Paul cradled their daughter in the crook of his arm. The baby looked tiny next to her father. Junie found it incredible that this little baby was something she and Paul had created together.

Paul smiled and looked at Junie. "Look who's awake." He glanced around the kitchen. "Do you have a bottle I could give her?"

"I'll heat one up and bring it in," Junie said.

When Paul came home from work, he liked to sit in the living room on the corner of the sofa, holding the baby and giving her a bottle.

Once the bottle was warmed, Junie inverted it and squirted some formula on her inner arm—as her mother had shown her—and decided it was not too hot. She carried the bottle into the sitting room.

Paul sat on the sofa, holding Nancy out in front of him on his lap so that her feet were against his abdomen. He smiled at his daughter and spoke softly to her. Nancy scowled, trying to get her hand out of the blanket, and succeeded and raised a fist.

Paul laughed and asked her, "What are you so angry about?"

Junie handed him the bottle and sat down in the chair next to his end of the sofa. She leaned her head against her hand, her elbow propped up on the arm of the chair.

Paul repositioned Nancy so that she was back in the crook of his arm, and he popped the bottle into her mouth. The baby sucked greedily at the bottle. Paul laughed and said to Junie, "She acts like you didn't feed her today."

"I know, she's a good eater," Junie said.

"That's my girl," Paul said to Nancy. He never stopped smiling.

Something was wrong, she could sense it. She knew he would get around to talking to her when he was ready. There was no sense in nagging him.

After Nancy had guzzled a couple of ounces, Paul laid a burp cloth over his shoulder and leaned the baby against his shoulder. He patted her firmly on her back until she let out a satisfying belch. Once the baby was back in position with the bottle in her mouth, Paul looked over to Junie.

"I went to the draft board after Nancy was born," he said quietly.

Junie's heart froze for a moment and then began an insistent drumbeat against her rib cage.

"And?"

Paul sighed and looked away. "I'm exempt from service."

Although she wanted to jump up and shout and cry with joy, she refrained. Paul's expression said he was not feeling jubilant.

"Why?"

"4-F," he said.

In the past year, Junie had heard all the different categorizations, with 1-A meaning fit for service. It seemed the majority of draftees were 1-A. Thelma's brother, Frank, had been 1-A. Barb's older brother had been deemed a 2-S because he was in med school.

All the numbers and letters made Junie's head spin.

"4-F?" she repeated.

"Yeah, not fit for service," he said.

"Why?" she asked. Although relieved that he'd been spared going to Vietnam, she was curious as to why he was classified not fit for service. Obviously, it bothered Paul, so it was best to temper her own glee.

"Remember when my appendix burst last year?"

Junie nodded. Right after they'd gotten married, he'd ended up in the emergency room with such terrible abdominal pain that he was bent over at the waist. Immediately, he'd gone into surgery. It had been distressing at the time, but the surgeon had assured them that Paul was young and healthy and would recover. He did but he'd had a long hospital stay and lengthy recovery at home.

"Because of that?" she asked in disbelief. But she wasn't going to look a gift horse in the mouth.

"Yeah, can you believe that? The armed forces don't want me, I'm not 'fit' enough to serve my country."

He looked down at Nancy, who was oblivious to her father's distress.

Junie hopped out of her chair and planted herself on the sofa next to Paul. She pulled her legs up beneath her and knelt.

"Oh, Paul, of course you're fit. You know how the armed forces are, they're buried under red tape."

He looked at her, searching her face. "I bet you're glad."

Junie chose her words carefully. "Relieved is a better word."

"The ironic thing is that when Nancy was born, I'd changed my mind. There was no way I could leave the two of you to fend for yourselves. So, when I appeared before the draft board, I was going to see if I could get an exemption due to the fact that I had dependents. But I had to wait until Nancy was born."

Junie nodded. She wasn't sure what the difference was; an exemption was an exemption, but maybe it was the principle of the thing. Leaning over, she kissed his forehead.

"I know you're disappointed, but sometimes things have a way of working out for the best," she said softly. That's what she truly believed in that moment.

Later, when they went to bed, she would kiss that scar on his belly.

CHAPTER TWENTY-THREE

Lily

The parish hall was all lit up later that evening when Lily arrived. As it was still dusk and a pleasant evening, she'd walked over, deciding she could use the exercise. She'd brushed back her hair and put on some small pearl stud earrings and had gone with a turquoise-colored maxi dress that dropped to her ankles. She brought a cardigan with her in case the air conditioning was turned on as the extreme heat continued.

There were plenty of cars parked out front, and it hit home how many widowed people there were in Hideaway Bay. She paused for a moment and stood there. She too could be a member of this group and wondered if the invitation to help Simon had been only a ruse to get her there. It didn't matter; she wasn't joining any group.

The din of conversation and subdued laughter floated out to her from the parish hall like bubbles on the wind. Lily stepped inside and was relieved to see not much had changed since she lived in Hideaway Bay as a kid.

The hall was paneled in warm maple and still smelled of furniture polish and Pine Sol. Some of the men from the group were pulling down tables and chairs from the stacks by the wall and setting them up.

Lining the paneled walls were official portraits of every mayor the town had ever had, going back over one hundred years. In a far corner stood the American flag along with the flag of New York State and another with the Hideaway Bay crest on it. Not only did the hall serve for community events but civic ones as well.

She caught Thelma's attention and made her way in that direction. She surveyed the group and decided it was what you would expect from a group of widowed people: the majority of them were over seventy, most of them with gray or white hair. There was one woman who appeared fiftyish but after that, Lily was the youngest.

"What do you need me to do?" Lily asked.

"You're here, that's great," Thelma said with a smile. "First, there's Simon, you can ask him if he needs anything. He might need help setting up. Just show him where everything is."

Lily didn't want to point out the obvious: that she didn't know where everything was. She said nothing, thinking she'd figure it out.

Thelma saw someone, lifted her hand, called out the other person's name, and excused herself.

Lily was left with no choice but to find Simon Bishop. She hoped he wouldn't mention anything about the job. She was embarrassed that she hadn't taken him up on it and didn't want to be called out on it.

Simon was out in the parking lot, unloading things from his trunk.

"Hello, Simon," she greeted him.

He lifted his head out of the trunk and smiled when he recognized her. "Oh, Lily, I didn't know you'd be here tonight."

"Thelma asked me to give her a hand." She spotted a few bags at his feet. "Can I help you carry some of this stuff inside?"

"That would be great," he said. He handed her a bag that wasn't that heavy.

"I can take something else as well," she said.

"Nah, I'm good."

As they walked inside, Simon stepped back to let her enter first.

"Are you doing a PowerPoint presentation?" Lily asked.

"No, I hadn't planned on that," he said. Then with a laugh he added, "I thought I'd keep it simple. I hope they weren't expecting something like that."

"I think they'll be fine," she said truthfully. It dawned on her that she might not be needed after all, but she decided to stick around.

The parish hall had been set up with numerous card tables, and members of the group had taken their seats. Some had brought notebooks and pens to take notes. Some had water bottles or cups of takeaway coffee.

Under Simon's direction, she helped him by passing out stapled sheets of paper. The cover read "Creative Writing."

When he was ready, Thelma stood at the front of the room and introduced him, and there was a round of enthusiastic clapping. Lily took a seat at the back, at one of the empty tables. The talk only lasted an hour, and Simon was interesting. He had a stockpile of stories to illustrate everything he was saying. At times, he was quite humorous. It had started out as a discussion on how to write a memoir but soon devolved into writing in general and how to get published. The group was fascinated.

One of the members raised his hand and stood when Simon called on him. He said he'd already written a memoir about his year spent serving in Vietnam. Simon appeared interested and said it would be an honor to read it. Lily visualized everyone in Hideaway Bay dropping off their manuscripts—finished and unfinished—at Simon's home.

At the end of it, Lily stood to help Simon pack up. The group members were eager to get down to the business of playing cards. Soon all the tables were filled and as Lily followed Simon to his car with his stuff, they were intercepted by Thelma at the door.

"I hate to ask, but I need another favor."

Lily didn't jump and say yes like she had the first time. She wanted to hear what was needed before she committed.

"What do you need, Thelma?" Simon asked.

"We're two players short for pinochle," Thelma said.

Gram had said when they were growing up in the city, playing pinochle in the park had always been one of Thelma's favorite things to do.

Lily made a face of uncertainty. "Oh, I don't know how to play pinochle."

"How can you be a granddaughter of Junie Reynolds and not know how to play pinochle?" Thelma teased.

"I don't know either," Simon said.

Lily figured that would be the end of that, but not so. Thelma instructed them to return as soon as they loaded up Simon's car. She waited for them in the vestibule.

"Follow me," she directed.

Lily and Simon ended up at a card table set up for four with Thelma and Mr. Lime from Lime's Five-and-Dime. It was odd to see the old man without his apron. Despite the warm evening, he wore a cardigan over a dress shirt.

"I found these two, they'll do," Thelma said.

"They sure will."

"Okay, Lily, you can be Augustus's partner. Sit across from him. Simon, you'll be my partner."

Before Simon sat down, Thelma grilled him. "Can you pay attention to what cards have been played?"

"I'll try."

"And one more thing, no crazy bidding. Remember, we can only get a certain amount of points with the meld. That's why I always hated playing with Ruthie as my partner. It was always more important to her to win the bid than to win the game. You can't operate like that."

Augustus Lime piped up. "I don't think Ruthie was familiar with the rules according to Hoyle."

Thelma nodded agreeably.

Lily and Simon exchanged a smile and took their seats.

Mr. Lime went over the instructions, and both Lily and Simon nodded. It sounded straightforward, but Lily knew it would be anything but. Mr. Lime reassured her, "Remember, it's only cards. We're just here to have fun."

Pinochle involved a special deck of forty-eight cards. There were all four suits, but they ran from nine to ace, and there were two of each in every suit. After a while, Lily caught on, as did Simon, and the next two hours flew as they played hand after hand. Thelma kept score with a pencil and a scrap piece of paper. Even Lily had to admit, it was enjoyable.

At the end of the card playing, the kitchen out back—a big, high-ceilinged affair with stainless steel appliances and countertops—was opened, and Lily offered to help, not in a hurry to return home yet.

As other members busied themselves in the kitchen like bees in a hive, Lily helped bring out the refreshments and line them up neatly on the designated table. She set up bottles of water and carried out the urns of coffee and tea when they were ready. There was sugar and creamer brought out, as well as small china cups and saucers. Everyone had brought some kind of dessert or snack to share, and Lily felt bad that she hadn't thought to bring anything. She spied Simon deep in conversation with the Vietnam veteran.

Several people approached her to reminisce about Junie or to offer their condolences. After two cups of tea and a couple of quarters of sandwiches, she helped with cleanup. Because there was a lot of help, it didn't take long.

Although it was dark out, the night sky was brilliant with stars. Lily kept looking up at the sky, marveling at it, until she tripped on an uneven portion of the pavement because she wasn't paying attention. Crickets chirped in the background.

She hadn't been walking long when a car slowed beside her, its headlights illuminating the road in front of them. A little nervous, Lily was now sorry she'd walked. Although Hideaway Bay was safe, that didn't mean crime couldn't happen.

She heard the window roll down and slowly, she turned to see who was following her.

"Lily!"

It was Simon. Relief flooded her. "Hey, Simon," she called back.

"Do you need a ride home?" he asked, leaning over the passenger seat.

"No, that's all right," she said.

"Come on, I'm going that way on my way home, it's no problem."

Lily was about to protest a second time when something large flew over her head. Something with a wingspan of three to four feet. It had happened so quickly she didn't know if it was a bat or a barn owl. She hurried to the passenger door.

"You know what, I will accept your offer," she said, opening the door and sliding into the seat.

"Good."

As he pulled back onto the road, she asked, "Did you ever find an assistant?"

"No, as a matter of fact," he replied. He looked over at her. "Any chance you'd give it serious consideration?"

Lily laughed but said nothing.

"This would only be for three months," he said after a few moments. "You could name your price."

"You must be desperate," she said.

"I am. I've got this deadline I'm going to miss if I don't get someone to help me organize."

"I'd hate to commit and then have to leave and go back to California," she said.

"Look, come over in the morning, I'll tell you everything the job entails, and you can decide for yourself if you're interested," he said smoothly. He pulled up in front of Gram's house.

Lily contemplated, her hand on the door handle. She supposed it couldn't hurt to see what it was all about.

"If you decide it isn't for you, I'll never bother you about it again," he said evenly. "And you can bring Charlie with you if you'd like."

That did it for her.

"All right. What time?"

CHAPTER TWENTY-FOUR

1966

12465 Star Shine Drive

Junie

As they drove out to the lake on Saturday morning, Junie held the baby in her lap, brushing her hair off her forehead. Nancy leaned against her mother. Junie couldn't get enough of her. She kept looking over at Paul, narrowing her eyes. The tinny sound of music came from the car radio. Junie loved riding in the car with the windows down and music playing, especially on a warm summer's day. She hummed along with the Mamas and the Papas' "I Saw Her Again."

"What are you up to?" she finally asked her husband. She kissed the top of Nancy's head, reveling in the fine, soft baby hair.

He turned to her, his smile bright and generous. "Me? Nothing."

She chuckled. "You're up to something, I can tell. Your feet haven't touched the ground since you got out of bed this morning."

"I'm looking forward to going out to the lake today," he said. He reached over and gave her thigh a squeeze. He flashed her his smile and she felt herself soften.

The last week had been difficult. Her sister's marriage continued to deteriorate. Margaret had broken her arm and although Junie and her parents suspected that Bill was the cause of her injury, Margaret had vehemently denied this, saying she fell down the basement stairs. Junie wondered if he'd pushed her but was afraid to say that out loud, even to Paul, although she suspected it was what everyone was thinking.

Junie had looked forward to this day at the lake with Paul and the baby. Just the three of them. She'd packed a lunch of cold chicken sandwiches, fruit salad, and macaroni salad. There was a cooler of bottles of Coke packed in ice. The weather was nice—not too hot, and there was a gentle breeze blowing in from the lake.

The time away from Margaret and her never-ending drama would do her some good. As soon as she saw the city in the sideview mirror, she began to relax. Although he didn't vocalize anything, Paul was annoyed with the whole situation, but Margaret was her sister and Junie needed to support her parents. She loved Paul and how protective he was of her. He'd been a good choice for a husband. And she could never imagine him raising a hand to her. He barely raised his voice. He was no pushover either. Actually . . . he was perfect. This brought a smile to her lips as she stared out the window at the passing scenery: the acres and acres of vineyards, purple grapes ripe and plump on the vines, the sweet smell in the air.

It was still early when they arrived in Hideaway Bay, and Paul was able to secure a great parking spot beneath a massive oak, which would provide shade for the day.

Junie held the baby on her hip while Paul put quarters in the machine to rent a stroller. Once the money was paid, the metal rack released the stroller and Paul pulled it free. She laid a cotton blanket down on the seat as sometimes the metal could get sticky with the heat. Once the baby was in the stroller, Junie pulled the diaper bag out of the back seat and set it in the tray behind the stroller. Paul closed the trunk.

"Don't you want to grab the cooler and the blanket?" she asked, digging through the diaper bag for her sunglasses. She never bothered to bring her purse to the beach; it was one more thing to carry. But she did put a lipstick, her change purse, a teasing comb, and her sunglasses in a side pocket of the diaper bag.

"Not yet. Let's take a walk, I want to show you something," he said. Paul didn't look at her as his gaze was fixed on Star Shine Drive ahead of them.

She narrowed her eyes at him. Now what was he up to?

She pushed the stroller, and the baby pointed at things. She liked this part of the drive along the shore. It was an asphalt drive with giant oaks, and she could hear the breeze rustling through the leaves. Even from here she could smell the briny scent of the lake that she loved so much. A swarm of seagulls cried out above them.

As they walked on, with the beach to their left and houses to the right, it was a sight Junie never tired of. These had been the summer homes of the wealthy at the turn of the century. They were grand affairs set back away from the sidewalk, giving them some privacy. But more and more middle-class people were coming out and buying up the workers' cottages that were located on neat little streets off of Star Shine Drive.

Junie couldn't imagine living in a house such as these. To think that these grand old places were once people's summer residences to escape the heat of the city. Why, they were more than twice the size of the house she'd lived in with her parents. As they walked along the narrow drive, people approached from the other direction wearing swimsuits and shorts and sunglasses.

Laughter floated out from them. A car drove by and honked its horn. An arm extended and the hand banged on the top of the roof and called out, "Hey, Paulie!"

Junie laughed. There was only one person who called Paul "Paulie." "Was that Stanley?"

"Yeah, I heard he bought some property out here and is opening a business," Paul told her.

"Really? Stanley? Where'd he get that kind of money?" Junie asked. Stanley didn't seem the type to be able to buy anything.

Paul laughed. "Ol' Stanley has his first communion money."

"What is it you want to show me?" she asked. She peeked in at the baby, now sound asleep, her forehead sweaty. Still, Junie thought she looked so darn cute in her little pink romper.

"It's right up ahead," Paul said with a nod.

Junie followed Paul's gaze but found nothing to satisfy her curiosity. Just more houses that lined the drive. As they walked by, she looked at every one of them, wondering what it would be like to sit on the porch every evening and watch the sun set over the lake. Maybe drinking a Coke or even lemonade. She'd like a swing on her porch if she had one. She imagined beach towels hanging over the porch railing after a day of swimming and children with ice cream dripping down their chins.

She thought of her friend, Barb. Her family still had a summer home out here in Hideaway Bay, but it was located at the other end of town near the gazebo in the common and the war memorial. Barb had married the previous summer. She hadn't been married three months when her husband was shipped off to Vietnam.

As they neared the end of the road, Junie slowed down. Star Shine Drive ended when traffic was forced to hang a right onto Lakeview Drive. There were no more houses after the end of Star Shine Drive, only a sandy path that cut through the dunes to the beach. If Paul took her through the sand dunes, he'd have to push the stroller.

The second to last house at the end of Star Shine Drive was a derelict one. Junie always felt sorry for it. It was like the poor relation against all the other homes. The front yard was overgrown with weeds, and one of the giant oak trees was diseased and possibly dead as evidenced by its lack of leaves in the height of summer. Even now as she stared at the two-story house with its long front porch, she smiled, thinking all it needed was some TLC. And some new windows to replace all the broken ones. And the shutters to be straightened. And a paint job. And some weeding . . .

Paul stopped and stood next to her. He, too, looked at the house.

Junie looked over at her husband. She liked the way the sun played off his hair, showing off its rich darkness. "Now what?"

Paul didn't take his eyes off the derelict house. "What do you think?"

"About what?" she asked, looking around. The sun was hot; she felt it on the back of her neck and her scalp. A fly landed on Paul's shoulder and Junie shooed it away.

"Of that house there." He gestured to the derelict house.

"It needs some tender loving care," she said.

"That's what I thought."

"Paul, what's going on?" she asked.

He sidled next to her and slung his right arm around her shoulders. With his left hand he made a sweeping gesture toward the house.

"This house is on the market," he said. "And I think we should buy it."

She snorted. "Hold on, I'll get my change purse. I think I still have that dime you gave me." When he didn't say anything, she added, "Paul, don't tease me."

He looked at her and he wasn't grinning. "I've never been more serious in my life, Junie Reynolds."

"Oh," was all Junie could muster at first. "But, how would we afford something like this?"

Junie was scrupulous with their budget. She knew exactly how much money they had every week, what they spent it on, and how much they had in their savings account, which wasn't much. Plus, Paul was socking money away in a pension scheme through the electrician's union.

"It's being sold for a song because it needs so much work," he said.

She could hear the excitement in his voice. She didn't want to get her hopes up. It seemed unreal. A dream, really. But a good one.

"How do you know it's for sale?" she asked.

"Sal was talking about it at work, said if he were younger, he'd buy it and fix it up himself," Paul said.

Sal was another union electrician who'd been married thirty years to Marie, who was the most amazing cook. They socialized with them from time to time.

"I came out last weekend and looked at it with the realtor," Paul said.

"I thought you were working a side job."

Paul grinned.

"Why didn't you bring me with you?"

"Because I didn't want to get your hopes up," he said. "I wanted to make sure we could do this."

"Can we?" she asked. What if they couldn't? What if someone else snapped it up? She kept the lid on the bubbling-up pot of her hopes.

He told her the price and even though it was a steal and not anywhere near the mortgage they currently held on their small house in the city, Junie felt herself pale beneath the morning sun.

"Where would we get that kind of money?" she whispered, laying her hand over her chest, her fingers splayed.

Paul placed his hands on his hips. "My father is going to loan it to us."

"Oh, I don't know, Paul, you know how I feel about borrowing money," Junie said. Even though Paul's father was a sweetheart, she didn't want to borrow money from him.

"We discussed it at length. Dad thinks it's too big an opportunity to pass up."

"He does?" Junie knew nothing about real estate or opportunities; she'd rarely seen any in her life. She wouldn't have recognized an opportunity if it came up to her and introduced itself.

"Look, I get a lot of side work, Junie, you know that. I could do a full day on Saturdays and maybe a couple of nights during the week."

Junie didn't want that, either. She didn't want Paul working himself to death. "That's a lot to take on."

"We can come out here on Sundays and start working on the place. I can trade guys at work for side work.

I'll do an electric job for them, say, in exchange for plumbing. I can insulate and drywall it myself."

"I can paint and make curtains," Junie said, excitement taking hold and setting down roots.

"It needs a lot of work, Junie," Paul said. "It'll take us years to get it where we want it."

"We're young," Junie said.

He looked at her for a minute, his gaze settling on her in that way that always made her a little breathless.

"And someday, when our kids have gone off to live their own lives, we could move out here permanently."

Junie's mouth fell open. It was like all her dreams coming true.

"Well, what do you think?" he asked.

Overcome, Junie jumped up into his arms, almost knocking him off-balance. Paul laughed. Tears pooled in her eyes, her arms shook, and her heart thumped against her chest.

"Oh, I love it." She could barely breathe for her excitement.

"Wait a minute," Paul said, panic in his voice. "You haven't even seen the inside. It needs a lot of work. It needs to be winterized."

She laughed. "So what? We have the rest of our lives to make it ours."

Paul cleared his throat and pulled her into his embrace. Junie loved the feel of his body against hers. It was as if he was made just for her and she for him.

"Oh, I wish we could get inside to look at it," she said, pulling away and staring at the house. She bounced on her feet and clapped. Nancy, now awake, clapped her hands to mimic her mother and Junie laughed.

Paul reached into his pocket and pulled out a set of keys. "It so happens that I have the keys to the place. I told the realtor I wanted to show it to you."

CHAPTER TWENTY-FIVE

Lily

Lily drove out to Simon Bishop's home as she'd promised the night before. As she got further away from Star Shine Drive and with the town in her rearview mirror, she wondered why she was going to see about a job when she already had one on the other side of the country. It seemed that her feet were moving in one direction while her brain was heading in another.

Alice had made another magnificent breakfast of raspberry sweet rolls with a cream cheese icing. At this rate, Lily would be going up a size in her clothes very soon. Briefly at breakfast, Alice had mentioned again about turning Gram's house into an inn, but Lily had shut her down immediately, stating she had to get going or she'd be late for her meeting with Simon. There had been no sign of Isabelle. She barely showed her face before eleven most mornings and by the time Lily left, she had still not made an appearance.

Things had settled down between the sisters. Gram had only been gone two weeks, and it felt as if there was an uneasy truce between the three of them. Isabelle was due to leave shortly, and Alice was heading back to Chicago in another week.

Lily drove toward the bluffs with Charlie in the back seat. Outside of Hideaway Bay proper, the road began to ascend naturally until she found herself on Lakeshore Drive, where the big multimillion-dollar houses were situated. Although located high on the bluffs overlooking Lake Erie, most of the homes had wooden stairways that led down to the beach below.

Lakeshore Drive was a winding asphalt road that ran parallel to the shoreline. You couldn't see any of the houses from this vantage point as both sides of the road were lush with trees, now in full, dark-green foliage. The GPS advised that she had arrived at her destination, and Lily pulled into the driveway up to a pair of imposing wrought iron gates in the high stone wall. She rolled down her window and looked at the camera pointing at her from an angle on the wall. A voice boomed out of an unseen speaker. "Yes?"

"Um, it's me, Lily Ford, I'm here to see Simon Bishop."

There was no answer, only the responding electric hum of the gates opening. Charlie walked from one window to another in the back seat. She'd brought her dog, partly hoping his large size would quell any desire on Simon's part to hire her. Because that was part of the deal: the dog had to come with her. That was her only condition.

As she drove through the gates, rain came out of nowhere and spattered against her windshield. Lily'd forgotten how storms could arrive unexpectedly here. She couldn't complain; the weather for May had been exceptionally warm since she'd arrived.

The driveway was long, flanked by giant poplars on each side. At the end of the row of trees, it opened up into a circular driveway in front of a large mansion. She had to admit to being surprised. Somehow, she expected it to be a more contemporary home, made up of a lot of glass and steel. But this house was not dissimilar from Gram's home—well, now her house. Except that Simon's house was bigger. Much bigger.

It was a three-story white clapboard affair with black shutters on all the windows. Big bushes lined the lower wall of the front porch. Lily recognized the leaf as a hydrangea bush and could only imagine what the blooms would look like in two months' time. To the left of the house stood a three-car garage, also white clapboard, and to the right was a tennis court that looked to be brand new.

The front door opened, and Simon smiled at the sight of her. He descended the stone steps at a saunter, grinning, a set of dimples bracketing his mouth. He wore a powder blue short-sleeved polo shirt, caramel-colored shorts, and a pair of worn boat shoes.

Charlie jumped out of the back seat and trotted over to Simon, who talked to him and stroked him behind the ears. He didn't appear at all intimidated by the dog's size.

Simon extended his hand to her and when she slipped her hand into his, her hand immediately became dwarfed.

"Thank you for coming. You have no idea how much I appreciate this."

"I'm here to see what it's about. No promises or anything." She didn't want to lead him on.

"Sure." He turned his attention to Charlie. "So, this is your work partner."

"Yes, for the most part, he's pretty laid-back, but he can be clumsy."

Simon regarded him. "I can see that. He's all legs."

"Yep."

"Well, come on in, and let's talk about this," he said with a wave of his hand.

"All right." She and Charlie followed him up the steps and into the house.

If the outside had surprised her by being more traditional than she expected, the inside surprised her too. It was contemporary in style and decorated in shades of black and white. The entryway featured a white marble floor and a glass and chrome console table. The railing on the staircase leading to the second floor was acrylic and steel. There was a large painting over the console table that looked like it was just splatters of black and white with dots of pink and turquoise paint on it. It was totally unexpected, and Lily's mouth fell open before she caught herself and remembered her manners. Her gaze circled around the room as Charlie bumped into a black acrylic pedestal stand that teetered in response, sending a large white porcelain vase crashing to the floor.

"Oh no!" she cried.

The dog, startled by the noise of the shattering porcelain, tucked his tail between his legs and ran behind Lily.

Immediately, Lily bent over to pick up the pieces, her face hot. "I am so sorry. I'll pay for it."

"Careful, don't cut yourself. I'll get a broom and dustpan."

She narrowed her eyes at Charlie. "Like I said, he's clumsy."

"You don't say," Simon teased.

Lily couldn't help but smile. "Why don't you get the broom and I'll sweep this mess up." She hoped the vase wasn't expensive, or she'd end up working for Simon Bishop for free.

Simon returned with a dustpan, swiftly brushed the pieces into it, and disappeared before returning again.

Lily was already having second thoughts. "You know, Simon, maybe this isn't a good idea. I don't think I can relax knowing there's a high probability Charlie is going to break things." Her gaze swept around the room, and she concluded there were a lot of things that could be broken there.

"Oh, don't give up hope yet," he said with a smile. "Besides, I don't work in the house. I have an office out in the backyard. I like to keep my workspace separate from my personal space."

Lily laughed. "You must be desperate."

Simon grinned. "Have I mentioned my deadline? So yes, I am desperate."

"All right then, show me what I would have to do if I should take the job," she said.

"Right this way."

Lily followed Simon down a wide hallway that opened up into a huge open plan area that included a gourmet kitchen and a family room. There was a large-screen television elevated on the far wall. Floor-to-ceiling

French doors lined the outside wall, offering a dramatic view of a sloping backyard and beyond that, Lake Erie. On the opposite wall to the windows, were ceiling-height bookcases crammed with books. The room was simply magnificent.

The kitchen was something else, and she couldn't wait to tell Alice about it. It was a baker's and cook's dream, a contemporary space with white cabinets and shiny black appliances. Cabinets, countertops, and surfaces gleamed. The space seemed awfully large for one person.

Lily and Charlie followed Simon through the kitchen and the family room, stepping through the French doors and out onto a large deck. Lily kept her eye on Charlie and where he was in relation to everything in Simon's house.

The rain had stopped by the time they stepped outside, only a passing shower. In the middle of the backyard, which looked professionally landscaped, was an in-ground pool. The whole area was breathtaking. The grass was a deep shade of green, and various flowers bloomed along the carefully edged gardens. There were numerous shrubs that Lily recognized: peonies, and rhododendrons, both with beginning blooms. In the height of summer, it must look magnificent, she thought.

The backyard followed the natural slope of the land down toward the lake. At the end of the property was a low stone wall and what Lily surmised was the top of a staircase that led to the beach. There was a paved brick area, and on it stood a wrought iron table with matching chairs. There was probably another beautiful view from that vantage point.

Simon headed off to the left, toward a small outbuilding. Remaining true to the main house, this much smaller building was also white clapboard with black shutters. French doors were situated in the middle of the building.

"Come on in," he said over his shoulder as he unlocked the door and threw both sides of the French doors open. "Don't worry about Charlie, he can't break anything in here."

Lily wanted to tell him not to hold his breath, that Charlie would probably find something to break, but she was too enthralled with the place to say anything.

This wasn't some garden shed converted into an office or some kind of man cave, but a purpose-built space for Simon Bishop's writing career.

A large outer room held a desk and a sofa and an easy chair. The windows were east- and west-facing and overall, the room was bright. There was a desktop computer on the desk. On the far wall were two doors, one leading to a small bathroom and the other to a kitchenette. Framed photos of Simon's book covers, more than ten in all, hung on the walls.

Simon showed her around his office, which was off the main room. Also a bright space, this room held more shelves crammed with books but after a quick inspection, Lily noted they were books to do with the craft of writing.

There was an old partner desk, mahogany with red leather inlay and gold trim. An electric typewriter sat on top of the desk. This she found curious. Off to the side sat a laptop open to the home screen. A series of windows faced the lake, and on the opposite wall another pair of French doors led to a smaller, enclosed garden. A paved brick area housed a bistro table and a pair of chairs. The space was enclosed by a high white-painted wall with lattice edging around the top. Climbing roses whose buds were just beginning to appear ran along the top of the wall, and bespoke birdhouses lined the fence at various heights.

"So, this is it," he said with a wave of his hand.

"What do you need me to do?" she asked.

"It would be full-time hours to start, as I am behind," he said.

She nodded.

"I usually type up my manuscripts on the typewriter. My assistant then keys the material into a Word document."

It sounded redundant, Lily thought. Why didn't he just type it directly into the computer instead of creating the extra step? But perhaps he was a creative type that had certain quirks.

He went over his routine, and Lily learned that he worked normal business hours: nine to five. He'd helpfully printed up a list of duties that the job demanded. It was more or less what she expected: proofread his work, keep in contact with his agent, manage his social media accounts and his weekly newsletter.

When he told her the wage, which included health insurance coverage, it was an offer almost too tempting to resist.

As she was leaving, he asked, "What do you think? Is it something you'd be interested in?"

"I'd like to think about it," she said.

He nodded. "Do you know how long you'd need? Because I need someone yesterday and if you're not interested, I'm going to have to start looking outside Hideaway Bay."

Lily understood. She certainly couldn't hold him up, even if she was afraid of making a decision. It wasn't fair to him.

She drew in a deep breath and said, "How about if I call you tomorrow morning and let you know either way. Would that work?"

"That's great, I appreciate that," he said with a smile.

He walked her and Charlie back out front to her car and as Lily looked around, she thought it might not be a bad place to work. But she did want to think about it and not make a rash decision. When she pulled away from the house, her thoughts swirled around: stay in Hideaway Bay or return home to California?

<center>~~~ele~~~</center>

Lily didn't wait until the following morning. She called Simon within a few hours of their meeting to let him know she'd take the job. Simon sounded delighted, and they agreed she'd start in two days' time.

Before the phone call to Simon, she'd rung her boss in California, requesting a three-month leave of absence for personal reasons. She apologized for any inconvenience she might cause with this time off, and her boss was gracious but told her he'd only be able to give her three months and no more. Lily said she understood. Her next calls were to her friends Cheryl and Diana to let them know of her plans and to ask them to forward any mail that might look urgent.

When all the phone calls had been made, Lily relaxed, happy with her decision and proud of herself for finally making any decision at all.

CHAPTER TWENTY-SIX

October

1969

Junie

It had been a good day, but Junie was beat. She'd been more tired with this pregnancy, more than she had been when she was carrying Nancy. But she still had five more months to go. Paul thought they should slow down with the work they were doing on the house on Star Shine Drive, but Junie wanted to work up until the snow fell and get as much done as possible.

She pulled on Paul's letterman sweater, which she had resurrected from an old trunk when they married and wrapped herself up in it. She carried bags of garbage out to the trunk of their car. Paul's parents were babysitting Nancy. She and Paul had come out early in the morning to do some painting, and they'd spent the morning taping off the kitchen. They'd chosen a soft yellow color, and Paul cut in along the corners and ceilings while Junie managed the roller.

She'd never been out to Hideaway Bay other than in the summer. In late October, the place was altogether different. The summer residents were long gone, and the population had been reduced to only the permanent residents. The air was cooler, the beach was all but deserted, and the lake was too cold for a swim. With the leaves gone from the trees, the little town looked barren. But her affection for the place hadn't altered one bit; she still loved it.

"I think that's all we can fit for now," Paul said, looking at the pit of their trunk, which was packed with tools, painting supplies, and brown paper bags of garbage.

"That's one room finished," Junie said, pulling two bottles of Coke out of the cooler and uncapping them with the bottle opener. Together, they leaned against the trunk of the car, facing the beach. Junie still couldn't quite believe it that this was to be her view. She had to pinch herself sometimes. She never grew tired of it. The sun was a watery orange ball in a dark blue sky.

"I suppose we should get on the road and head back," he said. He reached over, wrapping his arm around her shoulder and pulling her to him, kissing the side of her face.

Mondays through Fridays, Paul was expected to be on the jobsite by seven in the morning. Then he worked side jobs on Saturdays, and they'd been coming out every Sunday since they closed on the property to do some work. It was slow, and oftentimes it felt like three steps forward, two steps back, but they had one room done and all the windows had been replaced, and that was how progress was marked. A friend of Paul's who was a plumber had been laid off and was coming out to redo all the plumbing in the bathroom and kitchen. That would be a big job and would take most of the winter. Once they had running water and a flushing toilet, they could begin to stay out there. Junie didn't want to wait until next summer for that. She wanted to see what the place was like in January. It might be bleak in the winter, but it would still be beautiful. She was sure of that.

They finished their Cokes, and Junie laid the empty bottles back in the cooler. There was always so much cleaning up to do when they got home, between washing out all the paintbrushes and running the drop cloths through the washing machine, but Junie never minded. It was all for a good cause.

When they pulled out onto the highway, the farmer's stand caught her eye. She was surprised to see it still open. In the summer, the small white-painted shack sold strawberries for the three-week season in June, blueberries from July to September. And now, there were huge pumpkins lining the top of the stand and running along the bottom of it.

"Oh, look, let's get a pumpkin for Halloween," she said. She'd never seen pumpkins that large.

Paul pulled in and they got out of the car.

An elderly man—he was well into his eighties—stood behind the counter of the stand in a pair of dungarees and a brown flannel shirt over a thermal undershirt. Next to him stood a teenage boy wearing jeans, a blue plaid shirt, and a baseball cap.

"I didn't know you were open in the fall," Junie said.

"We're open all year round," the man replied with a broad smile. "I'm Ralph Anderson and this is my grandson, Ben."

The young boy looked up at them shyly from beneath a cowlick of blonde hair.

Junie frowned. "What do you sell in the winter?"

"Turkeys in November, but you have to come up to the house for those and choose your own. Christmas trees in December, and then we sell jars of canned goods from January until May or until they run out."

Junie's eyes widened. He was a true businessman. She liked that.

"We'll take three of the large pumpkins," she said.

"Pick out the ones you want," he said with a smile and a nod.

Once Junie chose the three largest pumpkins he had—one for her house, one for Thelma's son, and one for Margaret's boys—Paul paid for them and put them on the floor in the back seat. Within minutes, they were back on the highway.

"Next week, I'd like to put down contact paper on all the shelves in the kitchen cabinets and the pantry," she said. Margaret had taught her how to do it with a razor and a ruler so there were never any bubbles or creases. That would take her most of the day.

"I'm going to start pulling down that plaster in the attic," Paul said.

Junie nodded and looked out the window, content. The fields that had been profuse with cornstalks through the summer were now barren and plowed over. The cycle of life.

They took a slow, leisurely drive back to the city, quiet but content about the progress they'd made on the house out in Hideaway Bay. Junie thought it was coming along nicely and she could imagine herself, Paul, Nancy, and the new baby spending the summers out there when it was finished. She hoped Margaret would bring the boys out and stay; it would be a nice break for her nephews and maybe even Margaret to get away from their home if Junie could convince her to leave the city for a few days.

It was dark by the time they pulled up in front of Paul's mother's house. Paul parked in the driveway behind his parents' car. Junie was anxious to get Nancy home and give her a bath and put her to bed. She looked forward to bed herself. Every bone and muscle in her body ached. Once Nancy was in bed, she'd soak in the tub for a while.

By the time they went in through the side door, Paul's mother was waiting for them, looking pale. Junie's heart nearly stopped. Immediately, she asked, "Is the baby all right?" She put her hand to her chest, fearful.

Paul glanced from his mother to Junie, frowning. "Is something wrong?"

"Nancy's fine. Junie, your mother has called several times . . ." Her voice trailed off and she twisted a handkerchief in her hands.

Somehow the words in Junie's mouth managed to crawl out around the lump in her throat and in a whisper, she asked, "Are they all right?"

Mrs. Reynolds nodded. "They are but . . . it's Margaret. And Bill. They're in the hospital."

"What happened?" Junie asked, leaning against the wall, her knees buckling.

Mrs. Reynolds shook her head. "There's been a car accident."

The breath leeched out of Junie, and she was out the door and running toward the car.

Paul was behind her.

"Junie!"

But Junie ignored him, fumbling to open the car door, her only thoughts being to get to her parents and her sister.

"Whoa, hold on, hold on," Paul soothed in her ear.

Junie pushed him away, trying the door handle again, this time tearing her fingernail. Tears welled in her eyes.

"It's locked," Paul said gently, sticking the key into the lock and opening it.

Junie threw open the door and slid in behind the steering wheel.

Paul shook his head. "You're not driving. No way. Move over, Junie, and I'll drive you."

She scooched over, waving him on impatiently. "Hurry up, Paul. Come on, let's go."

He backed the car out of the driveway. "The hospital or your parents' house?"

"Let's drive by my parents' house on our way to the hospital."

Although they weren't particularly close because sometimes Junie didn't understand what made Margaret tick, she was still her sister. They were family.

Junie knew Paul was not a big fan of the Margaret-and-Bill drama, and he preferred Nancy not to be around any of it, but what was Junie supposed to do? Not see her sister, her nephews, and her parents anymore? This had been going on for more than ten years and not that Junie was used to it—she didn't ever think she'd get used to it—but it had become a part of the fabric of the Richards family. She tried to have Margaret's boys over as much as possible to give them a break. To show them what normalcy looked like.

Paul slowed down in front of the house Junie grew up in, but it was darkened. There were lights on next door in Mrs. Krautwein's house.

"Pull over, Paul," Junie said, opening her door before he'd even put the car in park. "Mrs. Krautwein might know something."

Junie trotted up the steps of their neighbor's house and knocked on the door and rang the bell. The door was immediately opened by Mrs. Krautwein, and she held it open for Junie, her face grim.

"What's going on?" Junie cried, feeling her face crumple.

"It's that husband of Margaret's," the older woman said. Everyone in South Buffalo knew about Margaret and her husband. "They were fighting, of course, and they got into the car, still fighting, and he wrapped the car around a telephone pole." The older woman's eyes filled with tears, and she retrieved a hankie from the pocket of her shirtdress and wiped at her eyes. "They're in the hospital. The police came to your parents' house."

"Where are the boys?" Junie asked, panicked.

"They're with Bill's sister, Betty."

Junie nodded, relieved. Betty and her husband, Martin, were good eggs as her mother was apt to say, and although they had no kids of their own, they doted on Stephen and Peter.

"I better get up to the hospital," Junie said.

Mrs. Krautwein reached out to her. "She has to leave him, Junie. He will never change. And she will end up dead."

A shiver ran down Junie's back. She could only nod. She thanked Mrs. Krautwein and headed down the stairs and got back into the car.

"Take me to the hospital."

On the way over, Junie told her husband what Mrs. Krautwein had said. Paul didn't say much, but there was a grim set to his lips. The hospital was only six blocks away, and Paul managed to find a parking spot on one of the side streets.

They ran as fast as they could to the emergency department, only stopping for Paul to open the door for her. With Paul in behind her, Junie approached the reception desk but pulled up short when she spotted her parents huddled together in the corner of the waiting room. They were leaning on one another, the sides of their heads touching. Junie froze. From where she stood, she could see her mother crying, and her father's body shook. Tentatively, she approached them, swallowing hard, and whispered, "Ma? Daddy?"

Both her parents looked up and Junie noticed they were holding hands. They never did that. She hadn't been raised in a family that showed open affection. It wasn't that Junie didn't feel loved; they just weren't demonstrative. It had taken her a year into her marriage to get used to Paul hugging her, kissing her goodbye in the morning when he left for work, and kissing her hello when he came home in the evening.

Her parents stood up slowly, as if they were unfolding themselves and working out the kinks. As if they were over a hundred years old.

Her mother started to say something, but tears pooled in her eyes and fell, and she shook her head several times. Her father spoke and when he did, his voice shook.

"Margaret is dead," he managed to get out.

"What?" Junie said. How could that be? Margaret wasn't even thirty. Her children weren't even grown-ups. She repeated, "What? What are you saying?" She was aware of Paul beside her. She heard his blown-out sigh at what her father said.

This didn't make any sense to Junie, and she felt many different things at once. Mainly disbelief, that someone as young and vibrant as her sister, with her flair for the dramatic, was now dead. Junie felt the blood drain from her face then from her extremities until her legs buckled, as if they could no longer support her weight. Her arms remained lifeless at her side.

A low, keening wail escaped from her lips as her knees gave out beneath her, but Paul caught her as she went down, and the last thing she heard was her mother's sharp cry.

Chapter Twenty-Seven

Lily

The morning of Isabelle's departure was cool with a slight mist. The warm weather that had spoiled them for two weeks was gone. Sundresses, bathing suits, and cotton tees were laid aside in favor of jeans and long-sleeved shirts.

For once Isabelle was up early. Alice had prepared a breakfast of scrambled eggs, bacon and sausage, and home fries browned to perfection with fried onion. When Lily entered the kitchen, Alice was hovering over the toaster.

Isabelle was already at the table, tucking into a plateful of food. She lifted a piece of crisp bacon in her hand and said, "I told Alice if she cooked like this every day, I might be tempted to stay."

"I wish you would!" Alice said. The toast popped up and she turned her attention to the two slices, slathering butter over them.

Lily fed Charlie first and refreshed his water bowl. Once she poured herself a cup of coffee and took the plate Alice handed her, she made her way to the table, where she sat down across from Isabelle.

"Are you all packed and ready to go?" she asked. She was sorry to see Isabelle go. Aside from a few tense moments, for the most part, the three of them had gotten on fairly well. Their mother and Gram would have been proud. Lily was afraid they would go back to the way it was before: not seeing each other and hardly even keeping in touch.

The previous evening, she'd told her sisters about her decision to stay on at Gram's house for the next three months and take the job with Simon. Both had been supportive.

"I am and I'm ready to get on the road," Isabelle looked around the sunny kitchen. "I'm really glad the house won't be empty," Isabelle said.

"And you're sure you don't mind me staying here in the house for the next few months?" Lily asked again. She wanted to be sure, and she didn't want to take advantage of either Isabelle or Alice.

"Of course not!" Alice said. "It's your house as much as it is ours."

"And while you're here for the next three months, you can think about my idea to turn the place into an inn," Alice said excitedly.

Lily exchanged a look with Isabelle. When Alice got an idea into her head, it was sometimes hard to dissuade her. She'd been like that since she was a child. But Lily had enough to think about besides redefining the purpose of Gram's home. She caught herself. It was their home now.

"Do you think you'll ever come back to Hideaway Bay?" Alice asked Isabelle, spreading apricot jam over a piece of toast.

Isabelle shrugged. "I don't know. My life plan is to see the world, satisfy my curiosity, and then maybe return to Hideaway Bay someday when I'm ready."

"But you're not ready," Lily guessed.

"No," Isabelle said. "I always thought Gram would be here when I came back. I don't know why I was under that delusion as she certainly wasn't getting any younger, and no one lives forever."

"Wouldn't it be nice if we all ended up staying in Hideaway Bay? Permanently?" Alice said, taking a bite of her toast.

"You're going back to Chicago next week, aren't you?" Isabelle asked.

Alice rolled her eyes and sighed. "Unfortunately, yes. But I feel like I never left. I've been bombarded with emails and texts."

"But you're on vacation," Lily pointed out.

Alice shrugged. "It's the nature of the beast. I knew that when I took the time off, that I'd be harassed."

"It sounds like you're unhappy," Isabelle said.

Alice went to say something but then closed her mouth. She stared out the window for a moment as if gathering her thoughts. "It's not that I'm unhappy. I do love my job, but the hours are relentless. I have no private life because I'm always working."

"That's no way to live," Isabelle said.

"I'm starting to figure that out for myself."

Isabelle finished her breakfast, stood up from the table, and gulped down the last bit of her coffee. "I better get on the road."

"Are you heading straight for Taos?" Lily asked.

Her older sister shrugged. "I'm not sure yet. I'll see where the road leads me. Sometimes, I like to go off the beaten track." Originally, Isabelle had purchased an airline ticket for Taos but canceled it days ago, stating she'd prefer to drive across country. Having just done that sort of thing, Lily wanted to warn her that it wasn't all it was cracked up to be. But she knew Isabelle wouldn't stay on the main highways. She was too much of an explorer.

Lily wished sometimes she could be more spontaneous like Isabelle, but it wasn't how she ticked. She preferred to have a homebase.

Isabelle carried her dishes over to the counter and laid them in the sink. She made a quick trip to the bathroom and met her sisters at the front door, where her suitcase and backpack stood. Before stepping outside, she put on her sunglasses, which Lily thought was futile as there was no sun out, unless they were worn to hide emotion. Lily, Alice, and Charlie followed Isabelle outside, where she stowed her gear into the trunk of her car. Once she slammed the trunk closed, she bent over to Charlie and lavished him with attention.

"Be careful, Clumsy," she said to Charlie.

The dog wagged his tail and gave a little whine.

When she straightened up, she held open her arms, and Lily and Alice stepped into them, the three sisters embracing each other.

"I wish you didn't have to leave," Alice said. Tears pooled in her eyes. "I like it when we're all together. It feels like I have a family."

"You do have a family, sparrow," Isabelle said, calling Alice by a name their Granddad had called her. A name that Lily hadn't heard used in years. Her throat tightened and hot tears stung her eyes.

Isabelle wrapped them tight in her hug and then planted a kiss on each of their cheeks. Lily laughed, but a tear escaped.

Isabelle pushed her sunglasses onto the top of her head, and Lily saw that her eyes were wet with tears as well.

"Look, I'll keep in touch," she said, clearing her throat. "I promise. No more not knowing what's going on in each other's lives."

"Really?" Alice said, her face full of hopeful expectation.

"Yeah, really."

"That would be wonderful," Alice said.

"It's only a text or two, Alice." Isabelle looked quizzically at her youngest sister. "It's really that important to you that we all be together?"

"Of course it is. Now that Gram's gone, all we have is each other."

Lily smiled at Alice. "There is some truth in that."

Upon further reflection, Lily realized that now that Gram and Jamie were gone, her sisters were the only family she had left. It was a sobering thought.

Finally, Isabelle made her way around to the driver side door and climbed in. "All right, be good, you two and stay out of trouble. Remember, I know where you live." She laughed when she said this.

Lily and Alice stood at the edge of the driveway with Charlie between them and waved goodbye until Isabelle's rental car disappeared from sight.

ece

Isabelle

Isabelle did not look in the rearview mirror as she pulled away from Gram's house. She couldn't. If she got even one glimpse of her younger sisters standing in the driveway in front of the white clapboard house, she might give in to the impulse to remain in Hideaway Bay and see how life played out. But it went against her nature to not be spontaneous, not be impulsive, so it was quite difficult not to glance back over her shoulder.

Once she turned the corner and she knew the house to be out of sight, she bit her lip and sniffled. She told herself that this wasn't who she was. She was a traveler. A wanderer. She didn't put down roots.

Being in Hideaway Bay had stirred up memories, not all of them bad, some of them good. That had surprised her. For a long time, she had equated Hideaway Bay with the trauma of their father's disappearance from their lives. But once back in the bay, she realized there had been plenty of happy memories there. Gram and Granddad had stepped up to the plate and filled in as best they could. And Mom, always well-intentioned, had tried her best. Mom had never spoken of Dad's disappearance. She never married again, never left Hideaway Bay. The romantic in Isabelle thought she never left because she was waiting for their dad to come home, wanted to be there in case he reappeared. But he never had. Isabelle herself hadn't stuck around, deciding from there on out that she'd be the one who did the leaving. Never again would she give a man a chance to leave her.

She supposed what she was in need of was a good therapist, but she figured it was too late for that now. She was who she was. Back to traveling the world now. Pushing all thoughts of her family out of her mind, she turned onto the main highway, thinking about her next destination. Excited about where she might end up and what she might see.

Chapter Twenty-Eight

1970

Junie

Junie was vaguely aware of Thelma being there. She could hear her rooting around in her kitchen, opening cabinet doors and closing them. Thelma spoke to her son Donny in a low voice. There was the whine of Nancy, who was now five and who would be starting kindergarten after Labor Day.

Junie knew she should try to get out of bed, but that would require energy she didn't have. Besides, Thelma was there. She'd look after her and the kids. Paul had left early for work. He was on a big job out at the university; he'd already been there for a year and there was at least another year's work.

She rolled over and looked toward the window. Again, she thought of getting out of bed, but then thought better of it. It was hot, though, and the sheets were sticking to her. The windows were wide open, but there was no breeze and thus no relief.

The previous evening, despite all sorts of coaxing on Paul's part, Junie refused to get out of bed. So Thelma and Paul had taken Donny, Nancy, and Margaret's two boys, Stephen and Peter, down to the baseball diamond to watch 4th of July fireworks. Watching her nephews navigate the world without their mother and with their father in a nursing home caused Junie a lot of pain. Some days it was more than she could bear. Every day, she managed to get to her parents' house to make sure they were eating and surviving. That daily visit sapped every bit of energy Junie had left and when she returned home, she'd take to her bed.

The door to her bedroom opened, creaking. Junie sighed. How many times had she asked Paul to put some WD-40 on those hinges? How many more times would she have to ask him?

Thelma sat on the side of the bed. "Come on, lady, time to get up."

"I will in a bit," Junie said. "What time is it?"

"It's almost one. I gave the kids SpaghettiOs and bread and butter for lunch," Thelma reported. She crossed her arms over her chest, draped one leg over the other, and began to swing her foot in time to some internal music.

"That's fine." There was a blessed relief in knowing she didn't have to worry about getting Nancy her lunch.

"I heard from Barb," Thelma said. Her leg continued to swing, and she stared at some unknown spot on the carpet. "She's coming home for the summer."

"Is she? That's nice," Junie replied, her voice flat.

It'd been a few years since Barb had come home. They still kept in touch, but Barb's life was out in California now. Her first husband had been killed in Vietnam and she had since remarried. Ever the romantic. Junie wondered how she'd found the strength to carry on.

She thought about it for a moment and asked, "Why is she coming home now?"

"Because I called her and asked her to."

"Why did you do that?" Although Junie already knew. Her current state of depression must have frightened a not-so-easily scared Thelma if she'd reached out to Barb. She'd often been caught in the middle of the two of them. They were like oil and water. But maybe not all the time. Maybe not now.

"How is Barb?"

She expected Thelma to make some caustic remark about Barb's golden lifestyle, but she didn't. "She's good. Still trying to get pregnant."

More than anything, Barb wanted a baby, but that dream was proving elusive with two husbands so far. *We all have problems*, Junie thought.

There was hope for the three of them yet. But still, she didn't rouse from her bed. She couldn't. Her body felt like it was weighted down.

Thelma let out a long, exasperated sigh. "Look, Junie, as your best friend, I'm telling you it's time to get out of bed and get on with your life."

Tears stung the backs of her eyes. How could she get on with her life? Her sister was dead. She'd miscarried the child that was due, and now there would be no more children. That one senseless tragedy had ripped her family apart. Her parents were shadows of their former selves. Her nephews were practically orphans. It broke her heart to look at them. It was easy for Thelma to say move on with your life. How did you move on with your life when it was a big, black hole?

Junie chose not to respond. If she stayed quiet long enough, Thelma might get the hint and leave, and then she could go back to doing what she wanted to do more than anything: sleep.

Thelma lowered her voice until it was almost a whisper. "I'm not saying what happened wasn't awful. It was horrific, but you not getting out of bed is not the solution. Nancy needs you. And those boys need you. They need all the support they can get."

"Don't say that!"

"What good are you to them lying in bed all day?"

"I can't do it," Junie wailed into the pillow.

Thelma nodded her head. "You can do it. Because you have to. You have no choice." Junie knew that Thelma had experience with this.

"I have no energy, Thelma," Junie said.

"I know. But go to the doctor, get some pills or something, or whatever they're doing these days."

"How did you ever manage to go on after your mother died?" Junie asked.

Thelma didn't reply right away but when she did, she didn't look at Junie. "I was young and didn't know how to deal with it. I just put one foot in front of the other and kept doing that day after day."

"I don't think I can," Junie said, overwhelmed with the thought of having to exert herself. She lowered her voice and added, "Paul has been sleeping on the couch."

Thelma snorted. "Because you stink! Junie, when was the last time you bathed?"

"I don't remember."

Thelma stood up and clapped her hands, startling Junie. "All right, that's it. I'm going to run you a bath, and you're going to get in it."

Junie made a face of displeasure. "Not today. I'll do it tomorrow."

"Nope, you either get up and get in the tub or I'm going to put you in it myself and scrub you with a wire brush!"

Junie didn't doubt Thelma's threat. She knew she would follow through. Being forced out of bed made her cranky, but she pulled the sheet back. "Okay, bossy."

Thelma laughed and left the room. "I'll give you five minutes."

Junie dragged herself out of the bed, wrapped her cotton bathrobe around herself, and headed toward the bathroom. In the living room, she spotted her nephews sitting quietly on the couch. Nancy and Donny played together on the floor with the can of Lincoln Logs.

"Hi, Aunt Junie," Peter said.

"Hi boys, are you hungry?"

"Thelma gave us SpaghettiOs, and she said she'd take us to the corner store for ice cream."

Their four young faces looked at her, expectant, and there was a tug on her heart. Thelma was right; they needed her. It wasn't their fault what had happened. She wanted to cry as the memories of that horrible day came rushing back to her.

Thelma was behind her, carrying a bath towel and a washcloth. "Come on, lady, bathtub." She nudged Junie gently in the small of her back, propelling her toward the bathroom.

The tub was full of water, and Junie hesitated in the doorway. She felt exhausted.

"Take a long soak, wash that hair, and I'll take the kids up to the corner store," Thelma said. "Before we go, I'll strip your bed and put on clean sheets."

"That isn't necessary," Junie said.

"Yeah, Junie, it is," Thelma said. "Get into that tub and we'll be back in half an hour."

She closed the door behind her and left Junie staring at the tub full of water. Eventually, she stepped into it, her body sinking down into the water. It actually felt good because it was so hot outside. The fog she'd been in cleared a tiny bit.

By the time Junie emerged from the bedroom after getting dressed, Thelma was returning with four kids in tow, all with ice cream cones in their hands.

Thelma stood there with her hands on her hips and stared at Junie. "Now, doesn't that feel better?"

Junie nodded. It did feel slightly better. It was a step in the right direction. She ruffled the hair of her nephews. Her heart ached and broke for them.

Thelma hung around for the rest of the afternoon, doing laundry and folding it and putting fresh sheets on the bed. At five, she glanced at the clock and announced, "All right, I've got to get this kid home and give him some dinner."

"I don't want to go home," Donny whined.

"We'll come back another day," Thelma said.

"How's Bobby?" Junie asked.

Thelma's marriage hadn't been turbulent like Margaret's, but she knew Thelma was unhappy, or she had been months ago. They were likely the most mismatched couple this century.

Thelma rolled her eyes. "As long as he stays out of my way, we're fine."

That was no way to be married, Junie thought. "What is it exactly about him that bothers you?" She couldn't imagine living like that with Paul.

"He breathes. That's what bothers me," Thelma said sharply. "All right, come on, Donny, we've got to get home."

Junie walked them to the door and thanked Thelma for her help who brushed off her gratitude.

It was too hot to be cooped up in the house and she encouraged Nancy and her nephews to play outside. She stood at the door as Thelma and Donny walked down the driveway.

"Will I see you tomorrow?" she asked. Maybe if she knew Thelma was coming over, she'd have a reason to get out of bed.

"Yeah, sure," Thelma said. "Will we take the kids out to the lake?"

"I don't have a car," Junie said.

"I know you don't," Thelma said. "I'll drive. We'll make a day of it."

"Doesn't Bobby need the car for work?"

"He can take the bus or walk."

Junie couldn't imagine telling Paul to take the bus to work while she drove off to the lake. Paul probably wouldn't even mind, but she wouldn't do something like that. But then things were different in Thelma's house.

Junie waved goodbye, sorry to see her friend go. She dug around in the kitchen closet for the box of chalk and handed it to Stephen, telling him he was in charge. She left the three kids out front on the sidewalk, on their bellies, drawing with the chalk.

She glanced at the clock; Paul would be home shortly. For the past eight months, he'd been coming home from work and cooking dinner. They'd eaten a lot of eggs and bacon or hamburgers and baked potatoes. Feeling like lead, she made her way to the kitchen. It felt like walking through heavy snow and by the time she reached the refrigerator, she felt a fine sheen of perspiration on her brow.

Paul arrived right on time. You could set your watch by him, she thought, thinking there was some comfort in his being so dependable.

If Paul looked surprised to see her in the kitchen going through the motions of making something for them to eat, he didn't show it. He put his hand on the small of her back and kissed her forehead. It made Junie want to cry.

He set his lunchbox on the counter and removed his thermos. He emptied the remnants in the sink, rinsed it out, and set it on the counter.

She didn't know what to say, so she said, "Dinner's in five minutes."

"Let me wash up, and I'll be right out."

She called the kids inside and seated them around the table after she wiped off their hands and faces. Their fingers were covered in chalk dust. She filled their glasses with milk and laid bacon, lettuce, and tomato sandwiches on toast in front of them. She knew Margaret's oldest, Stephen, loved these, and he'd end up eating two.

When Paul appeared in the doorway, she stammered, "I only have this. I didn't have time to make something proper."

"It's perfect. Too hot to turn on the oven," he said. He pulled out his chair and sat down.

Junie laid his plate down in front of him. She'd made him two BLTs with mayonnaise. He most likely would have a third one when he finished.

He reached for her arm, taking her gently by the wrist. She looked down at him.

"It's nice to have you back," he said softly, and he lowered his head and kissed the inside of her wrist.

Junie nodded, her chin quivering, and said nothing. She grabbed her plate and sat down next to him. For a brief moment, in the midst of her heavy grief, she knew a moment, a flicker, like a newly lit match, of peace.

CHAPTER TWENTY-NINE

Lily

"I'm glad you decided to take the job," Simon said when Lily arrived at his house early in the morning.

Lily was actually glad to be there. Since Isabelle had left yesterday morning, Alice had been quiet and moping around the house. She'd remained holed up in her room and the kitchen was still. No sounds of the mixer running or the low hum of the oven. It had been oddly distracting.

Charlie stood at her side and now that she was committed to the job, she hoped he wouldn't break any more valuables or anything else for that matter. She'd keep him by her side and keep a close eye on him. Alice had offered to watch him for the day, but Lily figured it was best to break him into his new routine as soon as possible.

"Well, it's only for three months, and it's kind of nice to be back in Hideaway Bay," Lily told him.

Simon nodded. "That's great. Let's head back to the office and we'll get started."

Lily and Charlie followed him out back.

"Before you leave tonight, I'll give you the code to access the security gate outside," he said. He walked with his hands in his pockets, his shoulders hunched against the light rain. Lily wore a rain jacket over her clothes. "And tomorrow, once you let yourself in, park your car out front and walk around to the back. Sometimes I start early."

"Did you want me to start earlier than nine?"

Simon shook his head. "No, nine will be fine. I always stop at five. Sometimes I have to force myself, but it's important to shut it off. When I first started writing, I'd write all day long, seven days a week."

"But not anymore?"

He shook his head. They were outside the office and Simon pressed buttons on the numerical keypad, disabling the alarm. He opened the door, stepped back, and allowed her and Charlie to enter first.

"Thanks," Lily said, stepping inside and removing her raincoat.

"In the top drawer of your desk is the code for the alarm for this office as well as the gate. Keep them handy but safe."

Lily nodded. "Of course."

He was kind of cute. Tall, broad-shouldered, with a short mop of curly brown hair. She'd bet it tended toward unruly if he didn't keep up with his haircuts. His smile was kind of lopsided and when he grinned, two dimples appeared as if by magic, highlighting his smile.

Simon clapped his hands and Lily jumped.

He laughed. "I'm sorry, I didn't mean to startle you!"

"No problem," Lily said with a smile.

"Now, don't take offense, but I work with the door closed. I'm easily distracted."

"No offense taken."

"If I need anything, I'll let you know," he said.

For a moment, Lily had an image of him constantly calling her name and her getting up ten to twenty times a day to see what he wanted or needed, like maybe his pencil sharpened or something.

Simon must have read the expression on her face because he said hurriedly, "But I promise not to be a pain. Would you prefer to be in the main house instead?"

"No, this is fine," she said truthfully. There was a beautiful view of the garden and the pool from her window, and enough space for Charlie to curl up on the floor. Briefly, she wondered if Simon would be okay with her bringing a dog bed for Charlie. She gave him a quick, reassuring smile, "Really, it's fine."

"Would you like me to make coffee?" Lily asked. Suddenly she felt nervous and hesitant about starting the job. But coffeemaking would be something to do and she could build from there.

"I've got a machine . . ." he said, lifting his hand up to indicate she should wait, then did a half spin and headed off to the kitchenette, leaving her no choice but to follow him.

"This arrived late yesterday afternoon," he said, and he stood back to allow Lily a look.

There was a brand-new, shiny coffee machine that took up most of the space on the small counter. In the bright overhead light of the kitchenette, the new appliance gleamed. Lily imagined the cost had been astronomical. It looked like a high-grade machine you'd find in a specialty coffee shop.

An instruction book was on the counter next to it, and there was a display of sample bags of coffee lined up against the backsplash.

He pulled out the brochure and studied it as if he were going to settle down and figure it out. Lily wondered if he expected her to learn how to use it. Looking at the monstrosity of a machine, she decided it might be easier to pick up coffee on the way in. But she watched, curious, as he leafed through the brochure, a frown of focused concentration etching his features. Because she felt sorry for him as he realized the error of his ways and the folly this machine represented, and because she thought it would be a colossal waste of money for this machine not to be used, she found herself saying, "I'll look through it and see if I can make some sense of it."

He looked up as if remembering she was there. "Are you sure?"

"Like I said, I'll take a look," Lily told him. "I make no promises."

"Of course not," he said, handing her the brochure.

It certainly was thick enough, and Lily tried not to be discouraged.

Simon handed her the instruction book. Stapled to the front of it was a business card.

"That's the rep's phone number if you have any questions. There's also a website with videos if you'd like to view them first. He left us a variety of samples, so we can try them and see what we end up with. Then you can order them from the website. I have a credit card for business expenses that you can use. Keep the receipts organized in a spreadsheet, because I can write it off."

Lily nodded, taking it all in. It was outside her realm of reality to be able to pay someone to learn how to use a major appliance you'd purchased. Hopefully, the learning process with the new machine would not be an exercise in frustration. She reminded herself to take her time and not to rush.

Once that was sorted, he went into his office and returned with a stack of paper, which he handed to Lily.

"This is what I've got so far," he said. "Transcribe it into a Word doc and remember to save it. Here's how I like my documents saved." He indicated a sheet of paper on top of the pile. "How to title them and what folders to put them into."

"Wouldn't it be easier for you to skip the electric typewriter bit and start your book in a Word doc?" she asked.

"Well, of course it would be, but I like using the electric typewriter," he said by way of explanation, which was really no explanation at all.

Lily didn't pursue it, thinking it was only for three months. She wasn't going to be there long enough to get that involved and wonder about his quirks and eccentricities. She nodded and took the pile from him. There had to be hundreds of pages there.

"All right, I'll leave you to it," he said. He stepped into his office, and before he closed the door, he said, "If you have any questions, just knock."

But Lily knew she wouldn't disturb him if she could avoid it. If he closed his door because he didn't like distractions, he might not appreciate the distraction of her knocking on it.

Once the door closed behind him, Lily looked at the stack of paper in her hands with the instruction guide set on top. Yep, between this and learning how to run that coffee machine, she would certainly be busy her first day.

— ele —

Learning how to work the new coffee machine had not been a simple task and had taken almost two hours of her day. She practiced by making several cups of coffee. The first two had to be thrown out, but the third one had been promising. She was beginning to think the job might suit her fine. She'd done plenty of thinking and overthinking these past seven months, so certainly didn't want anything mentally trying. As it turned out, she'd only had to disturb Simon twice: once to ask him if he'd like to try a cup of coffee, and the second time was to ask him if she was supposed to put dropped words into his manuscript.

Simon had looked up from his typewriter and appeared thoughtful. Finally, he'd told her to add the dropped word and highlight it.

She spent the rest of the day working on inputting his draft into the Word document, listening to the *clack-clack* sound of Simon's electric typewriter keys and the *ding* of the carriage return in the background. By the end of the day, she'd learned his system: the typewriter went for thirty minutes, then there was ten minutes of silence, and then the noise from the typewriter would resume. She surmised that he took little breaks. It hadn't taken her long to figure out his routine.

She and Simon had agreed that she would take two fifteen-minute breaks and a half-hour lunch. Of course with the rain, she timed her morning break in between the showers so she could take Charlie out to walk him around the grounds. Charlie trotted around the backyard, investigating and sniffing everything. She took her lunch at one and, not wanting to disturb Simon, she left a note on her desk saying she was taking her break outside. By then the rain had cleared, and she and Charlie headed toward the table and chairs at the end of the sloping lawn. She laid her rain jacket down on the low stone wall and sat on that. She slowly ate her turkey sandwich, pulling off pieces and sharing them with Charlie. When that was finished, she moved on to a blueberry muffin that Alice had baked the previous night. Blueberries exploded in her mouth, juice squirting everywhere. Not for the first time, she thought if Alice ever left the law, she should open a bakery. The lake was turbulent: greenish-gray in color and resplendent with foamy waves. The surf was deafening as it crashed on the beach. It certainly wasn't a day for swimming or boating.

As she sat there, she got lost in thoughts about Jamie. She wished things had ended differently for him. For them. Wished he'd survived and wished they had worked together on his gambling problem. But most of all, she wished he hadn't hidden it from her. Her life felt so upended. Taking Isabelle's advice, she was determined to make some decisions while she was here for the next three months. She didn't know where she'd go next in her life or even what the rest of it would look like. It certainly wasn't going to look like anything she'd imagined.

There was no sense in getting down about it. But it was hard not to.

Charlie approached her at the stone wall. He'd been investigating something beneath the rhododendron bush so that only the lower half of his body remained visible.

"Well, Charlie, will we go back to work?"

The dog wagged his tail in response. Lily picked up her garbage and stuffed it into the brown paper bag. As they walked back to the office, Lily admired all the different flowering bushes. She thought she might try to make herself a cup of coffee in that new machine.

Later, when she arrived home from work, she asked Alice to mind Charlie.

"I want to go up to that hobby shop in the strip mall I saw on my way in," Lily explained.

"No problem," Alice said. "Actually, I found a recipe for dog cookies, and it involves peanut butter and pumpkin. You don't mind, do you?"

"Of course not," Lily said with a smile. It was thoughtful of Alice to want to bake Charlie cookies. And she was pretty sure that the dog would appreciate the effort.

"What are you looking to pick up at the hobby shop?" Alice asked.

Lily shrugged, digging through her purse for her car keys. "I don't know. I just know that I'll know it when I see it."

"You going to do some crafting?"

"Maybe. I have the itch to do something with all that beach glass," Lily said with a nod toward all the containers on the porch floor. Since she'd started collecting, she'd had to buy more containers because there was a plenitude of brown and bottle green beach glass. She paused, holding the car keys in her one hand, doubting herself. "That's a good sign, right?"

Alice nodded. "I think so. I'm sure you'll think of something to do with it all. Who knows, you might end up creating a cottage industry."

"You know the old shed out back?"

Alice snorted. "The one that's falling down?"

Lily laughed. "Yeah, that. I was thinking of turning that into a little workspace, if that's all right with you and Isabelle."

Alice shrugged. "It's fine by me, and Isabelle won't care."

"Maybe I should check with her first," Lily said, biting her lip, unsure.

"No, just do it!" Alice said. "In fact, you should call that guy that runs Hideaway Bay Home Improvement to come out and make sure it's safe."

Lily paled. "I couldn't afford that."

"Don't worry about that, I'll pay for it."

Lily's eyes widened. "I can't ask you to do that! I wouldn't be able to pay you back, and that's not fair."

Alice rolled her eyes. "Stop it. Let me do this for you. You don't have to pay me back. The thing is, when you work a high-paying job but spend every waking moment at said job, you really don't have time to spend all your money."

Lily smiled, thinking that this was what sisters were supposed to do: help each other.

Touched by Alice's support and encouragement, Lily threw her arms around her sister and hugged her, surprising her.

"You're just going to the store, right? You're coming back," Alice said with a laugh.

Lily pulled away and said, "I'll be back. Thank you, Alice."

CHAPTER THIRTY

1972

Christmastime

Junie

Sometimes, Junie felt like she was going through the motions of life, especially now as she laid tinsel, one strand at a time, on the Christmas tree. Nancy helped by picking up the glass ornaments carefully and hanging them on the tree at various intervals like Junie had taught her. Paul was outside hanging large-bulb Christmas lights off the gutter. He'd been laid off for a week and although he didn't seem concerned, Junie couldn't help but worry. She had taken a seasonal job at a department store downtown, and it gave her some satisfaction to be earning her own money.

Fortunately, they had a Christmas club at the bank, so there would be no worry about presents. Still, she'd have to cut back somewhere to make sure they wouldn't end up short paying two mortgages or the utilities. Her father-in-law had been right: it was nice to have the upstairs tenant helping to pay the mortgage on the house.

Nancy chattered on about her list for Santa Claus. Since December landed, Nancy's feet had barely touched the ground, so excited was she about Christmas. Nancy had Paul's sandy brown hair and his piercing blue eyes. Thelma always said it looked like Paul spat Nancy out of his mouth.

But if Nancy pulled out that Sears catalog one more time to look at toys, Junie thought her eyes might cross.

As Nancy spoke nonstop beside her, Junie's thoughts drifted to Margaret and her parents. Not even thirty, Junie felt like an orphan. Within six months of Margaret's death, her mother had dropped dead in the Park Edge grocery store on the south side, right in the middle of the produce aisle. After that, her father seemed barely to cling to life. When the end came for him, it was quick: Burkitt's lymphoma, a rare and aggressive form of cancer. From diagnosis to death, there had only been six weeks.

She swallowed hard. Nancy asked her a question and Junie looked at her daughter, coming back to the present. Nancy waited, expectant, a big smile on her face. It was contagious, because Junie found herself smiling despite her sadness.

"I'm sorry, Nancy, what did you say?"

"Can we make Christmas cookies when we're finished decorating the tree?" she asked.

Junie nodded. The holiday season was going to be as normal as possible for Nancy. She wasn't going to infect her child's Christmas with her own sadness. Nancy responded by clapping her hands excitedly.

They finished decorating the tree and Junie plugged in the lights and stepped back, pleased with the overall look. Beside her, Nancy jumped up and down. "It's beautiful, isn't it?"

"It sure is," Junie said. Overwhelmed, she reached for Nancy and pulled her into an embrace. "You did a great job, honey."

"Let's go make cookies," Nancy said, and she skipped off to the kitchen before Junie could respond.

By evening, after the cutouts were cooled and iced and the dinner dishes were washed and put away, Junie sank onto the sofa, tired. She kicked off her shoes and flexed her toes, stretching them.

Paul sat down next to her, sinking into the sofa cushions. He pulled his handkerchief from his back pocket and wiped his nose, which seemed to run continually during the winter months.

"How are you doing?" he asked.

She nodded and said, "We're in good shape for Christmas. Most of the presents are bought and wrapped—"

"And hidden in the attic from a nosy eight-year-old," Paul finished with a laugh.

"That they are. Just some last-minute stuff to get," Junie said.

"Where is Nancy, by the way?" he asked.

"She's upstairs writing another letter to Santa Claus."

Paul laughed. He laid his arm along the back of the sofa and automatically, Junie scooted over until she was sitting in the crook of it.

"Want to have a few drinks later?" he asked.

"Oh, do I," she said.

When Paul had been working, they went out every Saturday night. The teenaged girl from next door, Jodie, came over and watched Nancy. But when Paul was laid off, they'd started having a few drinks at home instead. Nothing much. A few bottles of beer and for Junie, a highball or two. She would put on an album and sometimes, she preferred it to going out to a bar or nightclub. She'd gotten a new Christmas album in keeping with her habit of buying a new one every year, and she thought it would be nice to listen to that as they sat in front of their lit-up Christmas tree with their drinks in hand.

"I've been thinking about something. A lot, lately. And I want to run it by you to see what you think," Paul said.

Junie looked up at him. There was some slight graying at his temples. It occurred to her that they'd been together for over ten years. And so much had happened.

"Tell me," she said softly.

Paul leaned forward, his elbows on his knees, and looked over his shoulder at her. His shifting of position forced Junie to sit up straighter.

"What do you think of moving to Hideaway Bay permanently?"

Junie blinked. They'd always talked about moving to Hideaway Bay once Paul retired. As it was, the house was more or less finished. There were still little things to be done. The garden was a work in progress, and there were some unused bedrooms that were full of wallpaper equipment and tools because it was easier to store it in the house rather than drag it all the way back to the city. Junie and Nancy had spent the last two summers out in Hideaway Bay. Paul had driven back and forth to the city every day for work. Thelma would bring Donny out on the weekends. And Junie had loved it.

"But what about our life here? What about this house? We've still got almost twenty years left on the mortgage."

"We'd keep this house, rent out our place, and then we'd have two tenants paying the mortgage. It'll be a nice little income when we're older," he explained.

Junie said nothing. It sounded like Paul had given this some thought. But that was Paul. He wasn't impulsive by nature. He liked to deliberate about things. Junie liked that about him. He'd never made any rash decisions as far as the three of them were concerned.

"Are you happier here or at the house in Hideaway Bay?" he asked.

"You know the answer to that. But there's so much to consider. It's a huge move," she said. "What about your parents?"

"Junie, we have to do what's best for us and for Nancy," he said. "We're not that far away. And my sisters are still here."

"I don't know. I know there's no one left in my family, but I have to consider Stephen and Peter."

The current arrangement was that Stephen and Peter, almost teenagers now, had gone to live with their father's sister, Betty, and her husband, Martin. The boys' father had suffered a traumatic brain injury as a result of the car accident and no longer recognized anyone, and he remained in a nursing home for long-term care. Junie liked Betty, a friendly sort, and it seemed the boys were happy living with her and her husband. But in the summers, the boys spent a lot of time at Junie and Paul's. It was important to Junie that the boys remained connected with Margaret's family.

Paul shrugged. "They could come out and spend the summers with us at the lake. I think that would be a nice lifestyle for young boys. Betty's an agreeable sort, she'd see it too. And God knows we've got the room; Betty and Marty could come out and stay as well."

"We love Hideaway Bay, but will we love it year-round?"

"I thought about that too," Paul said. "We've only been out there in the summertime. Let's go out the day after Christmas and stay until Nancy has to go back to school."

"But I've promised Stephen and Peter they could spend New Year's weekend with us," Junie said.

"So, we'll bring them with us," Paul said. "Call Betty and ask her if they can come out with us. And if it's too much, I'll drive into the city and pick them up for New Year's weekend and then drive them back. Whatever the boys want to do."

Little sparks of excitement ignited inside Junie. This idea seemed to have come out of the blue. Although their long-term plan had been to end up there in about twenty years, they had never discussed moving out there permanently any sooner than that. Certainly, at the end of summer, she hated packing up and coming back home, but didn't everyone say that at the end of a vacation?

"Why is this so important to you?" Junie asked.

Paul didn't hesitate. "It's been a rough couple of years for you, Junie. And now with your family gone, I don't think there's anything left for you in the city. I think a major change of scenery would do us good. Nancy's getting older, and we don't want to wait until the point where she's in high school with friends she doesn't want to leave."

"Can I think about it?" she asked.

"Of course. I'm not going to do anything without you."

"What about work?" she asked.

He shrugged again. He made it sound like it would be easy, but he would be the one bearing most of the hardship, with his family still here in the city and the drive back and forth every day for work. That wouldn't be pleasant in the winter. It would get old real fast.

"Let's go out after Christmas and see how it goes."

"Good."

"Because we might absolutely hate the place in the winter."

Paul looked at her pointedly. "You? Hate Hideaway Bay in the winter? Ever?"

CHAPTER THIRTY-ONE

Lily

The late afternoon rain had cleared, and the air was redolent with the smell of wet earth. Rainwater fell in singular drops at intermittent intervals from the edge of the porch roof. The rain had been good; it had accelerated the opening of the blooms, so Hideaway Bay was looking pretty spectacular at the moment with all the burgeoning colors of pink, yellow, white, and purple.

Lily sat on the two-seater on the front porch, sifting through her beach glass. She'd picked up a batch of a hundred round ceramic disks and a tube of industrial adhesive as well as a few other odds and ends over at the hobby shop. Everything was laid out in front of her on the coffee table, and containers of green beach glass sat at her feet, within easy reach.

She was making ornaments. After watching a few YouTube videos, she'd learned how to drill a small hole at the top of the circle without cracking the disk. Granted, it had taken her four attempts, but the broken pieces were carefully set aside to be repurposed later. For what, she didn't know yet. Carefully, she arranged pieces of green glass on the outer edge of the circle so it resembled a wreath. Once the glass was set in place, Lily glued a small red ribbon at the base of it. She held it out at arm's length, pleased with what she had done.

She didn't know what she was going to do with all these ornaments, but she supposed she might give them away. All she knew was she enjoyed what she was doing. There was a sense of satisfaction to it.

Alice joined her on the porch. Isabelle had been gone only a week, and Alice was returning to Chicago in two days. Lily would certainly miss her company.

"What have you got there?" Alice asked. She picked up one of the ornaments from the table and studied it. "These are beautiful, Lily. Are you going to sell these?"

Lily shrugged, her face a study in concentration as she carefully glued a tiny piece of green glass to the ornament she was currently working on.

"They have that Christmas fair here at the parish hall in November. You could sell them there," Alice said.

"Hmm." Lily considered Alice's idea.

Spurred on by Lily not protesting, Alice said, "You could even market them as authentic Lake Erie beach glass," Alice said. Then she eyed Lily and asked, "Are you thinking of staying after the job with Simon ends?"

"I am," Lily said honestly. She'd decided she'd stay for the year until they had to make a decision about the house. She'd contacted her boss and given her notice.

Alice sat on the top step, tucked her bare feet beneath her, and stared at the lake across the street.

"Are you all ready to go back to Chicago?" Lily asked.

Alice had made it abundantly clear that she was no longer as enchanted with her job as she first was when she joined the law firm. And this worried Lily.

"I suppose it's time to face the music." Alice paused, leaned off the porch, and grabbed a daisy growing in the grass. She plucked at the petals as she spoke. "Actually, they asked me to come back to work five days ago."

Lily paused. "What?"

"The case I'm working on had its trial date moved up earlier."

"What did you tell them?" Lily asked.

"I told them I was still dealing with my grandmother's estate," Alice said.

"How'd they take that?" Lily asked, bracing herself. It wasn't like Alice to shirk the responsibilities of her job.

Alice shrugged. "As could be expected. They weren't happy. Said I was letting the team down. That I had dropped the ball. Blah, blah, blah."

"Oh boy."

"What makes me angry is that I'm on approved vacation, and I had three bereavement days at the beginning. And yet they bombard me with texts and emails on a daily basis."

Lily scowled. "That doesn't sound right. It sounds like your firm has some boundary issues."

Alice snorted. "I'll say. The morning of Gram's funeral, they texted me to ask me something about a brief I'd prepared before I left."

Lily was appalled. If her job had called her after Jamie died, she would have quit. She'd been fortunate in that regard, her boss and the company she worked for had been nothing less but accommodating.

"Will you get in trouble for not going back?" Although she knew Alice didn't like her job anymore, she certainly didn't want for her to get in trouble once she returned to work.

"Probably. A slap on the wrist or something. By not being there these last three weeks, I've lost a lot of billable hours for the firm," Alice said quietly. She played with the stem of the daisy she'd plucked. "So any chance of making junior partner has flown out the window."

"Does that upset you?" Lily asked.

Alice shrugged and stretched back on the porch floor, her legs hanging off the steps. "I don't know. When I first started working, more than anything I wanted to be made junior partner. But I missed it last year and the year before that. The bloom has gone off the rose, as they say."

After a comfortable silence, Alice said, "I wish I could stay here with you! I love it here."

"I wish you could, too, I'd love that," Lily said honestly.

She would miss Alice when she left. She'd enjoyed these past few weeks with her. Although the circumstances in which they'd reunited were sad, she'd enjoyed Alice's company. It turned out it was nice to share meals, walks, and long conversations into the night with your sister. Begrudgingly she had to admit that she missed Isabelle as well. True to her word, Isabelle had texted a couple of times since she left, telling them where she was and where she was headed next.

A Ford F-150 pickup truck pulled up in front of the house. On the side was a sign that read "Hideaway Bay Home Improvement." Dylan Satler jumped out of the cab, as did Sue Ann Marchek.

True to her word, Alice had called Dylan and had him come out to give an estimate on winterizing and updating the shed in the back yard for Lily, and he'd already started working on it, although they weren't expecting him today.

"Hello, ladies," he said. He stayed at the bottom step and looked up at the gray sky. "Thought I'd stop by and do a little more work on the shed."

"We didn't expect to see you today."

"One small job I want to do back there," he said, and he was off.

Sue Ann approached the porch steps and said hello. Alice invited her to sit down and asked her if she wanted anything to drink but she declined, saying she and Dylan were going out to eat when he finished here.

Sue Ann made herself comfortable in the wicker rocker and nodded toward Lily. "What do you have there?"

Lily held up one of the ornaments. "This?"

Sue Ann nodded and leaned forward, reaching her hand out. Lily placed one of the ornaments in her hand.

Sue Ann sat back and studied it. "Did you make this? It's clever!"

"Keep that one," Lily said.

"I'd like to buy a few for Christmas presents," Sue Ann said.

"Take as many as you want," Lily said.

Sue Ann rolled her eyes. "That's no way to operate a business."

Lily laughed. "It's not a business, it's only a hobby."

"Maybe you should rethink that," Sue Ann said.

"I told her the same thing," Alice piped in from her position on the stairs.

"Seriously, Lily, these are beautiful," Sue Ann said.

Lily blushed at the compliment.

Half an hour later, Dylan returned from the back shed. "All set. I'll see you on Monday."

"Okay, thanks, Dylan."

Sue Ann stood and said, "You're sure you don't mind if I take a couple of these?"

Lily nodded. "Sure, help yourself, take as many as you'd like."

Sue Ann picked up three ornaments and tucked them into her purse. She pulled out her wallet. Lily looked alarmed and waved her hands. "No, Sue Ann, I don't want any money."

"Nonsense. At least cover the cost of your supplies," she said. She laid a crisp twenty-dollar bill on the table.

"Thanks, Sue Ann," Lily said.

CHAPTER THIRTY-TWO

1982

Junie

"Where is the rest of that dress—still in the bag?" Paul asked Nancy. He wore a look of bewilderment.

Their seventeen-year-old daughter stood before them in a sundress with skinny straps and a skirt that just grazed the top of her thighs. Her hair had been curled and teased to kingdom come and she'd played it heavy with the purple eye shadow and the black eyeliner.

Paul stood slowly from his easy chair, holding his newspaper in one hand and his other hand on the small of his back. He leaned to one side as his back had been bothering him recently, leaving him with a slightly crooked stance and making him irritable. "No daughter of mine is going out of the house dressed like that." He paused and asked, "Where are you going? And who are you going with?"

"I'm meeting some friends down at the beach," Nancy responded with a lift of her chin. Her cheeks were tinged with pink. Her lips shone with lip gloss that smelled like bubble gum. Nancy had inherited her stubborn streak from her father.

"You're not meeting that punk Dave Monroe, are you?" Paul demanded. He threw his newspaper down on his chair.

"Maybe I am and maybe I'm not," she said tightly. She folded her arms stiffly in front of her, her purse hanging from its long strap off her shoulder.

Paul pointed to the staircase. "You're not going anywhere until you put something respectable on. Now get back upstairs, young lady."

Nancy rolled her eyes. "It's summer, Dad!"

"So what, we all start walking around naked?" Paul glanced toward Junie. "Junie? Have you got anything to say? Are you okay with her looking like this and going out in public?"

Junie stepped in. "Why don't you go upstairs and put on that lovely lavender sundress you have."

Nancy rolled her eyes a second time and stomped up the stairs, slamming her bedroom door. The house shook as a result.

"Why does she always have to slam the door?"

"It's like an exclamation point," Junie said.

"If I'd slammed a door like that growing up, my father would have knocked me into the middle of next week."

Within five minutes, Nancy ran down the stairs. She didn't stop, but she had changed into the dress her mother had suggested.

"That's better," Paul said quietly, settling back down into his chair. He picked up the newspaper and reorganized the sections.

She ignored them and flew out the front door, letting that one slam behind her as well.

"She better not be seeing that Dave Monroe," Paul said, his voice tight with fury. He shifted around a bit, trying to get comfortable. Junie picked up a small pillow off the sofa and tapped Paul on the shoulder. He leaned forward and Junie tucked it low behind the small of his back. Her husband leaned back, shifted a bit, and then sighed.

Paul didn't approve of Dave Monroe. And as Nancy's father, his reason was valid. The kid, Dave, had dropped out of high school in the eleventh grade and worked odd jobs around Hideaway Bay. Paul had plans for Nancy to go to college. He'd been saving for it all her life.

Although Dave Monroe dropping out of school bothered Junie, at least he seemed willing to work. He worked nearly every hour the good Lord gave him, and Junie begrudgingly respected that. His home life was not ideal. Raised by a single mother, the kid had no positive male role model.

"Maybe we should send her back to the city to stay with my parents," Paul said absently.

"He drives. He'll only drive up to the city to see her," Junie pointed out.

"I don't like this one bit, Junie," Paul said, holding the paper to his side. "What does she see in him?"

"She's a teenager," Junie said. "I suppose he's a rebel, or whatever they're calling boys like that these days."

Paul eyed her and frowned. "You never went through that stage, did you?"

Junie shook her head. She had remained loyal to her crush, to whom she was now married. Thank goodness for that or she'd still be living in the city.

"Can I make a radical suggestion?" she asked, treading carefully. She stood in front of him, put her hands in the pockets of her jeans.

"What?" There was weariness in his voice. She knew his back problems aggravated everything tenfold.

"I think we should back off. Let it run its course. And it will. She'll grow tired of him. It will get old real fast."

But Paul shook his head. "No, Junie, I disagree. What if she remains enamored with him? Tells us she doesn't want to go to college but wants to marry him. That would give me a heart attack."

Junie took a deep breath. "I think if we keep telling her no, keep harping on it, it will just drive her to him even more."

"You mean out of spite? What kind of girl did we raise that she'd do that out of spite?"

Although Paul was very intelligent, he tended to see things in simplistic, black-and-white terms. Nancy was a good girl, but she was also a teenage girl.

Junie drew in a breath and exhaled. A strong sense of déjà vu washed over her. Memories of growing up with Margaret filled her head. She looked at the doorway her only child had dashed through moments ago.

She verbalized her fears. "She reminds me so much of Margaret at that age."

Paul ran a hand through his hair. "Aw, Junie, please don't say that."

But she couldn't help how she felt.

CHAPTER THIRTY-THREE

Lily

Lily was at work when Sue Ann texted her the following day. Usually, Lily didn't bother with her phone until her break but when she saw Sue Ann's number pop up, she felt compelled to read it in case it was an emergency.

She read Sue Ann's text and then reread it three times to make sure she understood it right. In her texts, Sue Ann said that the olive oil shop, Bev's Bookstore, and the Pink Parlor all wanted to carry her ornaments on consignment. A thrill went through Lily. Sue Ann signed off with instructions for Lily to call her later when she got home from work.

She couldn't wait to tell Alice.

Simon emerged from his office as she was tucking her phone back into her purse. He was casual in a gray T-shirt, cargo shorts, and deck shoes. He rubbed the back of his neck, his glasses perched on top of his head. He set the next stack of pages down on her desk for her to transcribe.

"Can you get me chapters two and three? I need to go back through them," he said absentmindedly.

"Sure, give me a minute," she said. She opened up the file she'd created in Word and after a few clicks, the printer sprang to life.

Once it finished, she pulled the pages off the tray and handed them to him.

"Here you go," she said with a smile.

He looked through them, a frown forming on his face. "This isn't what I'm looking for."

Lily looked at him, not understanding. "It's chapters two to three."

He stared at the stack of papers in his hand. "I'm looking for the original. The original typed pages."

Lily went to say something then closed her mouth, gathering her thoughts. "Once I transcribed those, I shredded them."

All the color drained from Simon's face. "Shredded? They're gone?"

Lily nodded, realizing she might have made a mistake. She swallowed hard. "Was I not supposed to do that?"

"No," he said, running his hand through his hair. "I save all the originals because I write notes in the margin and sometimes—like now—I have to go back and jog my memory or maybe pursue a different thread in the story."

Lily stood up from her desk, her heart thudding, full of dread. And when she did, Charlie jumped up too, from where he'd been asleep. Had she made a costly mistake?

"I'm so sorry," Lily said. Her skin felt hot and prickly.

Simon ignored her apology. "I didn't tell you to save all the original typed manuscripts?"

Lily shook her head. "I don't think so." Her head filled with the image of all the original work she'd shredded over the last week.

"All right, what's done is done." He paused and looked around the room. "Going forward, will you please save all the typed work?"

She nodded. It was a mistake she'd never make again.

"The first file cabinet on the left is where I keep all my typed manuscripts of my books."

Lily's gaze traveled to one of four wooden four-drawer file cabinets that lined the wall.

She nodded, committing the instruction to memory.

Without another word, Simon disappeared into his office, closing the door behind him. It was several minutes before she heard the familiar sound of the typewriter.

CHAPTER THIRTY-FOUR

1983

Junie

It always amazed Junie how well a mother knew her child. How intuitively she knew her own daughter, Nancy. Whereas Paul would scratch his head and mutter something about teenage girls, Junie knew when to give her space, knew when to let her blow off steam, and most of all, knew when her daughter needed her mother.

It was a beautiful fall day and the pumpkins sat on the porch steps, waiting to be carved. Leaves were piled around the yard, and the tourists had gone home until next summer. This was Junie's favorite time of year: she could still sit out on her porch amidst the peace and quiet of the off-season.

Currently she was wrapped up in one of Paul's oversized sweaters and curled up in the wicker rocker. Paul had had to stop at the hardware store on his way home from work as he wanted to upgrade the lighting in the kitchen. Nancy sat across from her mother in the other wicker rocker, her back to the lake. Junie could never sit out here with her back to the water. She had to see it. Hear it. Smell it.

But Nancy was unusually quiet tonight. Her legs were curled up beneath her and she played with a strand of hair, looking at nothing in particular.

"Are you going out with Dave tonight?" Junie asked. Nancy continued to date him despite her father's protests. Junie didn't say too much, instead leaving the line of communication between them open.

Nancy shrugged. "I don't know. Maybe."

Something about her daughter's tone made Junie sit up and take notice. She had never seen Nancy so ambivalent about her boyfriend before. It left her wondering if they had had a fight or had broken up.

Junie leaned forward, placing the women's magazine she'd been reading onto the table.

She lowered her voice and asked, "Is there anything you want to talk about with me?"

It seemed to be the only opening Nancy needed, for she immediately swung her legs out from beneath her, her eyes pooling with tears and her chin quivering. Junie hadn't seen her like this in a long time—since she was a child, actually—and it alarmed her. She said nothing, waited for her daughter to speak.

Finally, Nancy blurted out amidst her falling tears, "I'm pregnant."

This shocked Junie. It was the last thing she expected. She'd had "the talk" with Nancy years ago, but she'd included the instruction that it was wise to wait until she got married before she engaged in sex. The thought of her daughter doing something so grown-up was eye-opening. She remembered how Thelma had found herself in the same situation and twenty years ago, it was a lot worse. Today it was a bit more acceptable but in the whole scheme of things, Junie had not wanted this for her daughter. For a moment, she was speechless. Then she was angry. Angry at the boy. Angry at Nancy for being stupid. But she reined in her ire; her daughter was upset enough, apparently, as the consequences of teenage sex began to sink in. As she should be. This changed everything.

Paul.

She closed her eyes and groaned. Paul's pride and joy was his daughter. Diligently, he'd been socking away money so his only child could go to college anywhere she wanted in the US. He had such big plans for her. Now that was all lost. Junie took a deep breath, trying to gather her thoughts and words.

"Are you sure?" she asked finally.

"You're not mad?" Nancy asked.

Junie sighed. "I'm not happy about the situation you've found yourself in, but we'll have to figure it out." She didn't know what exactly she had to figure out. She was still trying to process the news.

"How far along are you?" she asked.

"Four months," Nancy answered. The tears continued to fall.

"That far?" Junie asked. In five months, there'd be a new baby in the house. As far as she was concerned, babies were always welcome, but Nancy was only eighteen, with her whole life ahead of her. She was still a baby herself. Now what? Briefly, Junie wondered if this would have happened if they hadn't moved away from the city. It would be the only time in her life where she would question their decision to move to Hideaway Bay permanently.

Paul would surely go through the roof.

"Does Dave know?"

Nancy nodded.

"And what does he say about it?" Junie asked. What did the man that Nancy thought was the be-all and end-all think about becoming a father in less than five months?

Nancy shrugged again, and Junie thought that was ominous.

"You'll have to get married," Junie said, floating the idea out there.

Nancy flinched. "Do I have to? Couldn't I live here with you and Dad?"

Things were so different nowadays than they were twenty years ago, Junie thought. When she was Nancy's age, no girl would have been allowed to keep her baby. There'd only been two choices back then: get married or give the baby up for adoption. Times had certainly changed. Although she wasn't against Nancy keeping the baby and not marrying, she knew that Paul, whose values tended to be more traditional, would insist on marriage.

She pondered all of this, staring out at the lake, thinking how often she had looked at this same view when confronted with life's problems. There were times in life—pivotal moments—where one's reaction or choices dictated the trajectory of the rest of one's life. This was true for Nancy, and it was also true for Junie. Nancy was her only child, and she would do nothing to alienate her, nothing to push her away. She couldn't. Sometimes, she would look at Nancy and her heart was bursting, it was so full of love. And it wasn't because of anything that Nancy had done or said, it was simply because of her existence. She supposed it was like that for a lot of parents. There was nothing Nancy could do or say or be that would make Junie love her any less. It was impossible. In the whole scheme of things, that scenario could never exist.

"How do you feel about being pregnant at eighteen?" Junie asked.

Nancy seemed surprised at the question. She probably had expected Junie to blow up and tell her all the things she'd done wrong. Junie couldn't see the point. Besides, she knew that was all in Nancy's future once Paul found out.

Nancy didn't look at her mother; instead, she stared out at that same lake and whispered, "I'm scared."

Junie nodded. "We'll be here for you no matter what, so no sense in wasting emotion on fear."

"Will you tell Dad?"

"He's not going to be happy about it," Junie said. There was no way around this truth.

Nancy cried harder.

"Don't cry," Junie said. There'd be plenty of time for that later in life. "What does Dave want to do?"

"He wants to get married," Nancy said.

"Do you love him?"

"Yes."

There was no sense in telling her daughter that by the time she turned twenty-one, she'd be a different person from the one she was now, and that by the time she reached forty, she'd look back and not recognize her twenty-one-year-old self at all. It was hard to maintain a marriage when you were no longer the person you were when you first married. But that would be something Nancy would have to discover for herself. Junie had been lucky: during the course of their marriage, she and Paul had grown together. It had been a good, solid marriage.

Nancy pulled her knees up to her chest and hugged them. There had been no angry shouts. No hysterics. They just had to deal with it.

They were quiet for a while until Paul pulled into the driveway, home from the hardware store. Junie sighed. They were all in for an unpleasant evening, and Junie would be in the unenviable position of playing referee between her husband and daughter.

"Will you tell him now?" Nancy asked.

Junie looked at her, surprised. "Not now. I'll tell him after dinner." When she first married, one of the many pieces of advice her mother had given her was not to bombard your husband with all the problems of the day when he first walked through the door at the end of his workday. It was best to let him have his dinner and settle down first. Junie had stuck to that advice, and it had served her well.

"Come on, help me get the dinner on the table, and then disappear after dinner and I'll tell your father," Junie advised, getting up from her chair.

"I don't have to be there?" Nancy asked. Her relief was palpable.

"No, but come home early tonight. He's going to want to talk to you," Junie advised.

Paul stepped onto the porch. There were dark circles under his eyes, and he was in desperate need of a shave. He leaned in and kissed Junie hello.

"How are my two favorite people?" he asked.

"We're fine. How was your day?" Junie asked.

"The usual. What's for dinner?"

"I made sauce and a pan of lasagne," she said.

"Good. I'm starving," he said. "I'll go wash up and be down in ten minutes."

"Perfect."

Nancy hadn't said one word, but Paul hadn't noticed. They followed him inside. Paul headed up the stairs, whistling, and Junie and Nancy drifted toward the kitchen. Junie braced herself for the evening ahead. They might as well enjoy their meal.

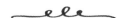

As they finished their dinner, the noise of a honking horn sounded outside, followed by a revving engine.

Paul looked up from his plate, unable to mask his dismay. "Is there any reason Dave can't come to the front door like a gentleman?"

Nancy refrained from making a smart remark and she stood, carrying her empty plate over to the counter. Without being asked, she rinsed it off and placed it in the dishwasher.

Without a word, she headed out of the kitchen. She'd been quiet all through dinner as Paul relayed some story about the new apprentice. Junie had laughed in all the right spots, but her stomach was in knots.

"Not too late tonight, Nancy," Paul called after her.

"No, Dad," Nancy said, her voice quiet.

Paul mopped up the rest of his sauce from his plate with a piece of garlic bread. "What's wrong with her? She didn't say one word during dinner."

Junie spooned sugar into her teacup.

"Trouble with Dave? Please tell me she's breaking up with him," Paul said, smiling. "Make my day. Make my year."

Junie took a sip of her tea. This was going to be more difficult than she'd thought. But it was best to get it out there as soon as possible.

"Nancy's pregnant."

Paul stopped eating, his chewing slowing down, his hand holding his fork midair. The color slowly drained from his face as what Junie said began to take effect. He didn't blink. He just stared. Junie did not take her eyes off of his. There had been difficult moments for sure in their twenty-year marriage, but this was certainly at the top of the list.

"What did you say?" he asked.

"Nancy's going to have a baby," she said, whispering.

"I'll kill him!" Paul said, the color coming back into his face, a bright red. He jumped up, his chair tipping over behind him. Junie stood up, a little unsure; she'd never seen Paul like this. "Where are they?"

"I don't know. She'll be home early," Junie said.

"Damn right she'll be! I am going to kill him," Paul said again. There was a muscle along his jawline that ticked furiously.

"No, you're not, I know you want to, but you're not," Junie said.

Paul rounded on her. "You were the one who said not to protest too much. 'Let it run its course' is what you said. And now look where we are!"

Junie took a step back. Surely Paul wasn't going to fault her?

"Her life is ruined!"

"Wait a minute," Junie said, putting her hand up but stepping back again when she saw the dark expression on Paul's face. "It's not ruined, it's just going to be different than what we wanted."

"What is this you're saying? Some crap you've read in one of your magazines?"

"Her life is going in a different direction than what we had planned for her," Junie explained, lowering her voice. She was glad they were having this conversation indoors and not on the front porch.

Paul's face crumpled as a realization hit him. "She won't be able to go to college." He collapsed into the kitchen chair and buried his head in his hands. Junie sat across from him. When he lifted his head, Junie was shocked to see tears in his eyes. She'd never seen him cry before, not even when his father died. He pulled a hankie from his back pocket and blew his nose loudly.

"She'll be stuck doing minimum-wage jobs for the rest of her life," he pronounced.

"She can take classes at night after the baby is born," Junie said.

Paul looked startled, as if he'd forgotten that there was going to be a new member of their extended family. "When is the baby due?"

"Five months."

He nodded as if trying to absorb all this information that was being flung at him all of a sudden.

"I know you're upset; I'm not thrilled either," Junie said, "And I hate sounding trite, but it could always be worse." She reached for him.

Paul snorted. "When in our twenty years of marriage has it been worse?"

That shook Junie, so much so that she pulled her hand away from him and placed it in her lap. Margaret came to mind; that had been worse. That was a whole other category of worse. There was no coming back from death, but this could be dealt with. Handled.

Paul stared at her for a moment and then extended his hand to her, trying to reach her, but Junie kept out of his reach. "Jeez, Junie, I'm sorry. That was thoughtless of me. It could always be worse."

Junie stood up from the table, a little numb. "I'm going for a walk on the beach. Whatever you do when Nancy comes home, don't yell at her. Yelling never solved anything."

Paul remained silent, and Junie left him in the kitchen and headed out. She needed to be near the shore, near the water, hear the gulls and the crash of the surf and smell the briny air. It would clear her head and help her figure out what to do next. Because no matter what happened, she was keeping her family together.

CHAPTER THIRTY-FIVE

Lily

It poured the morning of Alice's departure. It felt appropriate given the fact that a somber mood had settled on the house. There was a fierce wind that blew in across the lake, forcing the rain sideways so that sitting out on the front porch for one last cup of tea together was out of the question. Lily ran out and pulled the towels off the railing, but they were already soaked. Nothing to be done except to run them through the washing machine. Alice brought in all the cushions for the porch furniture and piled them up inside by the front door. The rain had turned the front yard into a swamp, and the pink tulips that lined the front of the house were no match for the onslaught of the wind. They were drooped over, their petals scattered all over the front lawn. It was what Gram used to call "a dirty day."

The lake itself was partially obscured by rain and mist, and it appeared as if you were viewing it through a gauzy filter. The weather report indicated that this particular front would last a few days.

Alice remained quiet, almost distracted. Lily offered to help her carry her luggage down, but Alice refused, stating she was quite capable of managing by herself. Charlie spotted the suitcase upright on the floor at the bottom of the staircase and paced and whined. Finally, after much reassurance from Lily, he parked his bum on the floor and stared at the top of the stairs, waiting for Alice to descend.

When Alice finally emerged from her room, she was slightly breathless, and her eyes were red-rimmed. Charlie stood and wagged his tail. When she landed on the bottom step, she rewarded him with a hug and a caress.

"Boy, am I going to miss you!" Alice said.

"He's going to miss you as well," Lily said. "You're the only one who makes him homemade dog biscuits."

Alice laughed. She dug through her purse and pulled out the keys to her rental car.

Lily looked at her sister. "You're leaving now? I thought we'd have breakfast together."

Alice shook her head. "I can't do a long goodbye, Lily. I'll just leave if you don't mind."

Lily's heart ached for her sister. She nodded. "Of course."

"What will I do with all the food?" Lily asked. "There's enough here to feed an army."

Alice smiled but there was no joy behind it. She'd spent the previous two days baking all sorts of cookies and cakes and pies. The house had the wonderful smell of vanilla, cinnamon, and apple.

"Invite Thelma over," Alice said.

"She and I wouldn't be able to put a dent into it," Lily said with a laugh.

Alice looked away. Her gaze scanned the living room as if she were trying to memorize every detail. She looked up the staircase.

"I hope you don't mind, but I've left some of my belongings in my room. On the off chance that I can get some time off, I don't want to have to drag my stuff back and forth with me."

"Of course. That makes sense," Lily said. "I hope you can come back soon."

"I'm doubtful. I'm so happy though that you've decided to stay," Alice said.

"Me, too. The job has worked out with Simon. I like what I'm doing with the beach glass, and I've settled in." She paused and added, "It feels right."

"I'm so glad to hear that," Alice said. Her posture relaxed. "Just to know that one of us will be here and that Gram's house won't be empty."

"Well, I'm here for the year," Lily said.

Suddenly, Alice's eyes filled with tears that quickly spilled over, and she sobbed. "I don't want to leave. I want to stay here in Hideaway Bay." She gasped, lowered her head, and with a quivering voice, she said, "I wish I could stay here with you."

"I wish that too!" Three weeks ago, Lily doubted she would have said words like that to either sister, much less believed them. But how things had changed in a short period of time.

Lily didn't know what to say to Alice, didn't know how to reassure her. She was hardly in a position to give anyone advice. She threw her arms around her younger sister and pulled her into a warm embrace. Alice grasped her tight and they held on to each other for a few moments. Then Alice pulled away, sniffled, wiped her eyes quickly and said, "I better get going."

They both reached for Alice's suitcase and Lily said, "Please, let me."

Alice relented. She took one final look around the inside of the house and stepped quickly through the screen door and onto the porch, where the rain continued to slam sideways.

"We're going to have to make a run for it," Lily said, raising her voice to compete with the howl of the wind.

They ran to the car and Alice popped open the trunk. Lily lifted her suitcase, put it inside, and then slammed it shut.

Alice opened the driver's side door and Lily hugged her hurriedly. They were both getting wet, and she didn't want her younger sister traveling in wet clothes.

"Call me tonight when you get home," Lily said.

"I will," Alice said, nodding.

"Go, or you'll get soaked," Lily said.

Alice got into the car, buckled up, and closed the door. Lily retreated to the porch and waved as her sister pulled out. Her heart ached and she felt her eyes fill with hot tears as her sister disappeared from sight.

For the rest of the day, she puttered around the house. Simon had told her to take the day off and although she felt guilty for taking time off from a job she'd just started, she was grateful to be able to spend the morning with Alice. But now that Alice was gone, the house just didn't feel the same.

She didn't know why, but she pulled out her phone and texted Isabelle. Surprisingly, they'd heard regularly from their older sister. And although Lily and Alice tried not to bother Isabelle too much with their texts, she always responded when they contacted her. Sometimes she sent photos of where she was.

Alice just left. Quite upset, Lily messaged.

It wasn't long before Isabelle responded, *I figured as much. Poor kid.*

They texted back and forth for a few minutes, and it felt almost normal, as if they'd always stayed in touch. Lily thought she could happily get used to it.

Isabelle wound up her conversation with: *I'll call Alice tonight. How's Clumsy?*

With that, Lily burst out laughing.

By evening, Lily was truly bored. She forced herself to stay out of the kitchen so she wouldn't eat any of the baked goods Alice had left behind. She'd distracted herself throughout the day with busy work: stuff that didn't necessarily need to be done but kept her mind off the fact that both her sisters were gone. Due to the inclement weather, she was limited as to what she could do. There'd be no foraging on the beach for glass, and sitting on the porch was impossible as it was covered in rainwater.

She'd heard from Alice late in the afternoon that she was home; the flight was fine, and she'd ended her text with a couple of sad-faced emojis. Lily offered to call her later, but Alice said she planned on turning in early as she needed to be at work first thing. Lily read between the lines and stepped back, giving her sister some space. Besides, Isabelle had said she'd call her.

After a small dinner of leftover ravioli, she set up shop on the dining room table and got happily lost in her beach glass art. Her newest creation used clay pots; she glued beach glass all over them as tightly spaced as she could.

Since Sue Ann had arranged for her to sell her Christmas ornaments on consignment, Lily had made another hundred to cover all the stores. When she'd lingered over the pricing and had settled on $4.99, Sue Ann had shaken her head and said no, $5.99.

By eight, her neck ached from sitting in one position too long. She stood from her chair, stretched her arms above her head, and yawned. It was too early to put the television on and although the rain had decreased to a mist, she was in no humor to go for a walk.

It was a Tuesday night, and Lily remembered that Thelma's card club was going on up at the parish hall. It would be a good idea to take all those baked goods over there to let other people enjoy them, and it would get her away from the quiet of the house.

She left Charlie sleeping inside and loaded all the baked goods into the trunk of her SUV, leaving the porch light on. There was still a slight mist, so she put her wipers on low and set off.

The parish hall was all lit up and cast golden shadows on the gravel parking lot. Cloud cover was heavy, and the night was dark. She pulled into a vacated spot near the back door. She thought maybe she'd sneak through the kitchen, drop everything off, and head back home.

There was no one in the kitchen when she arrived, her arms laden with trays of baked goods. There was minimal lighting, and all that stainless steel glimmered in the shadows.

One by one, she lined the trays up on the table. Across the way, coffeemakers gurgled and sputtered on the countertop. Coffee urns were lined up, ready to fill. Round trays of creamer and sugar were ready to be taken out.

Lily hurried as she wanted to leave undetected. Quickly, she glanced around for a sheet of paper so she could leave a note.

But the stainless steel butler door that separated the main hall from the kitchen burst open, and a hand flipped the light switch on. The room was immediately bathed in harsh fluorescent light.

When Thelma spotted Lily, she jumped back, startled, and put her hand to her chest.

"Lily, what are you doing sneaking around in the dark? You almost gave me a heart attack!"

"I'm sorry," Lily said. "I was just dropping off some baked goods and I didn't want to disturb you."

Thelma took in the sight of the trays laden with desserts. "Did Alice bake all this?"

Lily nodded. "She left this morning."

"I know she didn't want to go back to Chicago."

"No."

"Who knows, maybe she'll end up back here."

"Maybe," Lily said, although she suspected once Alice got sucked back into the vortex that was her job in Chicago, that probability would be less likely.

"Come on, you might as well help me set up," Thelma said. "Actually, we're one short for pinochle."

Lily waved her hands in front of her, frowning. "I wasn't staying. I just thought your group might enjoy these."

"Do you have plans?"

"Er . . . no," Lily said.

Thelma shrugged. "Then you might as well stay. You're a widow, so membership is open to you."

How had dropping over some baked goods become full-fledged membership? What had just happened?

Thelma checked the coffee, said nothing more as if the subject was decided (in Thelma's favor, of course), and picked up one of the dessert trays, carrying it out. Over her shoulder, she said to Lily, "Come on, don't just stand there."

Lily picked up a tray and smiled to herself, thinking it might not be a bad thing to spend the evening playing cards with other residents of Hideaway Bay.

CHAPTER THIRTY-SIX

1984

Junie

J unie sat with Paul, Thelma, and Barb in the living room at the front of the house. On her lap was her two-month-old granddaughter, Isabelle, whom Paul already referred to as Izzy.

Barb was visiting Hideaway Bay for the summer. With her was her nine-year-old daughter, Sue Ann. The little girl was her mother's replica with her blond looks. Barb was on her third marriage, and it was this marriage that had produced the little girl.

The girl was shy and sat right next to her mother on the sofa. When offered snacks, she shook her head shyly without speaking. Barb leaned into her, smiling, and said, "It's okay, Sue Ann. You can have pop and candy. We're visiting." The little girl broke into a smile that was just for her mother and then nodded her head vigorously.

"That's a good girl!" Thelma said enthusiastically. "I'll get it for her, Junie." She went off to the kitchen and returned shortly with a glass of Coke and some candy, which she handed to the girl.

"How's grandparenthood?" Thelma asked with a smile, sitting back down.

Paul beamed. "It's great! They're here all the time, so Izzy really knows us."

Junie looked at her husband and smiled. When the baby was born, Nancy and Dave weren't the only ones who'd been overwhelmed. Paul had been so awed by the infant that he couldn't hold her at first as he'd been shaking so much.

Nancy had married Dave in a small, quiet ceremony, and the reception had been held at her parents' house. Junie and Thelma had done a lot of cooking for it and Stanley Schumacher, who owned the Old Red Top, had supplied hot dogs and hamburgers.

The newly married couple had settled three streets over from Junie and Paul in a house that Paul bought for them. It almost killed him, but the money he had been putting away for Nancy's college, he'd used as a down payment on the small cottage. It needed a lot of work but like Paul told them, they had the rest of their lives to get it to the way they wanted it.

Junie loved being a grandmother. When the infant was brought home from the hospital, Junie had gone over and taught Nancy how to bathe the newborn, especially the creases of the neck where sometimes spit-up found its way and could end up stinky. She taught her daughter as her own mother had taught her. Even though it had only been a few months, this had been one of the best experiences in her life. Her baby had had a baby. No matter what happened, this baby was loved and wanted.

"And how are the newlyweds?" Thelma asked. "Has Dave got a job?"

"Finally," Paul said with a snort. Dave had a different idea of what constituted a good job than Paul did. "He got a job in the produce section of the grocery store."

"We all have to start somewhere," Thelma said.

"You know that, and I know that, but ol' Davy boy wants to walk in and start running the place," Paul complained.

"Not everyone was raised the way we were, Paul," Barb said, and Paul nodded in agreement.

"All right, Paul, but he's hardworking, you have to admit that," Junie said.

Paul turned to Barb and Thelma. "I wanted to get him a job as an apprentice in the bricklayers' union. It's a great job. You know what he said?" Barb and Thelma shook their heads in unison. Paul continued, "He said he didn't like cement. I was like, what? It's cement, for Pete's sake. There's nothing to like or dislike!"

"Let it go. He's working. If you keep it up, I won't let you hold Izzy," Junie warned.

"Ooh, Junie, that's a low blow," Paul teased.

"How's Donny getting on?" Junie asked. Donny was away at his third year in college, with one more year to go.

"He's doing great, made the dean's list last semester," Thelma crowed.

It was not lost on either Junie or Paul how well Donny had turned out despite his parents' unhappy marriage. Luckily, Thelma had chosen wisely with her second husband for he'd raised Donny and loved him as his own son. Things might not always start out right, but sometimes they turned out for the best.

"You did a great job, Thelma," Paul said. This was high praise indeed, thought Junie. Paul was rarely so effusive. But it was praise that was well-deserved, for Thelma had indeed done a great job. The death of her mother shaped her life. It proved to Junie that out of the most unpleasant or unhappy circumstances, some good could arise.

CHAPTER THIRTY-SEVEN

Lily

L ily finished transcribing Simon's next two
chapters, then walked the originals over to the file
cabinet and pulled open the drawer labeled "Original
Manuscripts." She leafed through the files until she
came to the hanging folder labeled with the title of the
current book he was writing. Preceding this file were
other folders containing the typed-up manuscripts for
his previously published novels. Curious, she fingered
the manila folders that followed the one housing
his current manuscript. Similar to his published
manuscripts, these were labeled with book titles but also
had "unpublished" added to the label. Her curiosity got
the better of her, and she lifted the first one out and
carried it over to her desk.

As she pulled out her chair, her eyes scanned the first page of the document. She sat down and pulled her chair closer to the desk, settling her feet beneath it. She read the first few pages of the manuscript. It surprised her. It wasn't horror; it was crime fiction, a story about a washed-up cop who'd been kicked off the force and was making ends meet through a half-assed detective agency. Lily could not put it down. For the rest of the day, she continued to read the manuscript on her breaks. When five o'clock rolled around, she thought about tucking it into her purse, but it wouldn't be right to take it without Simon's permission. She bit her lip, debating whether she should ask him or not. She was afraid he'd take it away from her or, worse, wouldn't allow her to finish reading it. And it was too late to allow that; she was hooked.

Finally, she decided she'd come in early the following day and pick up where she'd left off. Simon had a dentist appointment scheduled, so he wouldn't be in until later, but if he asked, she'd tell him she was just catching up on work.

The following morning, she arrived an hour and a half early. She parked her car quietly and with Charlie at her side, she made her way to the office out back. Inside, she made herself a chai latte with the expensive coffee machine and settled down on the sofa to finish reading Simon's unpublished manuscript.

When she'd finished, she put the manuscript down and stared at the wall for a bit. She was oblivious to Charlie, who snored at her feet. Sometimes you read something that was so utterly fantastic that you had to let it sit with you so you could digest it and think about all you had read.

This was that book.

Granted it was a rough draft, but the story was there. And what an incredible story it was.

She wondered why this one wasn't published. It was clear to Lily that Simon was a better crime fiction writer than he was a horror writer. Although to be fair, she didn't particularly care for horror, and some of the stuff she typed up was certain to give her nightmares. It was the only part of her job she didn't like.

Simon didn't show up until eleven. He bid her good morning and asked if it would be too much trouble for her to make him a single-shot americano. She stood and as he went into his office, she went about the task of making his coffee. As she went through the motions, she bit her lip, trying to figure out how to approach him and tell him what she thought of this other book. She knew he was under pressure with the current book he was writing, that it had to be almost perfect, and she couldn't imagine trying to write a whole novel with all that stress surrounding it.

She carried his coffee in and set it on his desk.

He'd already gotten in the "zone." Lily could tell by the way he had his pencils and his Wite-Out lined up to his right. Next to that was a stack of typing paper. He'd put his glasses on and was frowning at the sheet of paper in his typewriter.

Without looking up, his eyes still on the page in front of him, he said, "Thank you, Lily, I appreciate that."

She stood in front of his desk, hesitating.

Simon looked up at her. "Is there something else?"

"Well, yes," she said. "I don't know how to say this . . ."

"You're not quitting, are you? I thought we were working well together," he said. He appeared crestfallen.

"Oh, no, it's nothing like that at all," she said quickly.

"That's a relief." His shoulders sagged.

"One moment," she said, holding up a finger. She hurried out of his office and grabbed the unpublished manuscript from her desk drawer where she'd put it when he walked in.

When she reappeared in front of his desk, he eyed the stack of paper in her hand curiously.

Her words tumbled out as she handed it to him. "I found this in the drawer, and I read it."

Once he realized what it was, he looked up at her, his expression unreadable.

"Oh, Simon, it's absolutely wonderful," she said. "Your main character is so compelling! I won't apologize for reading it because it's just too good." Hurriedly, she added, "I couldn't put it down."

Simon broke into a smile to match her own. Lily thought he should do more of that: smiling. His eyes crinkled in the corners and the laugh lines became more pronounced, giving his face a look that said it was joyfully lived in.

Emboldened, Lily sat down uninvited in the chair across from his desk. Simon did not protest.

"Why is this manuscript unpublished?" she asked.

He set the stack of pages down beside his typewriter and looked at it for a moment. When he finally spoke, his voice was low and quiet. "I've wanted to be a writer since I was eleven. And I wanted to write crime fiction. But on an impulse, I wrote a horror book, entered a contest, won, and was awarded a publishing contract. The rest, as they say, is history.

"In a very short period of time, I have learned not only to trust you, Lily, but to value your judgment and advice," he said sincerely.

"Thank you," she said, feeling a flush of heat creep up to her cheeks.

Realizing that Simon was practically holding his breath as she made her pronouncement, she continued. "I love it. Really love it. The setting is so atmospheric and rich that I feel like I'm there."

He nodded and she went on. "But it's the main character that I am totally in love with."

Simon laughed. "Is it something I need to be worried about?" Realizing the implication of his statement, he turned red, cleared his throat, and said, "What else?"

Lily leaned back in her chair, relaxing, staring out at the lake. "Your detective is so well drawn that it, well, leaves me speechless, and leaves me anxious to read more."

"That's encouraging," Simon said.

"He's so flawed and has that great big wound that he survived but then has so much insight into life and the situations he finds himself in. And of course, he's so droll and witty. I don't even read crime fiction and I love it."

Lily turned to him. Simon wore a satisfied smile on his face.

She lowered her voice and said, "Simon, you have a winner here."

"I appreciate that, Lily."

"Have you written any more with this character?" she asked, hopeful.

He nodded. "I've written four books with that character."

"When did you find the time?"

He laughed an easy laugh, and Lily realized she'd been right to tell him what she thought about the book. Maybe he'd needed to hear it.

"In between all the horror books, I wrote those four. They more or less wrote themselves," he said.

"You wouldn't consider publishing them?" she asked. She couldn't speak for the others, but that first book needed to be shared.

He shrugged and his smile disappeared. "My agent thinks I should stick to horror."

"Maybe you need a new agent," she said.

He twiddled a pen between his fingers, and he said, "Maybe I do."

CHAPTER THIRTY-EIGHT

2004

Junie

J unie was still operating in a state of shock. She couldn't quite believe what had happened.

Paul was dead. How could that be? He wasn't even that old. Only sixty-six. Last week, he'd complained of terrible stomach pain. Finally, after much cajoling, Junie and Nancy managed to convince him to go to the doctor, who promptly called an ambulance and had him carted off to the hospital. A perforated bowel. He ended up septic and was dead within two days of his admission. Junie didn't think she'd ever be able to wrap her head around it. Just the week before, they had been making plans with Nancy and the girls. Paul wanted to take everyone to New York City. They hadn't been there since their honeymoon forty years ago, and Paul felt the girls should see it. He had said everyone should see it once.

The brochures still sat on the kitchen table back at the house. The luggage that had been brought down from the attic remained at the foot of the staircase, still waiting to be aired out. Paul had planned to do that.

She looked around the funeral home. Lots of family and friends from the city and from Hideaway Bay were here for the wake. Her gaze settled on Nancy. Their only child could not seem to stop crying. Junie's gaze traveled to their three granddaughters, who sat in the front row of chairs, directly across from the casket. The girls appeared red-eyed and numb. She worried about them. All three of them had idolized their grandfather. He'd been the only positive male role model in their lives. They were all young women now, beautiful, and Paul had been proud of each of them.

At the end of the evening, as the room cleared out, Nancy and Thelma approached.

"Come on, we'll go back to my house for something to eat," Thelma said with a nod toward the door.

Junie nodded. Tomorrow was the funeral. That was going to be a hard day, and she wasn't looking forward to it.

She looked at her best friend and her daughter. "I'd like a few minutes alone with Paul."

Nancy nodded and her eyes filled up again.

"Take your time," Thelma said. "I'll get the girls and we'll wait for you outside." She marched over to the girls and leaned over, gesturing toward the door. Junie smiled. Thelma would never change, and thank God for that.

"Will I stay with you?" Nancy asked. She rubbed Junie's arm.

Junie shook her head. She wanted one moment alone with Paul. That's all.

Nancy nodded and took one last look at her father, leaning forward and kissing him on the forehead. She left the room to join Thelma and the girls in the outer vestibule.

Junie approached the casket slowly. Of course, her husband didn't look anything like he had in real life. His body was like a shell. Paul, or the essence that was Paul, had gone on ahead of her. She wondered where he was, but was confident she'd see him again.

She stood at the edge of the casket with her hands on the brass rails. He looked so dapper in his navy blue suit. She thought it was a shame he hadn't worn a suit on more occasions, but then his job certainly hadn't demanded it.

A smile spread slowly across her face as she thought of their marriage and of him. How lucky had she been? Her granddaughters came to mind, and she whispered a little prayer that someday they'd each find a good man like she had.

She tried to think back to the first time she had noticed him. When she had first developed her crush. When was that? And where? Had she been twelve? Thirteen? It was so long ago she didn't remember. An avalanche of happy memories came down on her, and her tears flowed freely. She swiped quickly at her eyes with her bare hands. She'd gone through all her tissues, and her hankie was no longer usable.

She knew they were waiting for her outside, but she didn't want to rush. She couldn't. Finally, she reached into the pocket of her coat and pulled out a dime. She slipped it in along the inside of the blue satin lining of the casket.

"Call me," she whispered, and leaned over and kissed Paul goodbye.

CHAPTER THIRTY-NINE

Fifteen Months Later

August

Lily

"Are you sure you won't take that?" Lily asked her friend Diana. They stood in Lily's family room in her California house, contemplating one of the paintings on the wall.

The house had been sold and Lily had flown back to California to pack up her belongings and say goodbye to her friends. Charlie had been left with Simon and she maintained daily contact.

She'd arrived over a week ago and with her friends' help, had immediately divided her belongings into two piles: items earmarked for Hideaway Bay and things for the garage sale. Whatever was left had been donated to charity.

Diana hesitated over the picture.

"I'd like you to have it," Lily said. She'd already given Cheryl the flat screen television.

Diana looked at her and scrunched up her face, unsure. "You really want to part with that? It's so beautiful!"

"I won't be parting with it if you take it," Lily said philosophically. When Diana didn't say anything, Lily nudged her and said, "Take it, please, before I pack it up in the U-Haul."

"Oh, all right," Diana said. She stepped forward and carefully lifted the painting off its hook and carried it out to her car.

The three of them managed to transport Lily's boxed-up belongings to the back of the U-Haul. Somehow, Cheryl had managed to source a dolly, which made things a lot easier. Lily was not taking any big furniture back to New York there was no need to. There was plenty of furniture in Gram's house. But she did pack up anything that had meaning for her which included everything in her craft room.

Lily's plan was to leave first thing in the morning to start her three-day drive back to Hideaway Bay.

When the U-Haul was packed up and Lily had slammed down the metal door, the three of them stood on the sidewalk in front of Lily's house. The for sale sign was still there, with the 'sold' banner affixed across the top of it.

"Well, this is it," Diana said, her eyes welling up.

Lily nodded, unable to say anything.

"We'll be out for Memorial Day next year as promised," Cheryl said reassuringly. "We really want to see your hometown."

Tears slid down Lily's cheeks as she embraced her friends in a group hug.

"I promised myself I wouldn't cry," Diana said, her voice cracking.

"Me, too," Cheryl said with a laugh.

But Lily cried unabashedly. Her tears were a mixture of sadness at leaving her friends and happiness that she was lucky enough to have friends such as these.

"Now what?" Diana asked, when the three of them pulled apart.

"To the hotel, and then on the road first thing in the morning."

"Do you want to come back to my house and hang out?" Diana asked. "I hate the thought of you in a hotel room all by yourself."

Lily shook her head. She did not want to prolong the goodbye. Her evening would be spent in her hotel room, thinking about what was next for her in her life.

"Are you sure?" Diana asked.

"I am, thank you, I'm going to decompress before I get on the road," Lily said.

"All right, that's that then," Cheryl said stoically.

Lily hugged her friends one last time before they got in their cars and pulled away, tooting their horns. She stood on the apron of the driveway, waving goodbye to them.

She took in a deep breath, crossed her arms over her chest, and looked around the neighborhood, taking one last look and committing it to memory.

Finally, satisfied, she headed back into the house for one final walk through, to make sure it was all cleared out. Then she'd get on her way.

The house echoed loudly as she walked through the empty rooms, her home looking like a shell of its former self. Memories rushed her. Jamie carrying her over the threshold when they moved in and had only been married a few months, both of them laughing their heads off. Lazy Sunday mornings when Jamie would go out for papers, coffee, and bagels. The angry words about his gambling and their money problems boomeranged around in her mind. The sound of rain slamming against the windows as she sat at the kitchen table, leaning against the wall, trying to process the fact that her husband was dead.

There was good, there was bad, it had been their marriage, it had been their life, but it was over. It had been relegated to her past. She stood there for a few minutes at the front door, taking one final look. Satisfied, she pulled the door shut behind her, twisting the door handle to make sure it was locked.

She bounced off the one front step and jiggled the keys to the U-Haul in her hand, anxious to get home to Hideaway Bay and the next chapter in her life.

CHAPTER FORTY

May

Junie's Last Day

Junie

The sun shone bright as Junie headed out to the beach for her morning walk. She loved this time of the day, bright and early. May was her favorite month in Hideaway Bay. It meant summer was on the way and there'd be real warm days ahead. She'd already pulled out all the porch furniture from the shed and power-hosed it down. It was nearing eight, but the beach would still be empty. Another month from now, after the arrival of the tourists, she'd have to come earlier in the mornings for her walk or she'd be tripping over sunbathers on blankets. By July, she'd be out here by six. Thelma thought she was crazy, but Thelma was a late sleeper, especially since she'd retired. But not Junie. She loved the beach too much.

There was a strong breeze as she made her way across the street, looking both ways, as she'd done a thousand times over the years. The street was quiet. She looked to her left, toward town, and could see traffic on the main road. Hideaway Bay was waking up for another day.

The sun was climbing in the sky and gave off a diluted warmth. Still, it was enough for her. As she stepped up onto the curb on the other side of the street, she zipped up her purple fleece jacket and lifted her head to inhale the scent of the lake. A lone gull walked along the shore, staring out at the water, possibly searching for breakfast.

Since Paul died, her morning routine had been to go for an early morning walk on the beach, even before she had her breakfast. It was something she did that set her up for the day. Some people said prayers or read inspirational readings. Some people exercised, walking on their treadmill or doing yoga. And some people slept in until late morning like Thelma. But this was Junie's thing, and it would always be her thing. The beach and the water grounded her. It was the home of her soul.

There wasn't another person on the beach and Junie smiled. She liked having the place to herself. The lake was choppy today, and the waves thundered as they rolled in and crashed against the beach. There was one leisure boat off in the distance that rocked and bobbed on the lake.

As she walked along the shore—it was still a bit too chilly to remove her sneakers—her thoughts were preoccupied with her three granddaughters. It bothered her to no end that they weren't close. They hardly spoke to one another. It was no way to live, and it was no way for a family to act toward one another. Granted, she and Margaret hadn't been close, but she was still her sister and their families spent time together and she'd been devastated by her death. An image of Margaret came to mind, in a red dress, forever young. Junie winced. She'd been gone for more than fifty years but to Junie it sometimes felt like yesterday. Margaret would be so proud of her boys. They had turned out well. Despite the horrible tragedy, they'd grown up to be good men.

But again, Izzy, Lily, and Alice invaded her thoughts and took over.

The gull that had walked along the shore suddenly flew off, as if startled by something, and headed inland.

When Lily's husband had died and Izzy and Alice had flown out to the west coast, there had been a glimmer of hope for Junie that maybe the awfulness of

Jamie's unexpected death would draw the sisters closer. It hadn't, but maybe it was the first chink in the walls they had put up around themselves to keep the others out. She sighed. It was a bitter regret of hers that she hadn't tried harder to keep them together, forced them to be close. Especially after Nancy's death. Tears stung her eyes, and she knew it had nothing to do with the piercing wind. Her daughter's death was the one thing in her life she had never recovered from. It was an ache that wouldn't go away, a black hole that would never close, a wound that would never heal.

She thought about them all: Nancy, Paul, Margaret, the girls, her friends Thelma and Barb. If only the girls could have been as close as she was to Thelma and Barb, who were like sisters to her. Despite their differences, they'd always been there for each other. Hopefully, it wasn't too late for her granddaughters. What was it her mother used to say? As long as there was breath, there was hope.

She reached the end of her walk and turned around, starting toward home and her usual breakfast of Cream of Wheat and a banana and some orange juice.

She felt better than she had when she first started out, but that's the way it always was when she walked on the beach. Contentedness flowed through her. That's what this place did for her, what it had always done.

Her thoughts drifted back to her granddaughters. It was time to step in and get them to make peace, get them to see the importance of family. She wasn't going to be there forever, so it was best that she do something now.

She walked on, every once in a while glancing out at the lake and that boat bobbing out there along the waves. Shielding her eyes, she looked up at the sun. It was going to be a warm day.

A plan formed in her mind. She was going to bring them all back home. She'd ask them to come back to Hideaway Bay for two weeks. That was all. Lily needed a change of scenery. Alice was planning to visit later in the summer anyway, but maybe she could come sooner. She needed a break from that overly demanding job of hers. And it was time for Isabelle to come back home and recalibrate, if only for a bit. They were good girls. If she insisted, they would come. They could give her two weeks. It was time to put all this estrangement behind them. That's all she wanted, was for her girls to forgive and look out for one another and to be close. She knew she had her work cut out for her, but she felt excited about the task.

Ahead of her in the sand, she spotted something shiny, a red wrapper or something. As she neared it, she saw that it wasn't a piece of litter but a piece of red beach glass. She smiled and bent over and picked it up, turning it around in her hand. The blunt, smooth edges had been tempered by the lake and by time. Red was a very rare color in beach glass. You didn't see a lot of it. She took it as a sign from the universe and held it safely in the palm of her hand.

Her house came into view across the street, and she smiled. She loved that house, and it had been a happy one for the last fifty years. She fingered the piece of beach glass in her pocket, feeling confident that everything would turn out all right. It was time to get home, have breakfast, and start the day. And then she'd start making her phone calls to Izzy, Lily, and Alice.

She started across the sand toward the street when she was seized by a pain on the left side of her chest so excruciating it knocked her breathless and speechless. The pain radiated to her left arm and neck and Junie gasped, falling to her knees, wishing for it to pass. Dropping the fragment of beach glass, she clutched her chest with her right hand, her field of vision narrowing as she looked toward her home across the street.

The last thing she saw before everything went black was the house on Star Shine Drive.

CHAPTER FORTY-ONE

Lily

Simon stood from the wicker chair on the front porch of the house on Star Shine Drive when Lily pulled up in the U-Haul. She'd texted him earlier to say she'd be back in Hideaway Bay within the hour. He'd texted her back that he'd meet her at her house.

Charlie stood at the edge of the porch, wagging his tail as he waited for her. Simon walked over to him, reached down and petted the dog on the top of his head, and waved to Lily.

How nice is that? Lily thought, smiling to herself. She'd forgotten what it was like to come home to someone. She could very easily get used to it.

"How was the drive?" he asked, smiling and absentmindedly rubbing the back of his head.

"Long but thankfully, uneventful." She climbed the porch steps, leaned over and kissed Charlie on the head, then sank into the rocker. It was good to be home.

"I'm relieved to hear that," Simon said.

"How was Charlie?" she asked.

"He was fine. He's good at night and he's a great work partner."

Lily smiled. "I'm glad."

For a moment, they sat in silence, looking out at the lake. Lily wasn't sure what to say, suddenly very aware of Simon's presence beside her.

"You must be exhausted, would you like to go in and nap for a bit or relax? I could keep Charlie company," he said.

As tired as she was, she was also energized at being home. "I was going to take Charlie for a walk on the beach," she ventured. "Would you like to join us?"

He nodded. "Sure, I'd love to."

Lily dropped her purse inside, then patted the pocket of her sundress, making sure the housekey was there before pulling the door closed behind her and checking that it was locked. From the porch floor, she grabbed the plastic bucket she used to collect beach glass.

They headed across the street toward the beach with Charlie leading the way, the dog eager to go for another walk. Despite the fact that the evening was warm, the high heat that lingered as the summer days stretched into evening was missing. The seasons were beginning to change. Lily looked forward to fall in Hideaway Bay.

The sky was the palest pink and lavender. The sun, a pale orange, had already slipped halfway below the horizon. The walk wouldn't be too long as it would be dark in another thirty minutes. They walked as close to the shore as possible without getting their feet wet. Beach glass wasn't usually to be found right on the shore. The walk was companionable. They spoke of what projects she planned to work on next with the beach glass. Simon was a thoughtful listener, and she found she liked to bounce ideas off of him.

"What's next for beach glass?" he asked.

She told him all about the upcoming Labor Day festival and how she'd reserved a section between the stalls of the Pink Parlor and the one for the olive oil shop. She looked forward to it; hanging out all weekend with Sue Ann and Della promised to be good fun. There was a Christmas bazaar later in the year but she wanted to see how this upcoming festival went before she committed to that.

"That gets a lot of people, they come all the way from the city," he said. He did not look up from the piece of beach glass in his hand.

That excited Lily, a whole new set of eyes on her wares.

"Any news yet from your agent?" Lily asked.

A broad, generous smile spread across Simon's face. Lily automatically smiled. It was like basking in warm sunshine.

"I had a call from him this morning," he said with a satisfied grin. "The book is going to auction."

Lily dropped her bucket and jumped up and down, squealing. "Oh, that's wonderful, Simon, and so well-deserved!"

"I'm so glad I took your advice," he said.

"Me too!"

He'd spent the last year polishing the first three books in his crime series. It turned out his agent for his horror books wasn't interested, but he'd quickly found a new agent in New York City who was.

"When?" she asked.

"Soon. He didn't have the details."

She reached over and touched his arm. "I am so happy for you."

"Thank you, Lily."

He deserved this, Lily thought. She'd seen how hard he'd worked all year, getting the first draft ready to submit. She'd loved being a part of the process and watching his story take shape. Sometimes, after work, over a glass of wine, they discussed different aspects of his story. Lily was fully invested. She knew this book was a winner. She was kind of touched that he'd heeded her advice.

Simon bent over and picked up a piece of beach glass. "Look, an orange one," Simon said, holding out his hand to show her a smooth shard that was slightly bigger than a quarter.

Lily's eyes widened. In all her years of collecting glass at the beach, she'd only seen an orange piece once before. When he went to toss it into her bucket, she said to him, "Simon, you should keep that. Orange is a rare color, and it'll bring you luck."

He stopped walking and faced her. "I'm already lucky, Lily."

She got the impression he wasn't talking about his book going to auction.

"Besides," he continued. "I'd like you to have it." He held out his hand, and she plucked the tempered shard from his palm. Touched by the gesture, a smile spread across her face. But she didn't toss it into the bucket. Instead, she slipped it into the pocket of her dress, thinking she'd like to keep it on her nightstand.

As the sun continued to set, bathing everything in a pale pink light, Lily and Simon worked their way along the beach, collecting beach glass as they walked. When the bucket was full, they turned around and headed back, their conversation turning toward ordering takeout and opening a bottle of wine later on the porch. Lily looked ahead, smiling. It had been a long time since she'd felt as good as she did in that moment.

She didn't know how it happened or what instigated it, but as they walked next to each other, arms and shoulders sometimes bumping, her hand found its way into his, her fingers quietly interlaced with his, and they headed back to the house on Star Shine Drive hand in hand.

ALSO BY MICHELE BROUDER

Hideaway Bay Series

Coming Home to Hideaway Bay

Meet Me at Sunrise

Moonlight and Promises

When We Were Young

One Last Thing Before I Go

The Chocolatier of Hideaway Bay

Hideaway Bay Series Books 1-3

Escape to Ireland Series

A Match Made in Ireland

Her Fake Irish Husband

Her Irish Inheritance

A Match for the Matchmaker

Home, Sweet Irish Home

An Irish Christmas

Escape to Ireland Box Set: Books 1-3

Happy Holidays Series

A Whyte Christmas

This Christmas

A Wish for Christmas

One Kiss for Christmas

A Wedding for Christmas

The Happy Holidays Box Set: Books 1-3

Most books are available in ebook, paperback, and large print format.

Printed in Great Britain
by Amazon

33619699R00229